A gentleman stood before her, his clothing of the finest cut and his demeanor rather more lordly than that of a servant. "My lord, I beg your pardon."

Now she remembered who Dashiell Matthews, Viscount Carrington, was.

Adonis, she thought to herself.

Looking at the man was not unlike what Elena assumed mere mortals might experience if encountering the gods. His hair was, quite literally, spun gold. And she'd never been one given to flights of fancy, but his piercing blue eyes and sculpted cheekbones found Elena peering about for signs that they'd taken a wrong turn and somehow ended up on Mt. Olympus.

What is wrong with me?

"For what, Miss Barnes?"

Elena suddenly realized the man was slowly waving his hand in front of her face. "I'm sorry?"

Lord Carrington smiled with easy charm. "You asked that I pardon you. I was simply curious as to the offense."

Oh God, his mouth. His full, full mouth.

She shook her head and strained to take in anything but the sight of Lord Carrington. "For my maid's . . . For your rosebush, which will most likely require a serious pruning . . ." Elena paused, realizing belatedly that, in addition to making no sense at all, she'd also stopped the carriage short of the home's front door. A perfect start to what would surely be a perfect stay.

Perfect.

BY STEFANIE SLOANE

The Devil in Disguise
The Angel in My Arms
The Sinner Who Seduced Me
The Saint Who Stole My Heart

Books published by The Random House Publishing Group
are available at quantity discounts on bulk purchases for
premium, educational, fund-raising, and special sales use.
For details, please call 1-800-733-3000.

The Saint Who Stole My Heart

A REGENCY ROGUES NOVEL

STEFANIE SLOANE

BALLANTINE BOOKS • NEW YORK

Sale of this book without a front cover may be unauthorized. If this book is coverless, it may have been reported to the publisher as "unsold or destroyed" and neither the author nor the publisher may have received payment for it.

The Saint Who Stole My Heart is a work of fiction. Names, characters, places, and incidents are the products of the author's imagination or are used fictitiously. Any resemblance to actual events, locales, or persons, living or dead, is entirely coincidental.

A Ballantine Books Mass Market Original

Copyright © 2012 by Stefanie Sloane
Excerpt from *The Scoundrel Takes a Bride* by Stefanie Sloane copyright © 2012 by Stefanie Sloane

All rights reserved.

Published in the United States by Ballantine Books, an imprint of The Random House Publishing Group, a division of Random House, Inc., New York.

BALLANTINE and colophon are registered trademarks of Random House, Inc.

This book contains an excerpt from the forthcoming book *The Scoundrel Takes a Bride* by Stefanie Sloane. This excerpt has been set for this edition only and may not reflect the final content of the forthcoming edition.

ISBN 978-0-345-53114-8
eISBN 978-0-345-53444-6

Cover design: Lynn Andreozzi
Cover art: Alan Ayers

Printed in the United States of America

www.ballantinebooks.com

9 8 7 6 5 4 3 2 1

Ballantine Books mass market edition: May 2012

For my brother Michael.
We share a unique understanding of each other,
earned through the best of times and the worst.
Remember, what doesn't kill you makes you stronger.
And yes, I'll say it here for the entire world to read:
Rush is the *greatest* band of all time.
And their song "Xanadu" is, quite frankly, genius.

The Saint Who Stole My Heart

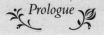

Prologue

Summer, 1798
AFTON MANOR
COUNTRY ESTATE OF THE EARL OF AFTON
SUSSEX

"Let it be known, Dashiell Matthews, that pulling my braids one more time will result in your untimely death." Ten-year-old Sophia Southwell tossed her head and the deep brown braids in question slipped over her shoulders as she turned back toward her familial estate.

Dash wiped at his brow and did his best to hide his laughter. As did his friends, brothers Langdon and Nicholas Bourne. The problem was, the angrier Sophia became, the funnier all three boys found her, which only made them laugh harder. And louder, unfortunately.

And the worst part of all was that Nicholas's laugh sounded very much like a bark of sorts. The four had not been able to agree upon whether it more closely resembled a sickly goose, a dog with a bone lodged in his throat, or an angry billy goat. But whatever the poor unfortunate animal, the bark was made even more entertaining when he tried to suppress it.

Which he never could do, in light of his extremely acute sense of the ridiculous.

This was one of those times.

Nicholas reached out to give the braids another good tug.

Dash slapped his hand away, and then punched him on the arm. "It's the heat, Sophia. You know it only brings out the mischief in us boys."

"By my own hands—bare hands, if you must know," Sophia threatened, not bothering to turn and look at them.

"Come now, Sophia, don't be cross," Langdon said gently. He bent down and yanked a handful of wild-flowers from the ground, offering them to Sophia like a real gentleman. "We didn't mean anything by it."

She turned and looked at them, eyeing the flowers as though she fully expected a snake to slither forth and disappear up the sleeve of her dress. "Is this an apology, then?" she asked with a suspicious frown, taking the flowers in her hands and tentatively sniffing.

The boys formed a half circle around her. They hesi-tated, each pushing the other and muttering things like "Go on, then," and "It was your idea, after all." Finally, Dash stepped forward. He licked his hands and slicked back his hair, then cleared his throat.

"I vow, Sophia Southwell, that these hands," Dash said dramatically, holding the offending fingers up and wiggling all ten, "will never, *ever*, touch your tresses again."

Sophia shaded her eyes against the sunlight and crowned him with her bouquet, bits of green leaves and white petals showering his shoulders. "First of all, you shan't get near any part of me with those spit-stained hands of yours or I shall kill you. Secondly, it's not just my braids, you ninny," she huffed, sweeping the three with an exasperated look. "It's your treatment of me this summer—as if I'm somehow different . . ."

"But you are, aren't you?" Dash asked, grinning. "Look now, you're wearing a dress, while we three," he paused, punching first Nicholas in the arm, then Langdon, "are attired in breeches. And shirts. Nary a dress among us."

Sophia brained all three with the flowers this time. "I've always worn dresses, you idiot—I am, after all, a girl."

"Precisely," Dash agreed, brushing daisy petals from his hair. "A girl, with . . . Well, that is to say . . . What I mean . . ." He felt his cheeks grow hot. "Come on, Sophia. Don't make me say it."

"With girl parts and such," Nicholas offered helpfully as he arched his eyebrows. "You've ten-year-old girl parts."

Suddenly, Dash and Langdon couldn't take their eyes off of a greenish-blue emperor dragonfly that'd presumably followed them up from the lake.

To watch the boys expire from embarrassment.

"Well, it's true, isn't it?" Nicholas added, scrubbing at his sweaty neck.

Langdon sighed and shoved his brother up the path. "We don't want to talk about your girl parts, Sophia— well, that is, we would. If it wasn't rude. But it is, isn't it?"

"Of course it is," Sophia agreed simply, apparently quite calm about such intimate references.

"Yes, of course. Anyway, it's just that we're all getting older," he explained in his steady way, belying his thirteen years. "You're ten now. Nick and Dash nearly twelve. And I'll be fourteen soon enough. We're growing up."

Sophia fell into line next to Langdon as Dash and Nicholas moved ahead of them toward the manor, the dust rising from the worn walk as they plodded along.

Langdon's response was true enough, Dash thought. They were growing up. The boys would head off to Eton while Sophia did whatever it was girls had to do to become proper ladies. Dash felt sorry for her—and glad for himself, which only made it that much worse. He'd have Nicholas and Langdon with him at school. Sophia would have no one—well, no one her age, anyway. Of course there were her parents. Lord Afton was a bit of a mysterious character as far as the boys were concerned, and no more than a congenial if absent father to Sophia. But her mother, Lady Afton, was different.

Dash kicked at a rock and watched it ricochet off a tree root and bounce into the heavy brush. Lady Afton was an angel. No one could convince him otherwise. She was the only mother he'd ever known, his own having died in childbirth. And she was perfect. Lady Afton let him wallow in the mud and never cursed when he tracked dirt in from outside. She read him adventure tales and laughed at his jokes. And when he cried, Lady Afton held him tightly and told him everything would be all right. Dash was happiest when he was with her. And that was enough for him. More than enough. Lady Afton loved Dash—loved all four of the children. And they loved her fiercely in return.

Nicholas nudged Dash in the ribs and laughed. Dash ruffled his hair in retaliation. Even Langdon and Nicholas, whose mother was hale and hearty after giving birth twice, preferred Lady Afton to their own flesh and blood. Dash couldn't blame them. Lady Stonecliffe seemed to like reading fancy French women's magazines more than mothering her sons.

He looked at Nicholas from the corner of his eye and wondered; was it better to have no mother at all than to have one who didn't seem to want you? He'd never dared to ask his friend. Nicholas was more likely to blacken his eye before he'd answer such a question. And anyway, Dash suspected that he already knew the answer.

Sophia's easy laugh reached Dash's ears and he turned to look back. Langdon was making a cake of himself as he watched the girl giggle. There was no need to ask the boy about his mother. He didn't seem to care either way. Oh, he adored Lady Afton, that was true enough. But his heart already belonged to Sophia.

Dash's stomach turned. How any boy could feel *that* way about a girl was beyond him.

"What will we do without you?" Dash heard Langdon say to Sophia.

"Get into trouble, I suspect. Speaking of which," she answered as they caught up with Nicholas and Dash, "I've a challenge for you three."

The devilry in her voice lifted the uneasiness of the moment and the boys smiled.

"Our excursion to the lake took some time—too much time, if I'm not mistaken," she said, looking at the sun's place in the sky.

"Hardly a problem, Sophia," Dash replied, kicking at a second rock in the path. "We'll sneak in as we normally do—through the library window and up the servants' stairs to the nursery."

Sophia looked back down and placed her hands on her hips. "Yes, you three will take the usual route. But I will enter through the front door."

Dash's jaw dropped. "You're putting us on. No one gets past Wilcox. Actually, no one's ever tried. And for good reason. Just what do you think will happen if he catches you? And he will, mark my words."

A butler with the keen sense of a hunting hound and the disposition to match, Wilcox never took his duties lightly, especially when it came to informing the adults of their children's transgressions. All four suspected that the man rather enjoyed catching them at their worst, which made them hate him even more.

"No one *has* gotten past Wilcox. I intend to be the first to do so. Right now!" Sophia announced excitedly, then took off running toward the front of the house, her long, thick braids flying over her shoulders as she disappeared around a corner.

The boys stared after her, and then looked at one another, hardly knowing what to do next.

"Well, come on, then," Dash finally said, following after Sophia.

Langdon and Nicholas caught up quickly, each thumping him on the head as they passed.

"I don't know about you two, but I'm not about to be beaten by a girl," Nicholas yelled, running even faster.

"Me neither," Dash shouted back, picking up speed as he raced toward the manor. "Right hot for a run, though."

❦

"She's probably up in the nursery right now, laughing at us," Nicholas muttered as the three boys took the servants' stairs to the fourth floor, the sounds from the house party muffling their movements.

Dash frowned. Nicholas didn't like losing. Dash didn't either, but he'd been the one who'd gotten stuck in the window and wasted precious time, so he could hardly commiserate with his friend.

"Girls," Nicholas added begrudgingly, his footfalls heavy as he trudged on, shame making his shoulders sag.

"She's upset about your talk of girl parts," Langdon said accusingly as they made their way down the hall. "She could hardly let such nonsense go without a setdown."

The three approached the nursery door, Langdon in front. "Apologize, and perhaps she'll be inclined to torture you only for a month rather than an entire year," he said optimistically, leaning toward Dash and whispering, "you might want to tell her about your window predicament—or not. Your choice."

He winked at Dash, then turned the door handle.

"Oh, all right," Dash began, following Langdon into the room with Nicholas close behind. "You win, I suppose—"

The sight before him stole the remaining words from his mouth.

Sophia sat on the cheery rose rug, feet tucked up beneath her wrinkled dress and arms wrapped tightly about her waist. Lady Afton lay next to Sophia, her head cocked at an impossible angle and a horrible red, jagged line running along her neck just below her chin.

"Sophia," Langdon uttered as he ran to her.

"I don't know . . ." Sophia whispered, looking first at Langdon, then at Dash and Nicholas. Her eyes were huge in her pale face. "She won't get up. She can't. I thought, maybe, that she wasn't . . . I screamed at her, pushed her—but she won't get up. Langdon, do something," she pleaded.

The boys watched Langdon hug Sophia tightly. Then Nicholas fell to his knees and sat back, his face turning ashen gray as he looked on with a dazed expression.

Langdon reached out and gently searched Lady Afton's neck for her pulse, his hand shaking. "Sophia, I'm so sorry. She's gone. There's nothing I can do."

"Don't say that, Langdon," Sophia begged, shoving him hard. "Don't you dare say such a thing." She savagely pushed him a second time, and then collapsed against him, hiding her face in his shirt.

"I'll find whoever did this, I promise, Sophia," Nicholas growled, his fists knotting at his sides. "I'll catch the—"

"Enough," Langdon choked out, tears welling up in his eyes.

Dash couldn't think. His head emptied of everything but the sight of Lady Afton. His heart beat loudly in his ears. He was waiting for her to rise. Expecting to hear her gentle laugh after pulling such a glorious prank. Wouldn't Langdon look the fool then?

Tiny beads of sweat broke out above Dash's upper lip and he wiped them away, still willing Lady Afton to move. None of it made sense. It couldn't. Because if it did, than Dash had to accept that it was real. That Lady Afton was dead.

Nicholas bent forward and beat his fists on the floor. Dash knelt down and hesitantly placed his hand on the boy's back, as much for himself as for his friend.

Nicholas recoiled at his touch. "Don't," he demanded low in his throat, his voice thick with tears.

Sophia began to sob and Langdon continued to hold on to her, the muffled sound making Dash's chest tighten painfully.

"Christ, Almighty."

Dash looked up pleadingly at the sound of his father's voice, as though the man could awaken him from the ghastly nightmare. "Father . . ."

Lord Carrington rushed to Dash and swept him up in his arms. "My boy, are you all right?"

Dash clutched his father's shoulders and tried to answer him. But his throat held tight to the words, allowing only a gasp to escape.

Lord Carmichael, a particular friend of the Aftons, entered the room. He braced himself on the doorjamb as he looked upon the scene. Uttering a guttural "no," he punched the paneled door and sent it crashing into the wall. The sudden noise seemed to prompt him into action and he began to move swiftly about the room.

"Answer me, Dash," Lord Carrington pressed, shaking his son.

But Dash could do nothing more than watch Lord Carmichael in silence. The man scooped Sophia up and pressed her small body to his chest, gently urging Langdon and Nicholas to follow him.

"Come, Carrington. The children must be seen to. And Afton . . . God, Afton. I'll fetch a footman and have him posted at the door. No one will disturb the room until we've had an . . ." He looked right at Dash, his jaw visibly tensing as though he'd done something wrong. "Now, Carrington," he finished, then strode from the room.

Dash threw his arms around his father's neck and held on for his very life. Lord Carrington squeezed him securely and followed Carmichael, leaving Lady Afton all alone.

1

"You're *quite* tan."

Honorable Nicholas Bourne looked across the card table at Lady Sophia Afton with a devilish grin. "Yes, well, exposure to the sun does tend to cause such things." He lifted his crystal tumbler in salute before draining it in one quick swallow.

"Nicholas," Sophia said reproachfully, in the same disappointed huffing of breath she'd exhibited while still in pigtails. "You're bluffing."

"I'm shocked," Dashiell Matthews, Viscount Carrington, objected, settling back against the gold patterned sofa. "Not Bourne," he admonished, a sly grin forming on his lips.

Next to him, Langdon Bourne, the Earl of Stonecliffe, stifled a laugh. "Come now, Sophia. Must you always be so suspicious?"

"Really, Mrs. Kirk," Nicholas commented as he looked at Sophia's companion with mock disapproval. "I'm greatly disappointed. The poor girl hasn't the first clue when it comes to scientific facts regarding the result of sun exposure on one's skin. What do you have to say for yourself?"

A quiet, intelligent woman, Mrs. Lettie Kirk had been hired as Sophia's nanny shortly after the death of Lady

Afton. And when her charge had outgrown the need for such things, she'd been persuaded to stay on as Sophia's companion, though it took very little to sway the woman, for she loved the girl as her own. She shifted her willowy frame in the chair across the room and adjusted her spectacles. "Lady Afton received the finest education a young woman could hope for, Mr. Bourne."

Sophia turned to Mrs. Kirk and arched an eyebrow. "Thank you, Lettie, for enlightening the man. But we both know the bluff I refer to is in his cards, not the sun in the sky."

She turned back to Nicholas and drummed her fingertips on the table. "Show me your cards."

"And *so* forward! Mrs. Kirk—"

"Now," Sophia ordered, pinning Nicholas with a lethal glare.

Nicholas threw down his cards, feigning outrage. Shoving back in his chair, he rose abruptly and carried his glass to the mahogany sideboard where the decanter sat, already nearly empty. "Do you steal away at night to a gambling hell and lighten the pockets of cutthroats?" he asked, pulling the crystal stopper out and pouring the rest into his cup.

"I needn't bother with such things," Sophia replied, her eyes narrowing as she assessed his cards. "Your behavior tells me all I need to know."

"What on earth is she talking about?" Nicholas asked, his words slurring slightly.

Sophia winced as the syllables slid into one another. "It's of no importance," she answered blithely, stacking the cards in a neat pile. "What matters is that you lost. I'll collect my winnings, now, if you don't mind."

Dash listened to the banter, letting his mind wander. He'd not set foot in Stonecliffe House since the night before Nicholas Bourne's departure for India. It hadn't changed a bit, the dark, masculine touches put in place by Langdon still evident throughout. Their mother had retired to the country upon her husband's death, eager to make room for Langdon and the wife and family she'd confidently assumed he'd acquire once he'd taken on the title.

Said wife and family were still breathlessly awaited by the Dowager Duchess. From what Dash knew of the woman, she'd wait as long as she had to, duty and responsibility far more important than dying ever could be.

"Yes, do pay up. I'll not have you besmirching the name of Bourne by denying what rightfully belongs to Sophia," Langdon chimed in, the cigar in his fingers giving off a mellow, smoky glow.

Nicholas finished off the brandy and leaned against the sideboard. "No, we wouldn't want that," he said sardonically, folding his arms across his chest. "Now, Sophia, these winnings. Remind me, what is it that we were playing for?"

"A promise," she answered so quietly that Dash thought he misheard her.

Nicholas stared at Sophia, his brow furrowing. "Well, that's rather vague, isn't it?" he replied, shifting his feet. "What, exactly, did I promise you?"

"Anything that I asked," she said, smoothly pushing back in her chair and standing. "Lettie, I'm chilled. Would you please fetch my wrap?"

Mrs. Kirk closed the book she'd been reading and rose. "Of course, Lady Afton," the companion replied. She walked from the room, gently closing the door behind her.

"Well, one lady alone with three men. This is scandalous," Nicholas jeered, waggling his eyebrows at Sophia. "Which I fully support, of course."

Dash couldn't put his finger on precisely why, but he knew a squall was brewing. He could feel it. "I'm eager to hear of your Indian adventures, Bourne," he interrupted, hoping to throw the storm off course. "Were there tigers? Oh, and cobras, of course. Wouldn't be a proper trip without a few snakes."

"My mother's death," Sophia said, as if Dash hadn't spoken. She twitched the silken skirt of her dress into place. "I want to talk about my mother's death. And how we're going to catch her killer."

Langdon stubbed out his cigar in a crystal ashtray and abruptly stood. "We promised to never speak of it—we all did, Sophia. I can't see the point in dredging up the past. It would prove far too painful for you."

Nicholas slumped against the sideboard, his composure markedly compromised. "Hell, Sophia. I'd no idea you'd ask for something so . . ."

"Yes?" she demanded, crossing her arms over her bodice. "What is it to you, Nicholas? What is it to *any* of you?" She pierced each one with a tormented gaze. "I know what it means to me . . ." she paused, clearly close to crying.

Dash didn't want to hear any more. All those years ago, Lord Carmichael had made the children promise to never speak of the tragedy. He'd assured them that doing so would only make the death harder to leave behind. They needed to forget if they wanted to move on, he'd reasoned.

Proper honor and respect was always shown for Lady Afton, but no one was ever able to explain what happened. No one even tried—not even Lord Afton. Or so it had seemed to him.

That is until his father and Lords Carmichael and Stonecliffe had invited Dash, Langdon, and Nicholas to join them and become members of the Young Corinthians, a clandestine spy organization that operated within the cavalry's Horse Guards. Nicholas had refused while the other two had gladly seen to their duty. Subsequent access to the files concerning Lady Afton's death had forced Dash and Langdon to accept that the less any one of them had known when they were children, the safer they all had been. The killer had made a habit of preying upon Corinthian agents and their families. No one had been safe.

The same was true today. Dash clenched his jaw as he thought back on all of the lies he'd told. The Corinthians had never come close to finding the killer, but Dash had kept the truth of the situation from Sophia. He'd played his part so well over the years that the guilt had nearly disappeared.

Or so it had seemed.

"Listen to Langdon, Sophia," he said. "He's right. It's ancient history. It would do more harm than good."

Sophia swallowed hard, not allowing one tear to fall from her eyes. "My dear, diplomatic Dash. Listen to yourself, would you? Hasn't there been enough harm done by the silence?"

She uncrossed her arms and walked toward him, reaching out to tightly grasp the settee. "Where did you go, Dash? Can you tell me? You've played at life so skillfully that I hardly remember who you were before my mother's death. Who are you, Dash? You're afraid. You know it and so do I."

"Dammit, Sophia, where is this coming from?" Dash lashed out, a sudden sense of exposure and vulnerability twisting in his soul.

"You'll not talk to Sophia in such a manner," Langdon ordered, his hard stare judgmental.

Sophia pushed away from the settee and rounded on the earl. "And why is that, Langdon? An overgrown sense of propriety?"

"I believe you're in need of rest. I'll call Mrs. Kirk—"

Sophia threw up her hands angrily. "This isn't fatigue, Langdon. It's a wretched, growing disease. And it's ugly and disruptive—and out of your control. When will you accept the truth?"

"She's gone, Sophia. I would do anything to change that fact—anything for you . . ." Langdon replied, his fists flexing at his sides.

"Then help me," she begged. "Help me find who did this to her. To us all."

"You cannot go chasing after a killer, Sophia," Nicholas ground out, frustration coloring his tone.

Sophia walked toward Nicholas until her skirts brushed his boots. She rested her palms on his coat, just above his heart. "Not by myself, no," she answered, her voice shaking. "Nor will you find peace all alone." She glanced meaningfully at the empty brandy bottle.

Nicholas stared at Sophia, as if he wanted to listen. Wanted to obey. Then his expression turned cold. He backed up and threw his crystal glass against the wall and watched as it splintered into a thousand pieces. "You've the wrong man, Sophia."

Mrs. Kirk came rushing into the room, Sophia's wrap in her hands. "I heard a crash, Lady Afton. Are you all right?"

Sophia lowered her shaking hands and folded them tightly together. "Right as a line, Mrs. Kirk. Right as a line."

Dash took a deep drink of the piquant brandy and contemplated her words. God, the woman *was* right. She deserved to know who killed her mother. They all did.

DORSET
Two weeks previous

"Elena."
Miss Elena Barnes, the only child of Henry Barnes,

Baron Harcourt, wrinkled her nose in unconscious protest when her father's voice intruded upon her reading.

"I saw that."

Elena smiled with warm affection. "You always do."

"And yet," he replied, taking a seat next to her on the chilly stone bench piled high with brocade pillows, "you continue to give yourself away. Attempting to deceive me is a hopeless habit, if there ever was one," he added amiably, settling his small frame comfortably on the makeshift settee and sighing with relief.

Elena slipped a satin ribbon between the pages to mark her place and reluctantly closed her book. Her gaze moved past the folly columns to the lake beyond and the white stone of Harcourt House shining brightly in the distance. "Really, one would think twitching my nose would be far easier to hide, even from you, considering that fact that everyone seems to agree that I always have my nose in a book."

Her father turned to her and cleared his throat, his eyes twinkling with wry disbelief.

"Oh, all right," Elena ceded with a smile, looking at the dear man. "It is true that I spend much time reading. It's my favorite indulgence. But must Lady Van Allen mention it at *every* dinner party? Even Lord Van Allen sighed when she brought it up again, and he never hears a word the woman says."

Her father reached out and took one of her hands in his, the weight and familiar feel acting as a gentle balm to Elena's stinging pride.

"Actually, I believe he does hear every word," she amended. "But it's not like the man to reveal that he's heard her comments, which only proves my point. Really, I have no illusions about my status as a bluestocking. Nor does anyone else in Dorset—or the whole of England, I would venture to guess. Perhaps even the entire world, though I would have to consult Lady Van

Allen on that point," she finished, winking conspiratorially.

Last evening's spring gathering had gone well and exactly as planned—with the glaring exception of Lady Van Allen's comment. The turbot had been braised to perfection, the wine her father's favorite, and those in attendance the best of friends. Elena adored every single person present, including Lady Van Allen, a bosom friend of her mother's before the baroness's death.

It was this very connection that drove the well-intentioned woman to say such things, Elena reminded herself. Lady Van Allen's conviction that Elena would eventually find her prince was both endearing and vexatious. Elena was all for perseverance. She thought it a commendable trait in the right situation. But when it came to her marital status, one would have to be an absolute lackwit to hold out any shred of hope for a happy announcement in the *Morning Post*.

She was five-and-twenty. If there'd been a prince for her, he'd long ago gone in search of a far more fair damsel, Elena thought philosophically. She calmly met her father's gaze, and then pointedly turned her attention to the fine day.

Brilliant yellow daffodils and creamy Lady Jane tulips bloomed in clusters about the folly. A sea of bluebells spread out before her, their minuscule heads bobbing on the breeze. And just past the lake, a doe and her speckled fawn nibbled at the sweet spring grass.

Elena contemplated the beauty of her pastoral home. She was content, in her own way. Hours spent relegated to the ranks of older women and wallflowers in ballrooms during her one season had firmly beaten down any hopes she may have harbored for a life in London. She'd been plain. And even worse, curved where she should have been straight. Heavy, when she should have been light. None of which had mattered a whit in Dorset.

But in London, *everything* about her appearance and comportment was taken into consideration.

And the women of the ton had judged her harshly—as if her inability to attract a man somehow made her completely undeserving of kindness or friendship.

She discreetly eyed a long curl of her brown hair where it lay against her shoulder, thoughtfully studied the formless moss-green muslin gown that hid her generous curves, and finally looked at the leather-bound book in her lap.

Bluestocking. Elena could still recall the first time she'd heard a fellow debutante call her that. She'd questioned whether the funds used to sponsor a young woman's season wouldn't be better spent on the poor. The room had fallen eerily quiet at her temerity, like a Dorset winter's morn after the first snowfall.

Elena mentally shook herself from the cold, crystalized memory. She'd left London shortly after. Turned tail, some surely said. Elena, in her darkest moments, might agree.

She'd been fully aware that returning to Dorset permanently would, most likely, end any chance of a suitable match. Again, perseverance was all well and good. But Elena was no fool.

Her father stretched his legs, the effort causing him to wince from pain.

The movement drew Elena from her musing and she slipped the cashmere shawl from her shoulders to tuck it around her father's. "What on earth possessed you to risk inflaming your gout by venturing this far afield? It is spring, but still cold enough to do you harm."

"The lure of seeing you smile was too great to resist," he replied cryptically.

Elena narrowed her eyes. "Come now, I do so all the time. Surely you could have waited until dinner."

"Oh, but this smile . . ." Lord Harcourt paused, grinning knowingly, "This smile will rival that of Euphrosyne."

Elena's heart leapt at the mention of the Greek goddess of joy. Her father knew better than to invoke one of her favorite mythological characters without just cause. "You've my complete attention. Please, amaze me with your news," she proclaimed eagerly.

Reaching into his waistcoat, he drew out a letter. He slowly opened the thick, cream-colored paper and began meticulously smoothing out the folds—every last one of them.

"You torture me for the fun of it, don't you?" Elena admonished, craning her neck in a vain attempt to read the inverted script.

Lord Harcourt chuckled and mercifully handed the letter to her. "Just a touch. You do make it so easy—and enjoyable. No one would blame me."

Elena righted the letter and began to read. The elegant handwriting was unfamiliar, but soon enough, the names mentioned within the lines began to make sense.

As did the message itself. Thrilling, fantastic, perfect sense.

"Am I to understand . . ." Elena asked, carefully setting her book on the bench between them before abruptly standing with the correspondence in her hand.

"I'm afraid I won't be of much use until you complete your sentence, my dear."

Elena reread the letter, turning in slow circles as she did so. "That the fifth Viscount Carrington has died—"

"Rather a sad fact for you to be so happily contemplating, wouldn't you say," her father interrupted to point out.

"Oh, of course," she agreed remorsefully, stopping in front of him. "He was a dear friend, was he not?"

Her father grinned again. "That he was, Elena. And he'd lived an interesting life, which is a blessing, indeed. I'd venture to guess the man is sitting at the right hand of the Almighty at this very moment, happily setting to work on one puzzle or another, as he was wont to do."

Elena realized he'd only been teasing her further and frowned at him before continuing. "Am I to understand," she began again, "that the fifth viscount Carrington died and his son has offered you the late lord's entire collection of antiquarian books?"

Lord Harcourt appeared to be contemplating her words. "Yes," he finally confirmed.

"Including the Paolini?" she ventured, not stopping to scold him as she held her breath.

"Including the Paolini."

Giacomo Paolini's *Abecedary Illustrations of Greek Mythology* dated back to the fifteenth century. A single copy had survived. And it resided in the Carrington library.

Elena felt the rush of excitement bubble from her belly to her chest, and finally her face.

"Ah, that is the smile I was waiting for," her father said, standing with some difficulty.

She automatically offered her arm just as the sun's rays began to slant toward the horizon. "When will you go?"

"Go where, my dear?" Lord Harcourt asked as he allowed Elena to assist him down the steps of the folly.

"To Carrington House in London, of course," she replied distractedly, her mind already contemplating where the valuable tome would be placed in the library at Harcourt House.

"Oh, there. Yes, well, you see, I won't be."

Elena stopped, forcing her father to do the same.

"What do you mean? Lord Carrington is expecting you."

He gestured ahead to where a cart and horse waited, and they set off once again. "That may be, but I can hardly travel with this gout plaguing me so. You will have to go in my stead."

"Father, is that really necessary?" Elena countered. "Could we not send Mr. Ghent after the book—that is, books?"

Lord Harcourt patted his daughter's hand. "And are you aware of my estate manager's knowledge of such things, my dear?"

"No," she admitted, already anticipating what would come next.

"Mr. Ghent knows no more of priceless books than a robin does," her father replied. "He's a good man, Mr. Ghent, but not the sort one sends to collect such valuables. Your expertise is needed, my dear."

Elena could hardly argue. She would not risk her father's health by insisting that he travel, and she'd not risk the safety of the books by employing Mr. Ghent.

Besides, there was no one more uniquely qualified to catalogue the tomes than herself. Their own library was a thing of beauty, if Elena did say so herself. From the time she could toddle along with the help of her dear nurse's hand, the baron had welcomed Elena into the enormous room that housed his most prized possessions. She'd come to love not only the books themselves, but the respectful process that was required for the care and safekeeping of the delicate volumes. They were an extended family of sorts to her, each one with its own unique place in her heart.

And Lord Carrington's books? Could she leave them in the hands of an unschooled individual? Elena envisioned rare books being tossed hither and yon, thrown into trunks without the benefit of even the most basic of lists to distinguish one collection from the other. It was too much to bear.

"I see," she answered practically, relishing the warmth of the sun's fading rays. "Of course, I'll go. We've no other choice, do we?"

"No," her father confirmed, patting her arm reassuringly.

Elena looked again at the letter in her hand. She'd met Dashiell Matthews once, which had been quite enough for her. She couldn't recall much about him, but she did remember the man had caught the attention of eligible females within the length and breadth of London—and quite a few ineligible ones as well. He was tall and broad, with golden hair and a face that could only be described as beautiful.

If you liked that sort of thing, Elena thought, feigning disinterest.

"And so I shall go," she agreed resolutely. They reached the aged farm cart and Elena allowed the groom to lift her onto the seat. She attempted to smooth her wrinkled skirt, ultimately accepting defeat and folding her hands tightly in her lap.

Returning to London had not been in her plans—ever.

But neither had acquiring Paolini's *Abecedary.*

She would travel as soon as possible, catalogue and pack the books, then return to Harcourt House before her father had time to miss her.

Simple. Straightforward. Just as Elena preferred.

"Good God," Dash muttered under his breath as he watched the landau bearing Elizabeth Bradshaw, Marchioness of Mowbray, pull to a stop in front of Carrington House.

Several heavy leather trunks were lashed to the conveyance, leaving Dash to wonder if there'd been room for the marchioness. He narrowed his eyes and peered through the window, fully expecting to find the interior filled with the familiar boxy shapes of yet more trunks.

Instead, he discovered a pair of bright green eyes watching him above a mouth that curved upward in a mischievous smile.

A footman dutifully opened the lacquered carriage door and lowered the steps, extending his hand. Lady Mowbray graciously accepted his aid and stepped from the carriage onto the pavers. She pulled her deep crimson pelisse tightly about her narrow shoulders and beamed at Dash.

"Lady Mowbray," Dash addressed the handsome older woman, walking to her side. "My dear lady, it's delightful to see you. And looking as beautiful as always, I must say."

The marchioness turned her cheek and allowed Dash to chastely kiss her soft, scented skin. "Yes, you must say, as I'm wearing a new gown. But 'delightful to see me'? Come now, my lord. Our shared history assures we may speak plainly, does it not?"

"You question my sincerity?" Dash asked with amusement, offering Lady Mowbray his arm. He waited while she adjusted her gloves, and then led her toward the wide, solid steps of Carrington House.

"Always," she confirmed, gracefully adjusting the pale yellow scarf tied jauntily about her neck. "That is why I'm your favorite aunt."

The irresistible woman was not his aunt, strictly speaking. But she may as well have been. Dash could not recall a time when Lady Mowbray had not been poking about his affairs, firmly asserting that her role as his mother's dearest friend gave her the right to do so. Not that the woman needed permission—at least not to her way of thinking. She could be incredibly opinionated and pushy, but Dash loved her all the same. Lady Mowbray knew him better than almost anyone else in his life. And so he overlooked her many annoying habits.

Though the number of trunks did give him pause.

"Now," the marchioness began, patting Dash's arm. "When does Miss Barnes arrive? I cannot wait to make her acquaintance. She is rumored to be quite intelligent—perhaps even as sharp as you, my boy."

The hair on Dash's neck prickled at the woman's words. "Do not even think on it," he warned.

"Think on what?" she replied innocently, gracefully lifting her skirts as they mounted the stairs.

Dash shook his head slowly in disbelief. "You know exactly what I'm talking about. Your attempts to secure a wife on my behalf are legendary."

"I would hardly call them legendary, my boy—"

"Lady Emma Scott?" Dash interrupted. The very mention of the woman's name quieted the marchioness.

A footman opened wide the oaken front door and stepped aside.

"That was simply a bit of bad luck," Lady Mowbray countered, sweeping into the foyer ahead of Dash. "How was I to know she was acutely allergic to flowers?"

Dash groaned and released her arm. "Precisely. Which is why you've no place dabbling in such matters—ever," he answered. "I do adore you, but come now. You've behaved so well since the infamous Scott scene. I thought you'd learned your lesson."

"Really, my lord, you haven't a clue as to how the female mind works, do you?" the marchioness answered blithely and patted him reassuringly on the arm.

Lady Mowbray handed her pelisse to a waiting servant and removed her poke bonnet. "Now, I would like to retire to my room. I would prefer to be settled before Miss Barnes arrives so that she might have my full attention. After all, it is my duty as her chaperone to provide instruction and guidance to the girl, is it not?"

Dash groaned a second time as the marchioness handed him the hat.

"We're in agreement, then. Splendid," she replied, clapping her hands together. "Tell me, where is my chamber?"

Dash stared at the bonnet in his hands. "The west wing. Bell will accompany you."

"And Miss Barnes? Will she be housed in the east wing—with you?" Lady Mowbray inquired innocently.

Dash gripped the hat in a death hold and cleared his throat. "Bessie . . ." he said warningly.

"Really, my boy. It's merely that the east wing affords a superior view of the city."

"Go," Dash commanded, pointing to the stairs.

"Yes, I believe I'll retire now," she replied amiably. "Bell, if you please."

Dash watched Lady Mowbray ascend the stairs until she disappeared down the hall to the western half of the house, realizing only after she'd gone that he'd fisted the blasted bonnet into an unrecognizable ball.

"Good God."

2

"You cannot be serious."

Dash stared at Stonecliffe with patent disbelief.

"Oh, but I am," Langdon replied. "When have you ever known me not to be?"

The two friends paused in the anteroom of London's Corinthians Club while a footman took their greatcoats.

It was only two o'clock in the afternoon, but Dash felt certain a drink was in order. "What man would bother wagering on me and Harcourt's spinster daughter? She hasn't even arrived in town yet."

Langdon had provided little information on their way over in the hackney. Apparently, the ton knew of Elena Barnes's imminent arrival. Dash assumed it was the work of Lady Mowbray, part of her grandiose plan to marry the two off.

A matchmaking marchioness *and* a bluestocking under his roof within the span of a handful of hours? Brought to *point non plus*—and by his own doing. Perhaps his mind was not what it once was, after all.

Bluestockings, Dash thought to himself, grimacing. A derisive term for women generally believed to be too learned, if he remembered the definition correctly. He didn't agree, of course. But he had to admit that no one tested his patience more than the few bluestockings he'd met.

"Carrington." Mr. Francis Smeade nodded in greeting as they passed in the oak-paneled hall.

Dash reciprocated with a stiff hello. A very distant relation, Smeade had clawed his way up in the social standings until he perched precariously on a respectable rung. He'd done so by any means necessary and made a number of enemies along the way. Even so, he'd convinced the Corinthian membership to allow him in, the mix of agents and civilians necessary and useful. Dash couldn't be bothered to devote the time required for such strong emotion, so he simply disliked Smeade. Nothing more and nothing less. He pushed the annoying man from his mind and returned to the problem at hand.

"Are you going to answer me or will I have to challenge you?" Dash asked impatiently, following Langdon to the back of the club.

"Ha!" Langdon snorted with marked disdain. Dash couldn't help but chuckle.

Dash's fighting skills were, in a word, unimpressive. He'd trained long and hard to reach the minimum level required by the Corinthians for all members. He possessed the strength to take a man down, but it would not be a pretty fight. He preferred it that way. Physical violence made Dash uncomfortable. And field agents frequently killed enemy operatives. He'd seen death firsthand. And he never wanted to again.

His strength and value to the Corinthians was his mind. Dash detected patterns in the clues that no one else saw. He could crack a code with his eyes closed. Strategize ten steps ahead of the enemy. And keep his wits about him with cool detachment the whole time.

They reached the gaming room and Langdon paused, holding a hand up. "I believe it would be better for you to see for yourself. Come this way."

Dash hadn't a clue what his oldest friend was nattering on about. He brushed past the man and strode into the middle of the room, taking in the scene before him.

Everything looked exactly as it should. True, there weren't as many men present as there would be later in the evening, but Dash could find nothing amiss among the small crowd of lords scattered about the gaming tables playing ecarte and commerce, all fours and casino.

And then his gaze landed on the betting chart hanging on the wall just beyond the vingt-et-un table.

"Is that my name?" he uttered to no one in particular, grinding his teeth. "And Miss Barnes's—in the same sentence containing the word 'marriage'?"

Langdon reached his side. "Quite right. Though, if I may be so bold, it's actually 'marriage/death.'"

"Meaning?"

"Odds are four to one that you'll marry Miss Barnes. And five to one that you'll expire from vexation."

Dash ground his teeth again, his jaw muscles protesting. "It was you, wasn't it?"

Langdon turned to Dash, his expression clouded with confusion. "I beg your pardon?"

"You're the one who proposed the bet involving the onerous bluestocking whom I've met but once, aren't you?" Dash accused.

"Come now, Carrington," Langdon replied with a grin. "I was only having a spot of fun. Besides, we've need of a distraction." He forcibly turned Dash about by the shoulders and gestured toward the cigar room.

Dash was almost afraid to ask what, exactly, his friend was referring to. "And why is that, Stonecliffe?"

He followed Langdon's lead and left the gaming room, his friend remaining silent until they were comfortably settled in deep, leather armchairs and each had chosen a cigar.

"Will there be anything else, my lords?" a liveried servant asked, lighting the fragrant cheroots with a nearby candle.

"That will be all, Jensen—for now, that is," Langdon replied politely. "Do keep a bottle of my special cognac on hand, please."

"Already taken care of, my lord."

"Good man," Langdon said, turning his attention to the cigar.

Jensen bowed and turned away, moving to assist Lord Reese, who'd just arrived.

"Your best cognac? And in the afternoon, Stonecliffe? This must be a piece of news," Dash pressed.

Langdon tilted his head back and blew a large ring of smoke into the air. "Sophia, Carrington. She's determined to pursue the matter."

"By 'matter,' you mean her mother's killer?" Dash asked in a low tone, inhaling the fragrant smoke.

"Precisely," Langdon murmured, looking thoughtfully at his cigar. "Such an exercise is . . ."

Dash could conjure a million words to end Langdon's sentence. Dangerous. Terrifying. Downright heartbreaking. But he kept them to himself, aware his friend would not publicly discuss the more intimate details of the situation. He exhaled, punctuating the air with his own ring. "And what do you propose we do?"

Langdon looked at him for a long while, his eyes bleak. A haze of smoke settled between them before he spoke again. "I haven't a bloody clue."

"Jensen," Dash called out.

The servant hastily made his way to where the two men sat. "Yes, Lord Carrington?"

Dash inhaled deeply, letting the tangy smoke fill his lungs, and then exhaled in one long breath. "We'll take the cognac now."

Jensen nodded and turned to collect the liquor.

"The bottle, if you please, Jensen."

"Of course, my lord."

CARRINGTON HOUSE
LONDON

Dash missed his father.

He sat in the late Lord Carrington's study, toying with a puzzle he'd found on the mahogany desk. The two interlocking keys refused to untangle, no matter how hard he tried. He pulled and prodded at the medieval style pieces, but the puzzle refused to reveal its secret.

He had loved his father deeply. The sole reason Dash had survived the shock and anguish of Lady Afton's death was the late viscount's refusal to give up on his son. And Dash had furnished countless opportunities over the years to relent. Yes, he'd loved his father, and let him in as much as he could. But it had never been enough for the late viscount.

Dash stared hard at the iron keys, but it was his father's face that swam before his eyes.

If he were still alive, the late viscount would have assured Dash the promise he'd made to Carmichael all those years ago was worth keeping.

None of the four had ever discussed the specifics of Lady Afton's case. But the specter had haunted Dash ceaselessly. It had inhabited his nightmares and colored his days until the only peace to be found was in his work.

There, he could become someone else entirely, allowing for little if any substantive, connecting seam between himself and almost everyone in his life. From the beginning, Dash's distinctive features had gotten in the way of his work. It was difficult to blend in, to not be seen or detected, when one drew the attention of every female between London and Scarborough. He wasn't particularly vain about the issue, but there was no point in ignoring the plain and simple facts.

The solution, as it turned out, was obvious enough: play the part. Everyone assumed that men with classic looks were dimwits. So he kept his mouth shut and allowed those who didn't know him to judge him unfairly. Those who really mattered knew the truth, such as Lord Carmichael and Bessie; well, that wasn't exactly true. Lord Carmichael knew the truth. And Bessie? When she'd pressed the point many years back, Dash had convinced her that it was nothing more than a game to him. She'd thought it rather tiresome, but had accepted his reasoning and hadn't questioned his behavior since.

Frustrated, Dash savagely pulled at each cast key, attempting to force them apart.

He'd kept his promise to his superior, all right. But he knew the Afton case by heart now. In between assignments, he'd pored over every last piece of information he could find in the Corinthian files. It hadn't been difficult; the leads and any real facts were few.

Early in his career, Lord Afton had encountered an individual known only as the Bishop. Any information pertaining to the man had long ago vanished from the files, but this much was known: Afton had come close to capturing the man. The Bishop had escaped—with his need for revenge fully intact. He'd bided his time and waited until Afton had let down his guard to strike. Then the Bishop had cut him to the core and murdered Lady Afton.

There had been more murders in the years following. Always a family member of agents who'd encountered the Bishop at some point during their service.

Dash threw the iron keys across the desk and watched as the puzzle skidded to a stop against a crystal paperweight.

It had become harder and harder over the years for Dash to keep his promise—and for the friends to ignore the ever-present specter of Lady Afton.

Nicholas had chosen to travel abroad rather than face yet another Yuletide hazed in regret and haunted memories. He'd stayed away for five years before his recent return, building his fortune in India, according to the few letters he'd written.

Dash drew a deep breath and reached for the puzzle, this time examining each key before moving it. Both bore the typical comb-tooth style bit, but their stems were topped with a fanciful "C" for Carrington.

He understood why Nicholas had chosen to leave. But that didn't make the situation any more tenable, especially for those left behind.

He turned one of the heavy keys clockwise while holding tightly to the other, but they continued to withstand his efforts.

Dash closed his eyes, remembering what his father had always sworn was true of puzzles:

"Deuced counterintuitive, puzzles. The more you think about the problem, the less likely it is that you'll solve it. Just like anything else in life, I suppose. Close your eyes, my boy. Clear your mind, and it will come."

Nicholas's return had brought back an old familiar pang. Dash could not say which was worse—the strange numbness that had settled into his soul during Nicholas's absence, or the deep, enduring ache that plagued his heart when the four were together. He could not remember what it was to feel light. Young. Alive.

It had been too long, Dash admitted, the feel of the metal keys slipping apart in his hands hardly registering in his mind.

Dash opened his eyes and looked down at the keys, one in each of his hands.

Clear your mind, and it will come.

Dash would find the Bishop. He had his answer.

A knock sounded on the panels of the partially open door and Dash looked up.

"Bell, my good man," Dash exclaimed, forcing all thoughts of the case from his mind. "Tell me, if you had to wager on a woman either driving me to marriage or driving me to death, which would you choose?"

The butler stood in the doorway, his face devoid of emotion. "I'm afraid you've lost me, my lord."

Bell had presided over Carrington House for more years than Dash could remember. He was loyal, intelligent, and supremely capable.

More important, he'd been a trusted friend to the late viscount. And while Dash didn't know the man intimately, there was something comforting in his presence.

"Nothing, Bell, nothing at all," Dash assured the man. "Now, what is it you need?"

"Miss Elena Barnes is due to arrive," Bell replied, the parted keys on the desk catching his eye. He paused. Then he blinked slowly and his emotionless gaze returned. "At any moment, my lord."

Dash reached for the two pieces and put them back together. "A puzzle man, are you, Bell?"

"Not in the slightest, my lord. But your father . . ." Bell looked at the floor.

Dash gently returned the keys to the desk. "Father did love a good 'stretch of the brain,' as he was so fond of saying."

Bell swallowed. "Quite right, my lord. Now, Miss Barnes?"

"Yes, of course. Miss Barnes. I suppose I should prepare to . . ." Dash let his words fall off, hopeful that Bell would excuse him from the impending welcome party.

"To meet Miss Barnes, my lord. Exactly," the butler confirmed.

"Exactly," Dash repeated. *Exactly.*

Bell offered him a hint of a smile. "I'll await you in the foyer, my lord."

Dash nodded as he watched the butler leave. "Of course. I'll be right there."

God. Miss Elena Barnes was the last thing he wanted in his life. And for that matter, the last thing he *needed* either. If not for his promise to his father that the books would be given to Lord Harcourt, Dash would have left them as they were.

It was the worst time to have the woman in his home. He couldn't have known that Nicholas's return would spur such action on his part. But Dash had already written to her father by the time he'd heard of his friend having sailed for England.

How was he to honor his father's request *and* get rid of the woman as quickly as possible? A bluestocking? Most of his acquaintance loathed those with a weak mind—especially men. Dash was accustomed to remaining silent and allowing others to assume his intellectual inferiority. But perhaps the situation called for him to play a more active role.

Dash reclaimed the puzzle, smiling as he did so.

He'd have Miss Barnes back in Dorset before her father had time to miss her. He'd bet his life on it.

※ ⚞

"I beg your pardon, Miss, but I think I'm going to be sick."

Elena had reason to take her maid Rowena seriously. The poor girl had already cast up her accounts several times during the three-day ride from Verwood to London. The stops between had done little to ease the agony of Rowena's sour stomach.

"Right," Elena said with brisk reassurance, thumping the roof of the carriage and calling for her father's coachman to stop.

The traveling coach slowed and came to a full stop. Elena turned the brass door handle and pushed hard, forcing it open.

Rowena dove from her well-appointed seat, landing safely on her feet, and vomited into a manicured patch of roses.

Elena rushed out after her, settling a supportive hand at the back of the poor maid's waist. "Oh Rowena, are you all right?"

"Might I be of assistance?"

Something coiled in Elena's stomach at the sound of the rich, deep male drawl. That, or she'd managed to secure Rowena's ailment for herself. "Yes, if you would be so kind," she began, rubbing Rowena's back lightly as she turned to look over her shoulder at the servant.

Only it was not the liveried form of a Carrington house footman that met her gaze. A gentleman stood before her, his clothing of the finest cut and his demeanor rather more lordly than that of a servant. "My lord, I beg your pardon."

Now she remembered precisely who Dashiell Matthews, Viscount Carrington, was.

Adonis, she thought to herself.

Looking at the man was not unlike what Elena assumed mere mortals might experience if encountering the gods. His hair was, quite literally, spun gold. And she'd never been one given to flights of fancy, but his piercing blue eyes and sculpted cheekbones found Elena peering about for signs that they'd taken a wrong turn and somehow ended up on Mt. Olympus.

What is wrong with me?

"For what, Miss Barnes?"

Elena suddenly realized the man was slowly waving his hand in front of her face. "I'm sorry?"

Lord Carrington smiled with easy charm. "You asked that I pardon you. I was simply curious as to the offense."

Oh God, his mouth. His full, full mouth.

She shook her head and strained to take in anything

but the sight of Lord Carrington. "For my maid's . . .
For your rosebush, which will most likely require a serious pruning . . ." Elena paused, realizing belatedly that,
in addition to making no sense at all, she'd also stopped
the carriage short of the home's front door. A perfect
start to what would surely be a perfect stay.

Perfect.

She stared at the servants standing on the broad steps,
all waiting awkwardly to dance attendance on her.

"For the vomit, Lord Carrington," she finally said, de-
ciding the most direct course was more than likely the
best at this point.

Lord Carrington looked at her, his brow clouding
with confusion. "But you've not cast up your accounts,
have you Miss Barnes?"

Ah, yes, it was all coming back to her now. Of course
she'd never been privy to the conversations of the more
desirable debutantes of her day, but Elena had heard
snippets of delicious gossip here and there when the girls
hadn't been aware of her presence.

This man was reputed to be as brainless as he was
beautiful.

Perhaps even more so.

"No, no, I have not, my lord," Elena replied, releasing
Rowena into the care of a footman who'd made his way
down the street.

Elena almost, *almost* wished Lord Carrington had not
opened his mouth.

"Shall we ride to the front door, Miss Barnes?" the
viscount asked, pointing to the carriage's open door.
"Seems a waste, after all. Wouldn't you agree?"

Elena watched as the footman escorted Rowena
toward the waiting servants, reassured by his solicitous
manner, before turning her attention back to Lord Carrington. "In the carriage, then?"

"Of course, Miss Barnes," he replied incredulously.

"I'd hardly ask you to sit astride one of your matching grays."

She peered deep into his blue eyes, searching for intelligence.

And deeper.

And found nothing.

Oh, dear.

Elena sighed. "Actually, if you would not mind ever so much, I do believe I'd prefer walking."

Lord Carrington shrugged his shoulders and gestured toward the house. "Then we shall walk."

The two walked in silence to the waiting servants. Lord Carrington introduced the principal staff in a leisurely manner, finishing with the butler, Mr. Bell.

The man bowed politely. "Miss Barnes, if you would allow me," Bell began in a low, firm tone, "may I make the proper introductions?"

The short, round man looked as uncomfortable as Elena felt.

Lord Carrington laughed. "Hardly necessary, Bell. We met—over there, just a moment ago. Couldn't you see from here?"

Elena looked at Bell with relief. "Yes, Mr. Bell, that would be lovely."

"Miss Elena Barnes, may I present Dashiell Matthews, Viscount Carrington."

Elena dipped into a graceful curtsy, then offered her hand to the viscount.

He executed a dignified bow and took her gloved hand in his, placing a chaste kiss against her knuckles. "A pleasure to make your acquaintance, Miss Barnes," he pronounced, his friendly smile accompanied by a wink.

Elena smiled warmly at the man, much the same way she did every time she encountered Peter Hoskins, a pig farmer who lived not far from Harcourt House. Some years before, Peter had made the unfortunate mistake of coming between a sizeable angry sow and her offspring. He'd never been the same in the head after that, nor would he ever be.

"And I, yours, Lord Carrington," she replied conspiratorially, noting yet again the man's devastatingly handsome looks.

Such a pity, she found herself thinking, though she could not imagine why.

3

Bessie stood just inside the foyer, willing herself to remain still. She cocked her head to the right in an effort to better hear the conversation taking place just on the other side of the viscount's front door. Blast, but Carrington and Miss Elena Barnes were practically whispering. Try as she might, the marchioness could hardly hear a detail of their conversation.

Oh, Dash, she sighed. It was true enough that her past efforts to find him a wife had failed. But it wasn't entirely her fault. The man's irksome habit of hiding his intelligence from the world had done little to help. She knew the truth behind his lie, of course. Lady Afton's death so many years before had made any meaningful connection with others almost beyond his capabilities.

Almost, that was. No, Bessie wasn't the woman to bring him to task. But she'd find the one who was. She loved him too much to accept failure; the memories of her own happy marriage comforted and strengthened the marchioness during dark times. And she longed for Dash to have the support of a loving wife.

Of course he'd mentioned Lady Scott, she reflected wryly. Cheeky boy.

But Miss Barnes's visit offered the chance of a new beginning. True, Bessie had little to go on. Not one of her friends had been able to provide any real information regarding the baron's daughter, other than that the woman was smart. Too smart, most of them commented, arching their brows for emphasis.

The door handle rattled, startling Bessie into action. She spun quickly and scooted toward the staircase, then turned back as though she'd just that moment descended.

Too smart, the marchioness thought. Well, she'd thrown women who were too pretty, too cultured, and too perfect in the viscount's path with no success whatsoever.

Perhaps intelligence would rule the day.

The door opened wide, the bright spring sunshine beaming across the gleaming floors to where Bessie waited.

Miss Elena Barnes crossed the threshold and paused.

But not in that dress, Bessie mentally made note. She was so eager to make Miss Barnes's acquaintance that she found it necessary to purposely slow her steps as she crossed the expanse of marble. She drew nearer and the girl pasted a smile on her face—one she clearly did not feel in either her heart or her head. It wasn't merely fatigue that marred her countenance. Bessie could hardly claim to know her thoughts, but the rise of Miss Barnes's chest as she drew a quick intake of breath indicated what, precisely? Surely not fear?

"My lady." Dash drew Bessie's attention away from Miss Barnes. "May I introduce Miss Elena Barnes?"

The girl dropped into a polite curtsy and bowed her head, giving Bessie an unguarded moment to take in the whole of her. The dress did not improve upon closer inspection, the puce color and ill fit truly a crime of fashion. But the form beneath the drab gown was decidedly spectacular—not unlike Bessie's own at that age. Her hair was a lovely mahogany brown, shot through with hints of gold. Unfortunately, the style brought to mind a terrifying governess Lady Mowbray and her sisters had endured during their childhood.

That governess and her particular hairstyle had met

with a most unfortunate accident involving honey, if Bessie remembered correctly.

Miss Barnes rose slowly and lifted her gaze.

No, Bessie thought with conviction, she'd not cover this woman in honey. But there was a great deal of work to be done. And much of it had nothing to do with frocks or coiffures.

For she was certain that was fear in the younger woman's eyes.

"Miss Barnes, this is Elizabeth Mowbray, Marchioness of Highbury. Lady Mowbray will act as your chaperone during your stay at Carrington House."

Bessie wanted to wrap her arms about the girl and assure her that all would be well. Instead, she acted the ever-respectable marchioness and nodded. "My dear Miss Barnes, it is indeed a pleasure to make your acquaintance. You see, I have no children of my own. I consider it a distinct honor to have such an opportunity. There is so much I would like to teach you."

"The honor is all mine," Miss Barnes replied, the placid smile remaining, though Bessie could have sworn she saw the girl tremble.

"Lady Mowbray, do refrain from frightening Miss Barnes, won't you?" Dash teased as he gestured for Bell to approach. "Bell, see Miss Barnes to her chambers—in the *west* wing," he ordered, his emphasis on the instructions not lost on Bessie.

Miss Barnes bowed her head once again. "Lady Mowbray, I look forward to seeing you at dinner. Viscount Carrington, I'm most eager to tour the library. Perhaps after I've settled in, you'd be so kind as to allow Mr. Bell to show me about the books?"

"Oh, that won't be necessary," Bessie replied before Dash could answer. "The viscount will do the honors."

She bit back a smile as Dash clenched his teeth and nodded in agreement. "I can't claim to know very much about the books, but I would be happy to show you the library, Miss Barnes."

"Very well," Miss Barnes replied. She started up the wide marble staircase after Bell, pausing and turning to look back. "I will return within the hour. And if you'd be so good as to secure some foolscap and a writing instrument, I would be most grateful."

She continued up the stairs, not waiting for Dash's reply.

Bessie looked at Dash, smiling with delight.

"Why are you grinning as though you've just escaped from Bedlam?"

Bessie clapped her hands and nearly crowed. "She's lovely."

"Hmph," Dash grunted in response.

"Oh, she needs a bit of love and care," the marchioness added confidently. "But just wait and see, my boy. Just wait and see."

*

"Rowena?" Elena exclaimed, entering her bed-chamber and closing the door on Bell with relief.

The young maid stood before Elena's open trunk, pursing her lips as she eyed the contents. "I'm afraid your dresses are creased something fierce, Miss."

"I don't care a tuppence about such things—as well you know," Elena replied, walking purposefully to the wan girl's side. "You've need of rest. And tea. A restorative cup of tea is just the thing."

Elena took Rowena's hand and urged her toward a charming pair of upholstered chairs. Pointing to the one closest, she waited until the maid settled onto the peach damask cushion before claiming the second chair.

"Now, tell me, are your quarters suitable?" Elena began. A silver tea service sat atop a low rosewood table. She prepared a delicate china cup with a splash of milk and two lumps of sugar, finishing it off with the aromatic tea.

She handed the cup and saucer to Rowena, ignoring

her friend's squeak of protest. "You're as white as lime-stone, Rowena. The least I can do is ready your tea."

Rowena reluctantly accepted the gently steaming cup and sipped. "Must you always be worried about my comfort, Miss? Shouldn't you be thinking about what dress you'll be changing into?"

Rowena had been abandoned on the steps of Har-court House as a newborn some twenty years before. She was rumored to be the by-blow of a local prostitute and a member of the aristocracy, though Elena's father hadn't bothered to confirm the story. His tender heart had found a child in need and for him, that was enough.

Five-year-old Elena had been instantly smitten with the baby, and her affection for Rowena had only increased over the years, as had Rowena's for her. The two motherless girls had bonded and become fast friends, despite the differences of birth and station in life.

"I'm a bluestocking, Rowena. Defending women's rights is what we do," she chided gently. Rowena's mysterious beginnings had always plagued Elena's mind. What would have become of her dear friend if she'd not been dumped on their doorstep? The possibilities were chilling—and unnecessary. Equality and enlightenment were needed in their world, and Elena wanted more than anything to be a part of accomplishing that goal.

"My room is neat and tidy, just the way I like it," Rowena assured her, adding, "I'm to share with Molly, one of the housemaids. Nice girl, if a touch talkative."

Elena readied her own tea and sank back onto the damask cushions, weary from the long journey. "Is that so?" She gestured invitingly at the plate of cucumber sandwiches.

"No, thank you." Rowena shook her head and took a second fortifying sip of the hot, sugared brew. "Molly went on and on, telling me about all the changes of late. Lord Carrington's only been in residence a short while.

He's nice enough, but keeps to himself. Now Lady Mowbray . . ."

Elena smiled at the twinkle in Rowena's sky-blue eyes. "Yes?"

"Well, *everyone* knows Lady Mowbray—or her story, I should say. She's terribly elegant. Invited to all the right parties and finest balls. How did Molly put it?" Rowena paused, appearing to consider her tea. "Oh, I remember now: 'Lady Mowbray is one of the most influential ladies of the ton.' The whole staff is in a dither over her presence."

Elena returned the rose-patterned cup and saucer to the silver tray, her tea having lost its flavor.

"Oh, and over your arrival, of course, Miss," Rowena added hastily.

"It's not that, Rowena, but bless you for the effort." Elena reached for a sandwich and took a bite, chewing contemplatively before swallowing. Her stomach rolled with worry and a growing anxiousness. "My last chaperone was a celebrated member of the ton, and as you know, that did not end well."

Lady Hastings had been persuaded to sponsor Elena's first season. Baron Harcourt had paid a moderate sum and the influential woman was engaged to take the awkward girl under her wing. Unfortunately, the widowed baroness forgot her duties all too soon, leaving Elena vulnerable to fellow debutantes who seemingly took pleasure in her unschooled ways.

Rowena set her cup and saucer on the tray and stood, her beautiful creamy coloring nearly returned to normal. "That was then, Miss. And this is now," she said firmly. "Have some faith. Lady Mowbray might just surprise you." She walked to the trunk and eyed the garments inside, a gentle huff of displeasure escaping her lips.

Elena sighed deeply. She hated surprises. They didn't

fit into her well-ordered, predictable world. The very word "surprise" made her anxious. "Bite your tongue, Rowena Smith. Bite your tongue."

⁂

Dash drummed his fingers on the arm of the uphol-stered chair as he looked about the library. He'd prom-ised to give Miss Barnes the grand tour of the massive room. Actually, Bessie had offered him up, and then conveniently disappeared upstairs.

He couldn't help but admire the man. *A right good agent Bell would have made,* Dash thought as he studied the room. Literally hundreds of books lined the shelves, the topics they covered as wide as his father's interests—which had been vast, indeed.

Mathematics, religion, astronomy, history—the list went on and on. Dash had always admired his father's thirst for knowledge, but his subsequent love affair with the mountain of volumes before him? That was some-thing Dash had never understood.

Oh, Dash devoured books as voraciously as his fa-ther—if not more, when it came to particular areas of interest. But once he'd read a book, he had no need of it any longer. His mind captured the information so pre-cisely that Dash could conjure up exactly what was printed on any given page at any time.

"How on earth will you be able to part with them?"

Startled, Dash looked to the entry. Miss Barnes stood in the doorway, her curvaceous form framed by the heavy oak molding. She looked at the room with won-der in her eyes.

"Easily," Dash answered, standing and walking to her side.

She nodded in understanding, a small, pitying "Oh," escaping from her lips as she took his arm and allowed him to escort her across the room.

Dash fought the urge to add "because I've read each

and every one—and committed them to memory, no less" but he didn't, of course. To do so would be counterproductive.

And why should he care what she thought of him, anyway?

He led Miss Barnes to the shelves where the books on mythology were housed. "The Greek gods and such live here," he explained in a bored tone, pointing to the volumes. "Well, they don't live here, of course," he added, laughing at the poor joke. "Romulus and Remus and all of that. Father said you were a student of such things. Is that true?"

Miss Barnes patted him gently on the arm before pulling away. "Romulus and Remus were Roman, my lord," she gently corrected. "But yes, it's true, I am a most enthusiastic student of mythology."

Dash watched as she reverently ran her fingers over the volumes, stopping on a deep blue book and carefully easing it from its place.

Of course he knew that Romulus and Remus were Roman. But she'd taken the bait. That was always satisfying when it came to deceiving the bluestockings.

And what a bluestocking she was. Her knot was so severely fastened that Dash wondered if she was actually able to close her eyes. The tension provoked by applying such a number of pins surely caused the skin about her eye sockets pain.

The color of the hair so ruthlessly imprisoned within the torturous style was not precisely muddy brown, as he'd originally estimated so many years before. Actually, it was closer to a rich sable, he realized, with hints of gold intertwined throughout. He decided it would no doubt be stunning if it were ever set loose and allowed to fall naturally about her shoulders.

Intrigued, he continued to study her as she returned

the book to the shelf and walked slowly down the long, carpeted aisle, unaware of his perusal.

Her face was more fetching than he'd given her credit for, her hair color reflected in her eyes. Large and fringed in thick, sooty lashes, they were expressive and quite striking. Her nose was charmingly pert, and her mouth . . . Dash paused at her mouth, noting the movement of full, pink lips as she silently read off the titles of books to herself.

She bent to examine the lower row of books, giving Dash a nice view. Her deliciously curved backside perfectly complemented rounded, firm breasts. An hourglass. A wonderfully proportioned hourglass with the sand in just the right spots.

Dash ignored the flash of heat that suffused him and focused on being annoyed. The chit's hideous dress was what he'd expected of her. Bluestockings were known for being bookish. And yet, he'd never once made the acquaintance of even one who'd ever cracked the covers of *La Belle Assemblée*. No, her unfashionable dress did not surprise him in the least.

But the curves? Now, that was completely unexpected. As were her lush mouth and the silky hair . . .

"Oh!" Miss Barnes exclaimed in a hushed tone, her excited intake of breath pulling Dash from his thoughts.

She rushed toward the end of the aisle, skidding to a halt in front of a glass case situated against the wall.

Dash couldn't help himself. Her enthusiasm was infectious, and he followed.

"Giacomo Paolini's *Abecedary*," Miss Barnes whispered, as though speaking a sacred prayer within the walls of a grand cathedral.

Dash moved closer to the case, studying the book. Its presence was wholly surprising. His father must have acquired the volume shortly before his death. "Have you read it, Miss Barnes?" he asked, breathing in her delicate floral scent as he did so. He couldn't readily identify the flower.

"Hardly," she replied, leaning closer to the case, her brow nearly skimming the glass. "This volume—the only one still in existence, mind you—was lost for years. Your father was incredibly fortunate to find it, my lord."

"Mmh," he replied, distracted. Rose? No, the scent was more complex than that. Lavender? He discreetly breathed deeper, dragging in more of her elusive scent, suddenly desperate to know.

Bergamot.

"Ha," he declared.

Miss Barnes jumped. "I beg your pardon, my lord?" she asked, looking at him as though he were mad.

Really. I'm not the one gushing over an old book.

Dash fought the urge to say the sentence out loud and instead, straightened his crisp cravat. "Funny that, wouldn't you agree? My father found a book that so many could not," he replied, looking at the volume with what he hoped was childlike glee. "Were there many people searching for it?"

"Oh, yes." Her voice brimmed with enthusiasm. "The late Lord Carrington was not the man who actually found the volume, of course. But we can all be thankful he had the foresight to provide such an admirable and efficient home for it. Look here," she gestured at the case. "See how it is perfectly situated away from the sunlight . . ."

Dash hardly heard a word she said. He couldn't pull his gaze away from the fascinating quality of her skin and the flush of color from her cheeks, down the curve of her throat, to the neckline of her dress.

"And the case? Why isn't it stacked with the rest of the books?" he wondered aloud.

He knew *exactly* why, of course. Direct sunlight would compromise the already fragile pages. But he wanted to watch her hands as she talked, gesturing and pointing this way and that, as expressive as the excited cadence of her speech and tone.

Dash wondered why he was noticing her hands. They were, after all, only hands. She possessed a pair just as nearly every other human being on the planet did.

What was he doing? He wasn't supposed to be interested in Miss Barnes. He just needed her to pack up the books and go back to Dorset, as soon as possible.

"Fascinating stuff," he interrupted her careful explanation, needing to be anywhere but next to Miss Barnes. "But I'm afraid I must be off. I'll leave you to your books."

She smiled at him shyly. "Of course, my lord. This must all be terribly boring to you," she replied, curtsying.

Dash bowed and turned to go.

"Thank you, my lord," she added. "You've no idea what these books mean to me—and my father, of course."

Dash paused, but did not turn around, fearful that she'd draw him back. "Oh, don't thank me, Miss Barnes. It's all my father's doing."

It was the truth, after all. Though Dash was having a hard time being thankful to his father for anything at the moment.

"I look forward to seeing you at dinner, my lord."

The woman could not bear to relinquish the last word. "Yes, Miss," he replied.

"Excellent."

Christ Almighty.

4

Elena was late to dinner. She'd been absorbed in her thoughts when Rowena had found her in the library. Earlier, she'd watched the viscount disappear through the doorway and sighed, only then realizing she'd been holding her breath. She'd pressed her hand to her bodice, right over the rapid beat of her heart, and frowned.

Elena didn't want to find the man attractive. As she'd explained the dangerous relationship between rare books and sunlight, her traitorous skin had blushed at his intent stare, a curious sense of pleasure lightening her limbs.

But then he'd abruptly left.

Elena knew Lord Carrington was quite the catch even if he was stupid. While she, though highly intelligent, was not.

She'd attributed the ridiculous notion to fatigue by the time she'd reached her room and found there was little time to change. As for fashioning her hair into a chignon or applying the rouge Rowena had begged her to purchase for the trip? It could not be done. And so she was late, quite possibly looking worse than she had upon her arrival at Carrington House.

And she'd smelled of vomit then.

Perfect.

Lady Mowbray smoothed her silken silver hair and took in Elena with a lively smile. "My dear, have you

any sisters?" she inquired, her feathered brows punctuating the question with a charming arch.

Elena mentally ordered herself to sit up straight and
quietly cleared her throat. "I'm afraid I cannot claim
siblings, unfortunately. I am my father's only child."

"Lucky girl," the marchioness sighed, her eyes soften-
ing as she appeared to contemplate such a singular state.

"You'll have to excuse the marchioness, Miss Barnes,"
the viscount said, cutting his slice of perfectly roasted
ham. "You see, her sisters—and Lady Mowbray, I may
add," he continued, aiming a vacuous grin at the marchioness, "are known about town as the Furies. They're
quite a force of nature, those three. Perhaps you've
heard of the trio?"

Elena shook her head and casually took a small sip
of claret. "No, I'm afraid the sobriquet does not sound
familiar."

"I knew I would like you," Lady Mowbray said with
happy conviction, sending a superior smile toward the
viscount. "You see, not *everyone* knows us as such."

Elena hesitantly allowed herself to appreciate Lady
Mowbray's comment. She set the crystal goblet beside
her plate and watched as the viscount acknowledged the
woman's victory with a smile and a good-natured shrug
of his wide shoulders. "Though I do live in Dorset, alone
with my aged father, on a vast estate," she added, suddenly feeling bold. "News from town nearly always
misses our isolated corner of the country, you see."

The viscount let out a bark of laughter and his eyes lit
with amused approval. "I believe I like you as well, Miss
Barnes."

Lady Mowbray's eyes grew round and she looked at
Elena with mock horror. "Why, Miss Barnes, I like you
even more now." Her peal of laughter could only be described as utterly charming.

Elena smiled a true, unaffected smile. She was quite

unexpectedly pleased. She had, of course, anticipated the worst from her chaperone. Not that all of the ton's matrons could possibly be as horrible as Lady Hastings had been.

But a marchioness? Well, Lady Mowbray's rank alone entitled her to treat Elena just as she pleased. Elena had expected minimal courtesy and politeness. She'd decided the resulting awkwardness and discomfort would be a small price to pay for the books, but she hadn't looked forward to the necessary social interaction with her host and chaperone. This conversation was making her question her assumptions.

"Now, my dear," Lady Mowbray began, winking conspiratorially at Elena. "What shall we do with you while you're in town? You've come at the perfect time, of course, with the season only beginning. But we must narrow the possibilities."

"Oh, no," Elena and the viscount said in unison, startling the marchioness.

"That is," the viscount continued, allowing a footman to clear his plate, "Miss Barnes has no interest beyond the books. Isn't that right?"

Elena looked at Lady Mowbray, whose disbelief was obvious in her expression.

She fidgeted with the lace overlay skirt of her jonquil silk gown, rubbing the fabric between her forefinger and thumb under the cover of the table. "Lady Mowbray, your thoughtfulness is most appreciated. But I'm afraid the viscount is correct. I must go home as soon as possible. My father is terribly anxious for me to return."

"But, surely a ball or two—"

"She hardly has the time for such plaguey things," the viscount interrupted, drumming his fingers on the heavy table.

"A musicale?" the woman offered hopefully, looking to Elena for agreement.

"The books, Lady Mowbray, require my full attention," Elena said with what she hoped was the right amount of regret.

The marchioness smiled in understanding, putting Elena's concerns to rest.

"I simply won't hear of such a thing."

Taken aback, Elena stared at the woman, as though she'd uttered the most deplorable of curses. "I'm sorry, my lady?"

"Come now, Lady Mowbray," the viscount muttered in a low tone, his fingers going still. "She wants nothing to do with your demmed social fluttering. Why won't you leave her be?"

"Have I ever, in your memory, let anything 'be,' my dear boy?" Lady Mowbray replied, giving the viscount a chastening look.

Lord Carrington let out an exasperated sigh. And his fingers began to tap once more in an impatient tattoo.

Elena thought longingly of the library. She was sure she heard the books calling to her.

"Now," the marchioness continued. "As your chaperone, it is my duty to ensure your general well-being. Obviously, one's social calendar is directly tied to this, yes?"

She considered protesting. But Lady Mowbray was so determined. And, Elena admitted with some regret, if she carried on, the marchioness would likely only require her to attend even more events.

Elena continued to worry the fabric of her skirt, an idea forming as she did so.

"Of course," Elena ceded carefully, "though I've very little in the way of fashionable attire, as you can see." She gestured at her gown. "Therefore, I can only commit to three outings, my lady. I'm sure you understand."

Lady Mowbray nodded solemnly. "My dear, a woman should never miss an opportunity simply because she does not possess a suitable gown. Therefore, I'll make an appointment with my modiste in the morning. The woman is an absolute wizard. She should be able to quickly create enough gowns for at least ten outings."

"Splendid," Elena muttered with feigned enthusiasm. She hadn't seen that coming.

She raised her glass to her lips and drank deeply, sensing that fortification would be in order.

Bloody books. Dash strolled the aisles of the library, the early morning sun illuminating the titles as he lazily ran his forefinger along the spines.

Bloody bluestocking, he mentally corrected himself, picking a volume randomly from the shelf and pulling it down. He opened it and leafed through the pages absentmindedly. The last six months had been difficult, with rarely a free moment. There'd been his father's death to deal with, then his move to Carrington House, and adjusting to the demands of his title. And of course his work with the Corinthians as well. All good reasons for Dash having failed to realize what a loss his father's books would be to him.

Then Miss Barnes had innocently posed a question. "How on earth will you be able to part with them?" she'd asked.

And now here Dash was, sentimentally fondling books as if doing so would somehow ease the pain of missing the old man. His father wasn't in the books. But they were a part of him, just as his heart and liver, lungs and brain had been.

"Bloody, bloody bluestocking," Dash muttered, his curse becoming an inquiry as he gazed down the end of the aisle to where the room ended and an alcove began. Its brocade curtains were pulled tight and a small object sat on the floor to the left of where the two fabric panels met. As Dash drew closer he realized it was a woman's shoe. Suddenly, a slender foot appeared beneath the left curtain. It pointed and then arched, as though the owner were relieving a touch of stiffness.

"You really do wear blue stockings," Dash exclaimed, ridiculously delighted by the discovery.

A squawk of dismay sounded from behind the brocade and the foot disappeared.

Dash waited for the woman to part the curtains.

And waited.

"I know you're there," he called out.

"I know that you know that . . ." Miss Barnes replied, a heavy sigh stealing the remainder of her words. "Really, my lord. Could we not both pretend otherwise?"

God, he'd embarrassed her. He'd awoken annoyed with the woman and now? Well, now he had to make things right. Blast, but living with women in the house was burdensome.

Dash closed the distance to the alcove. He reached out and brushed the brocade curtain three times.

"What on earth are you doing?" Miss Barnes asked quizzically, the curtain still firmly in place.

"May I come in?"

Dash heard an "oh" of understanding, then the swish of skirts before the curtain was slowly pulled back.

And there she was. Miss Barnes sat with her back propped against the wall of the alcove, her legs tucked beneath her and a book lying open on her lap.

"Good morning, Miss Barnes." Dash eyed her before taking a seat at the opposite end of the cushioned bench. "You're up quite early."

Miss Barnes gave him a nervous smile. "I'm from the country, Lord Carrington. We are accustomed to such things."

She smoothed a stray lock of hair behind her ear and cleared her throat. "And you? I was led to believe native Londoners never rose to meet the morning sun."

"True enough," Dash replied, his earlier vexation

with Miss Barnes dissipating. "Though you should know I've spent a fair amount of time in the country myself."

Miss Barnes leaned forward and closed her book, propping it against the window. "Is that so? What part?"

"Sussex. As a child I spent every summer there with my father," Dash replied, finding himself inexplicably angling forward as well. "It was idyllic, Miss Barnes. Bright, sunny days that seemed to go on forever. Starry midnight jaunts about the grounds. My friends and I, well, I suppose we were nothing more than young wild animals," he finished, an odd sense of embarrassment settling in his chest.

"It sounds utterly perfect," she replied, understanding in her voice. "And very much like my childhood in Dorset, though I know you'll find it hard to believe."

"But you're a woman," Dash countered without thinking. The realization that it was exceedingly easy to appear witless in front of Miss Barnes was not lost on him.

Her shoulders relaxed and an effortless smile lit her face, all nervousness gone. "Yes, my lord. But my mother died in childbirth. And after my fourth nanny resigned over a frog's mysterious appearance in her soup, my father left me to my own devices."

Dash slapped his knee in approval. "Miss Barnes, you are a *surprise*!"

She tensed and suddenly scooted back until she leaned once more against the wall, folding both arms across her bodice. "I don't know about that, my lord. But tell me, when were you last in Sussex?"

Dash stared at her, nonplussed at the abrupt return to wary reserve and desperate to discern what he'd done wrong. "Not for fifteen years."

"Why would you take so long to return?" she continued, her face revealing no hint as to what he'd done to offend her. Her voice was cool; her expression held only polite interest.

"A family tragedy, Miss Barnes. A dear friend's mother was killed," Dash began, still distracted by the loss of her earlier friendly warmth and unaware of what he revealed. "Too many memories in Sussex."

Miss Barnes's stiff politeness evaporated. She unfolded her arms and reached out as though she thought to take his hands, and her eyes filled with concern. "I am sorry, my lord. I should not have pried."

Dash leaned in farther, desperately wanting to take her hands in his, but reason forcing him not to.

God, what was he doing? This wasn't like him. Not at all.

He abruptly stood, pushing the brocade panels wider to fully reveal the world once more.

The sound of the brass curtain rings sliding against the rod startled Miss Barnes and she straightened.

"No need to apologize, Miss Barnes," Dash reassured her, his words clipped. "What is in the past is just that— the past."

She reclaimed her book and opened it, laying one palm flat against the smooth pages. "Of course, my lord. Good day."

Dash realized that having stood, he should move, preferably soon. "And good day to you, too, Miss Barnes," he replied, turning from the alcove and retracing his steps out of the library.

≈ ✻

The encounter with Lord Carrington in the alcove had left Elena with the oddest sensation, as though something of significance had happened. What that "something" was, she hadn't been able to identify. She'd eaten her breakfast, drank more tea than any one person should, and still the situation had continued to mystify her.

She'd decided she needed fresh air and a bit of exercise to clear her mind and set out with her maid for a walk.

"Londoners truly call this a park, then?" Rowena asked disbelievingly, holding up one hand and counting off one finger at a time. "Miss, I can count the trees standing—might need my toes to do it, but still."

Elena bit her lip to keep from laughing at her friend's exaggerated country accent and turned to take in Blooms-bury Square. Rowena was right—the quaint, tidy square of green couldn't hold a candle to Dorset's lush fields and wide, welcoming lanes. But it did afford Elena the opportunity to get away from Carrington House and think—even if doing so meant walking the entire park five times around.

"How do city people stretch their legs, then?" Rowena asked, hurrying to keep up with Elena.

"Well, perhaps *they* don't feel the need to do so," Elena answered, though she couldn't imagine such a thing. Without a good walk, Elena wouldn't be able to make sense of her multitude of tangled thoughts.

Such as when Lord Carrington had called her a "surprise" in the alcove. The word had startled her from the comfortable intimacy their childhood revelations had created and forced her to remember just who she was and why she was there.

Elena was a woman who hated surprises. She was in the viscount's home to see to his father's books. And that was all.

Then why was she still bewildered by the interlude?

"Or perhaps they don't worry quite as much as you."

Elena slumped momentarily against her friend, sighing when Rowena looped an arm about her waist and squeezed gently. She couldn't share her feelings regarding the viscount, not yet. But she couldn't lie. Luckily, there were a multitude of concerns on her mind. "Well, it involves Lady Mowbray. And anything having to do with a marchioness is quite worry-worthy, wouldn't you agree?"

"Is that even proper English, Miss? 'Worry-worthy?' It *must* be awful. Tell me, what has you so upset?"

Elena slowed her steps, the sound of Rowena's voice soothing her jangled nerves. "She's insisted that I attend a number of social events while we're in town."

"Heavens, that *is* the end of the world," Rowena teased, nudging Elena with her elbow. "You're not fresh from the schoolroom, Miss. You're older. And wiser."

Elena returned the favor and looped an arm through hers. "Older, anyway."

"What does the mistress of Harcourt House have to fear from these London swells? Don't forget who you are and how far you've come. Not now," her friend pleaded, resting her head on Elena's shoulder for a brief moment. "I believe in you."

"You are the dearest girl. Have I told you that?" Elena replied, her confidence bolstered by Rowena's words.

"Not today, no," Rowena answered distractedly, looking ahead as a gentleman approached.

Elena eyed the man critically as he drew closer. He was fashionably dressed in buff breeches and a deep blue waistcoat, his Hessian boots polished expertly and his snowy white cravat perfectly tied. A thin, white scar marred an otherwise ideal face. He was one of the most beautiful men she'd ever laid eyes on. And yet, there was something in his swagger, or perhaps his overly expressive eyes, that made Elena uneasy.

He fastened his gaze on Rowena and his lips curled into a predatory smile. Elena pulled her friend protectively closer and quickened their pace.

"Miss," Rowena begged, trying to put some distance

between them. "I can hardly walk without stepping on your skirts."

Elena patted her hand. "Never mind my skirts, Rowena."

The man was nearly upon them now. "Goodness," Rowena sighed, clearly having forgotten all about Elena's skirts.

"No, no! Not 'goodness,' Rowena," Elena admonished, the unsettling feeling inspired by the man only growing as he purposefully stepped directly in their path and bowed.

"Ladies." He smiled brilliantly. "A beautiful day, is it not?"

"Goodness," Elena muttered disgustedly.

Rowena squeezed Elena's arm and giggled.

"It is indeed, your . . ." Elena paused, as though searching for the correct address. "Well, I hardly know what to call you—which is why I find proper introductions to be infinitely useful in such situations, don't you?"

Somehow, the man managed an even bolder grin, eliciting a second giggle from Rowena. "You are correct, madam. But wouldn't you agree there are times when one simply cannot wait on propriety?" he countered, winking at Rowena.

"No, I would not," Elena replied succinctly, not even bothering to curtsy before dragging Rowena around the man and down the path.

Rowena looked over her shoulder and giggled again. "He's still staring after us, Miss," she said breathlessly.

"Let him stare," Elena said, her voice quivering from the encounter. "But a lady? Never."

Rowena obediently turned her head and focused on the path. "He was quite handsome, wasn't he?"

"Rowena, you must understand that men, no matter how handsome or charming, are dangerous—in one way or another."

The girl frowned. "Even Viscount Carrington? Because, to be perfectly honest, Miss, he doesn't seem smart enough to cause anyone trouble."

"Yes, especially Viscount Carrington—he's too dim to realize just how dangerous he is. And that makes him doubly dangerous," Elena replied earnestly.

She steered Rowena toward a bench and sat, relaxing at the feel of the sun on her skin.

"Well," Rowena began, settling in next to her. "If there's one thing I mean to look out for, it's men who are—"

"Dangerous," they said in unison, with the full and proper seriousness that the statement deserved. And then they collapsed against each other and laughed until their sides ached from the effort.

5

Dash had fled for an auction at Tattersalls after encountering Miss Barnes in the library alcove. Once there, he'd helped Langdon choose a chestnut Thoroughbred and purchased a bay gelding for himself. The friends had then found their way to the club, where Dash had been ever since.

Shifting in the straight-backed wooden chair, Dash stretched his legs out beneath the oaken desk. He turned his head from left to right, then again, attempting to ease the muscles aching from the strain of too many hours bent over the Afton case notes.

He'd read through the creased, worn papers so many times he'd lost count, hoping to find some clue he'd overlooked, although he had long ago memorized every single word.

Sounds from the floor above, within the Young Corinthians' club, drifted down to the rabbit warren of hidden rooms that comprised the organization's headquarters. Dash glanced at the candelabra set before him on the desk. The beeswax tapers had burned down to nubs, warning him the hour was late.

He closed his tired eyes and rubbed his temples. Miss Barnes was not what he'd expected—at least not entirely. Oh, she was certainly a bluestocking. But she was decidedly lacking in any of the superior airs that experience had taught him most women of her ilk normally displayed proudly.

She seemed quite willing to accept his intellectual inferiority with nervous grace and patience, which was a start.

He opened his eyes, staring impatiently at the flickering light from the candles. It was only the first day, he reminded himself.

Despite his appearance and place in society, the perception by the ton that he was one step above a dunce allowed him to be disregarded and thus, nearly invisible. This made him all the more valuable as an agent.

But Miss Barnes had *seen* him in the alcove. She'd unearthed a piece of Dash so intrinsically tied to his soul that he'd shuddered at his own vulnerability. And in turn, she'd blossomed before his eyes, only to close up once more for reasons only she understood. The encounter had left him breathless. Confused. And worse, distracted.

He held his forefinger above the candle's flame, lowering it, then raising it higher as the heat intensified.

"Do be careful with that candle, Carrington," a familiar voice commanded simply. "I'd hate for you to compromise your skills with a lock."

Dash looked up. Henry Prescott, Viscount Carmichael, had entered the shadowed room. Arms crossed, the older man leaned one shoulder against the wall, clearly at ease. "Please, Carmichael, I could take the crown jewels with my teeth," he answered with a dismissive shrug, abandoning the casual game with the flame.

"True enough, but I'd rather you not," the Corinthian handler answered, moving toward a well-worn leather chair. He settled his tall, wiry frame into the seat, his gaze fixed on Dash with unnerving intensity.

Dash gathered the sheaf of papers in front of him and smoothly slid them to the far corner of the desktop.

"What brings you to the records room so late? How many guineas did Williams fleece you for this evening?"

"I lost one time, Carrington. And the man cheated, I'm sure of it," Carmichael answered, his shrewd blue eyes sparkling with amusement. "And you? Not poring over the Afton papers again, are you?" he asked, though he certainly didn't have to. Carmichael was subtle in everything, but clear. He was disappointed and Dash knew it.

Dash slumped back comfortably and rested his elbows on the chair arms. "Well, unlike you, I made a small fortune off of Williams this evening. And when that became tedious, I wandered down here out of sheer boredom. Better this than to return home to Miss Barnes and the marchioness. They've overtaken the place, I tell you. Next thing I know, my room will be filled with tasseled silk pillows, fashion magazines, and Sèvres vases full of sweet-smelling flowers."

Carmichael smiled. "Lady Mowbray?"

"Precisely."

His superior shuddered slightly. "Well, that makes sense. But this Miss Barnes? Surely she's no match for your charm?"

"Harcourt's daughter. Do you know her?" Dash asked, hopeful that Carmichael's interest was piqued.

The other man frowned as he considered the name. "I haven't seen Harcourt in years. And I don't remember a thing about the daughter. Her mother died giving birth to her, I believe. But that's all I can recall."

"You're not the only one," Dash replied. "The chit spent very little time in town—just enough, from what I understand, for one miserable season. The poor thing didn't take at all. Then she returned to her father's estate in Dorset, never to be heard from again. Until now."

Carmichael nodded. "And how did she find her way

to your home? Seems a strange destination for the woman."

"Her presence is due to my father, I'm afraid. Willed his library to Harcourt," Dash answered flatly. "Not that I've any use for the books—read them already. But just how long do you suppose it will take a lady to pack up hundreds of rare and valuable volumes? One week? Perhaps two? Please tell me less than three."

"Having a lady in your home is quite dreadful, then?" Carmichael asked, his subtle sarcasm not lost on Dash.

"Quite," he said with emphasis. "And she's a blue-stocking to boot."

"Ah," Carmichael nodded in understanding. "No wonder you're wasting time down here—and on a case you've been ordered to stay away from. I could almost understand why you'd break protocol—almost, that is."

Any Corinthian worth his salt knew that when Carmichael used such a tone, you listened. "Just a bit of reading, is all."

"You know as well as I that the Afton case could never be 'just' anything to you—which is why you're not allowed near it," Carmichael replied, folding his arms across his chest. "You're a smart man, Carrington. I shouldn't have to repeat myself."

"I could say the same for you, Carmichael," Dash replied lightly, regretting the flippant comment immediately.

Carmichael toyed with the gold signet ring on his left hand. "You've seen him then?"

"Seen whom?" Dash asked, puzzled.

"Stonecliffe's brother."

Of course Carmichael would know of Bourne's return. But why he had to be so damn perceptive *all* of the time, Dash couldn't fathom. "Why do you ask?"

"Don't play coy with me, Carrington. Remember, I've known you far too long for such ploys to work. The four of you, together again? Won't be easy, I imagine. You must find a way to move on. One that doesn't include chasing after ghosts."

Dash stared down at the papers, the memory of Lady Afton's lifeless body flashing before him. "And you? Did you find your way?"

"In a manner of speaking, yes," Carmichael confirmed, standing from the chair. "Now, join me upstairs for a drink?"

Carmichael didn't understand. And Dash could accept this fact. But he wouldn't turn back now.

He placed both hands on the desk and pushed himself up. "Yes, I believe I will."

Elena rushed down the hallway to the accompaniment of the hall clock chiming the dinner hour. She stopped just short of the dining room and smoothed out the skirt of her hunter-green gown. The feel of the silk as she slid her fingers along it soothed her. She rolled her shoulders back, forced a pleasant smile, and proceeded into the room.

Only to discover Viscount Carrington was absent.

"Miss Barnes," Lady Mowbray exclaimed, waving her hand elegantly in the air. "Do come and sit next to me. Lord Carrington is at his club, so it is only us women this evening."

Elena walked the length of the Elizabethan table, attempting to make sense of her disappointment. She should have been relieved by the viscount's absence, considering that she'd yet to puzzle out just what, exactly, had taken place in the alcove that morning.

She waited patiently while a footman pulled out her chair, and then sat down, absently picking up the embroidered serviette and placing it on her lap.

Was it truly disappointment she felt? And if it was, why?

A delectable treacle sponge pudding was placed in front of Elena. She stared at it, utterly confused.

"It won't bite, my dear," the marchioness assured her.

Elena looked to Lady Mowbray for an explanation.

"Life is short, Miss Barnes," the marchioness said, taking up her silver spoon. "Whenever I am able, I begin each meal at the very end. Then I work my way back to the necessary bits. I suppose some would find this odd."

"I think it's terribly brilliant," Elena replied honestly, reaching for her own spoon and dipping it into the decadent dessert.

"Good," Lady Mowbray confirmed happily.

Elena brought the spoon to her lips and took a bite: the sweet treacle-soaked sponge seemed to melt on her tongue, delighting her senses.

"Now, tell me about your first season, my dear. I want to know precisely what happened."

Elena swallowed hard, the sponge pudding suddenly dry and tasteless. "With all due respect, Lady Mowbray, I don't see how that information could be of use. To anyone."

Her shoulders tensed of their own accord and her stomach rolled uneasily. Did the marchioness expect Elena would regale her with the humiliating tale simply to amuse her?

"Miss Barnes," the marchioness countered, setting her spoon down and looking at Elena with concern. "It is of great use to me, I assure you. How else am I to avoid repeating whatever disasters occurred that sent you running back to Dorset? You'll not fail a second time, my dear. Not with me as your chaperone." Her firm nod and determined expression clearly conveyed her conviction.

"Oh," Elena murmured, suddenly ashamed that she'd assumed the worst of the woman. "Well, I don't know that there was one instance in particular, my lady. But this," she paused and gestured to her hair, then her face, and finally her body, "did not help matters."

The woman was a marchioness, and apparently a kind one at that. Surely she'd politely avoid Elena's revelation and that would be the end of it.

"Am I to assume you believe yourself to be at fault?"

Or nearly the end of it.

"Obviously," Elena answered, lifting a second bite of pudding to her mouth and forcing herself to chew.

Lady Mowbray continued to stare at her. "I'll not lie, as it would only be a waste of my time and yours. Your gowns number among some of the most unfortunate I've ever set eyes on. And your hair? Well, it's glorious, but the coiffure is not. Tell me, who sponsored your season?"

"Lady Hastings," Elena managed to get out around the bite of sponge.

Lady Mowbray rolled her eyes in response. "Well, that explains quite a lot. Lady Hastings is atrocious. You're a beautiful woman with an impressive mind and a quick wit. It's all there, underneath the lamentable packaging. And now you have me. So there is nothing to fear, my dear. Nothing at all."

Elena wanted desperately to believe the woman. But she'd have to believe in herself first—in a way she'd never managed before.

"You look skeptical, Miss Barnes," the marchioness noted, taking a bite of her pudding and pausing to savor it. "What if we made a wager?"

Wagers always ended badly in books. In fact, Elena had never read a single volume involving a wager where tragedy had not struck the poor, unsuspecting mortal a mighty blow.

Still, she was curious. "What might you have in mind, Lady Mowbray?"

"My lord."

Dash swung about at the unexpected sound of Bell's voice. "Bell, I've just arrived home from the club, which explains my being awake at such a late hour. But surely you should be abed by now?"

The butler's hair was slightly mussed and his eyes bleary, as though he'd just been roused from sleep. "My lord, Cook sent for me. If there's anything that you require?"

Dash looked over the butler's shoulder, but the round, gray-haired cook was nowhere to be found. "Cook?"

"The woman has the uncanny ability to sense when someone is in her kitchen. I don't know how she does it. But she does—with regularity," Bell explained.

Dash turned back to the milk he'd poured into a tankard and added the almonds, egg white, brandy, and rum. "Just making myself a posset, Bell. Care for some?"

He walked to the fireplace and reached for the poker whose end rested in the low, glowing embers. Holding the tankard waist-high, he slowly lowered the tip of the poker into it, a satisfying hissing emitting from the fragrant brew.

Bell retrieved a wooden spoon and gestured for the tankard. "No thank you, my lord."

Dash handed the tankard over and returned the poker to the fireplace. "My father used to make this very posset for me when I was a child."

"And for himself, my lord," Bell replied fondly, sleep clearly having lowered his guard. He joined Dash at the table and began to beat the ingredients together with the spoon. When a foamy froth appeared at the top, he pulled the spoon from the tankard and gave it back to Dash.

Dash leaned against the table and took a sip, the

hot, creamy drink sliding easily down his throat. "Did he now?"

"Oh yes, many times," the butler confirmed with a hint of a smile. "You were very much alike, you know. Always with too much on your minds to sleep."

"Is that so?" Dash pressed. Talking about his father was strangely comforting after the long day he'd endured.

Bell carried the spoon to the scullery and returned. "Yes, my lord. You remind me very much of the late viscount."

"Well, let us hope I can live up to the old man's example," Dash answered, his words surprising Bell—and himself.

Bell turned back to Dash. "My lord, there isn't a doubt in my mind that you will. Nor was there in your father's. He told me so himself." The butler folded his hands together. "Now, if there's nothing else, my lord, I'll return to bed."

"Of course, Bell. Good night," Dash replied, watching the man's retreating form until he disappeared.

He took another slow drink of the posset and inhaled the heady almond aroma. They'd never discussed such things, Dash and his father. It hadn't occurred to Dash to do so, nor obviously to the late viscount.

So why did Bell's words hold so much weight with him now? Why was Dash turning soft at precisely the moment that he needed to be strong?

He drained the tankard and set it in the sink, wiping away a trace of froth on his upper lip. He'd let the drink work its magic, claim a good night's rest, and return to the Dash he knew and understood in the morning.

All would be right in the morning.

6

Elena lay in her bed, listening to the night noises floating up from the streets below. The clip-clop of horses' hooves and the roll of carriage wheels did little to distract her from Lady Mowbray's proposition. If Elena agreed to give herself over entirely to the marchioness and attend the selected events with "marked enthusiasm," she would be allowed to accompany Lady Mowbray to the Halcyon Society. The group had been organized to rescue women from prostitution and was known for its progressive techniques, even to those as far afield as Dorset.

Elena had long dreamed of providing such a service to her community. And Lady Mowbray's connections to the charity could make it all come true.

Despite her initial reservations, Elena had discovered she rather liked the marchioness. She was as demanding and, Elena felt sure, as difficult as any other woman of her rank. But she was kind, too, and in possession of a warm, sympathetic heart—very unlike her fellow matrons who had made Elena's debut season so painful. No, she was no longer afraid of Lady Mowbray.

But the viscount?

The very thought of the man made Elena's head buzz. She quickly jumped out of bed and donned a dove-gray linen wrapper over her plain night rail. She slid her bare feet into a pair of soft felt slippers and tipped a single candlestick into the remains of the fire, waiting until the wick burned to life. She stared at the orange flame, watching it twist and sway against the enveloping darkness. It was mesmerizing, the flame's rhythmic movements almost making her forget why she'd flown from her bed to begin with.

Almost.

An hour or two in the library would put her mind right.

Elena laid her palm against the door, its coldness on her skin broke the fire's trance. She proceeded to make her way downstairs. Slowly. And with great difficulty.

Elena's sense of direction could be called "limited." She wasn't bothered by her shortcoming—well, not severely so. But she was rather glad that she was alone.

"*Drat,*" she grumbled as she traversed the west wing's main hall.

This was hardly helping matters. At home in Verwood, Elena knew every shop and every street corner. At Harcourt House, she could find any room with her eyes closed.

But here? In London? Elena didn't know up from down—both literally and figuratively.

Elena spied a portrait of three superior-looking spaniels that were poised on a puce cushion, looking, to her way of thinking, as though they were readying to relieve themselves. She'd passed that very same painting before—mere minutes before, unfortunately. Surely there could not be another portrait of spaniels in need of relief, could there?

No. No one would make the mistake of purchasing two such paintings. Not even the viscount.

Blast, why was the man plaguing her mind so?

Annoyed, she turned, holding the candle aloft and marching back down the hall. In Dorset, everything was in its place—including Elena. But here, in Carrington

House . . . Well, Elena didn't even know how to finish the thought. What was she doing?

The stone floor, between the Persian runners that appeared intermittently, chilled Elena's slipper-shod feet. She gritted her teeth and picked up the pace, quickly arriving at an impasse. She'd thought for sure that continuing on in a straight line would bring her to the staircase, but her path had ended abruptly with the unfortunate appearance of a wall directly in front of her.

Right or left? Elena could feel her heart begin to race. A lightness threatened to overtake her head, and her cheeks burned.

Two days in the capitol city and she'd been reduced to wandering the halls at night, thinking on a man, of all things. A man most assuredly her intellectual inferior. And yet, a man whose heart mysteriously spoke to hers.

This was madness.

Elena resolutely turned right and proceeded down the darkened hall, the sight of the staircase buoying her courage. She confidently descended the stairs, her head held high. Reaching the marble foyer she stopped for a moment, closed her eyes, and concentrated. At least she'd had the good sense to memorize which door led to the library. She opened her eyes, proceeded to the front door, then turned, as though she'd just arrived inside. She looked to the right, counting the rooms until she came to the third entryway.

She tightened the silk sash at her waist and strode toward the spot, careful to take note of the portraits on the walls so she could find her way back to the stairs once finished with her work.

No portraits of spaniels this time, only long-faced relatives and tasteful country scenes. At the end of the hall she spied a large portrait, the candlelight seemingly drawn toward it. Unable to resist, Elena passed the third door and continued down the hall.

Closer now, she held the candle aloft and examined the portrait. The subject was the viscount, standing next to a large bay horse. One hand rested gently on the beautiful bay's neck while the other was held loosely near his waist.

Elena stood on tiptoe and moved closer, peering at his friendly smile. "You really must leave me be," she paused, wondering just what one could expect from a portrait, then whispered, "please."

"Why are you talking to the painting, Miss Barnes?"

The richly timbered voice caught Elena by surprise and she wheeled around, nearly igniting the viscount's coat with her candle. "Don't be absurd, my lord," she replied with false confidence. "I was merely noting the fine brushwork—aloud, yes. But to myself."

He reached out and gently caught her shoulders, steadying her. "Pity, that."

"And why might that be?" Elena asked, trying to ignore the warmth and feel of his hands on her.

The viscount released her and stepped back, turning on his heels and walking a few paces to stand in front of a portrait just to the left of the library entrance. "Well, you see, I talk to the paintings and had rather hoped I wasn't the only one."

"Are you toying with me, my lord?" Elena asked warily, joining him.

The viscount held up the candelabra in his hand and it bathed the portrait in light, revealing a stunning young woman. "My mother, Miss Barnes. She was beautiful, wouldn't you agree?"

She'd miscalculated the distance and now stood too close to him, the heady, masculine scent of sandalwood weakening her knees. Elena took two steps to the right, and then focused her attention on the portrait. "Oh," she sighed. The viscountess was exquisite. She wore a luxurious ball gown from some thirty years past. A glittering ruby necklace encircled her slim, ivory neck. And a playful smile artfully curved her lips. And her hair—the same spun gold as the viscount's. "You are quite right, my lord. She is beautiful, indeed. Do you miss her?"

The viscount looked at her, confusion creasing his brow. "Didn't you know? She died in childbirth. I never knew her."

"But you failed to answer my question," Elena countered without thought, regretting her words the moment they spilled from her lips.

He turned his gaze back to the portrait. "Because you already know the answer."

"Please, forgive me," Elena entreated, looking down at the floor. "Of course you miss her—the same as I miss mine."

She looked up and found the viscount staring at her. A muscle flexed along his jawline, and his eyes searched hers. Tension stretched between them. "There is something about you, my lord. Something that makes me act . . ."

"Strangely?" he finished on her behalf. He swallowed hard before continuing. "Perhaps it's that we share so much, Miss Barnes. A kinship, if you will," he finished in an amiable tone.

Kinship. Is that what he saw when he looked at her? A sister? Who was the foolish one now?

Elena examined her wrapper and night rail, embarrassment flooding her senses. "Precisely," she managed to answer. "Now, I believe I'll return to bed."

"Allow me to escort you," Lord Carrington insisted, placing his hand on the sensitive stretch of skin just beneath her elbow and guiding her down the hall. "Miss Barnes, I meant to ask you, why are you up at such a late hour?"

Elena yanked the two sides of her wrapper tightly to-gether and reluctantly accompanied him. "I could not sleep."

"Yet one more commonality between us," he re-marked, looking down at her and grinning. "And what kept you awake?"

"Flights of fancy, my lord," Elena answered, tears forming just in the corners of her eyes. "Nothing more than flights of fancy."

※ ✿

"My dear, did you sleep well?" Lady Mowbray ladled a second spoon of sugar into her tea and studied Elena.

Elena savored a forkful of bacon and looked across the breakfast table at the marchioness. Rowena had assured her that the dark smudges beneath her eyes were hardly noticeable. Clearly, Lady Mowbray thought otherwise.

"I'm afraid not," she answered, smoothing her hair. "Due to the unfamiliar sounds of the city, no doubt. I'm certain I'll grow used to such things soon enough."

The viscount lifted his teacup and stared into it, as though searching for something.

"My lord, are you in need of tea, or have you taken to reading the leaves?"

"Neither," Lord Carrington replied, examining the dregs at the bottom of the cup one last time before setting it carefully back on the table. "Simply thinking is all."

Elena turned her attention to the coddled eggs on her plate. Simply thinking? Was he contemplating their con-versation last night? Lord knew Elena had been—and still was, apparently.

"Hmm, now that I look at you more closely," Lady Mowbray remarked, "you appear rather exhausted, as well. Odd that both of you would have difficulty sleeping, and on the very same night," she continued, stirring her tea while she looked first at the viscount, then Elena, a certain gleam in her eyes.

A gleam that unnerved Elena.

"Come now, Bessie," the viscount said. He shrugged and returned his attention to his breakfast plate. "Nothing odd about it at all. A late evening spent at one's club tends to drain a man."

"Quite so," she agreed. "As does wandering about in the dark—together."

Elena dropped the forkful of eggs that she'd brought to her mouth and looked at the viscount expectantly.

The man's jaw tightened as he clenched his teeth. He said nothing.

Oh, that wouldn't do at all.

Elena tilted her head slightly to one side and arched her brows inquiringly as though she hadn't a clue as to what the marchioness meant. "I beg your pardon, Lady Mowbray?"

"Really, my girl, don't play coy with me," the marchioness replied, sipping her tea. She watched both Elena and Viscount Carrington over the rim of her cup, her eyes twinkling with suppressed amusement.

The viscount emitted a deep sigh. "One of your spies has been busy, I assume?" he asked.

"They are your servants, and it is their job to ensure the safety of all those who dwell within Carrington House," she replied simply, stirring a third teaspoon of sugar into her tea.

"It's not at all what you—or the servants, for that matter—may be thinking. Assuming—really either . . . Well, actually . . ." Elena fumbled to a halt and set her fork down. "I couldn't sleep last night, that part is true. So I thought to visit the library. Only, I became lost."

Lady Mowbray nodded in acceptance of Elena's explanation, though a hint of amusement remained.

"And I came to her rescue," the viscount added, quickly holding up his hand. "That is, I found her, returned her to her suite, and that's all there is to it."

"Really?" the marchioness said mildly, the gleam fading with each passing moment.

"Honestly," Elena promptly added.

The marchioness pursed her lips and set her cup down in its saucer, clearly completely put off her tea. "Well, that's a disappointment."

A wicked voice in Elena's head agreed, while the pragmatic side of her brain tsk-tsked at the very idea. Really, the marchioness was as misguided as Elena, hoping that there was more to the story.

"Lady Mowbray, you are my chaperone, are you not?" Elena asked, folding her hands in her lap.

Lady Mowbray did the same, a supreme look of defeat upon her face. "I am."

"Should you not be relieved to hear that nothing . . ." Her words trailed off, as they were wont to do when speaking of something she'd rather not.

"Really, my dear girl, I feel you may be confused as to a chaperone's duties." The woman's voice was feminine but firm. "Let me explain. Midnight meetings with just anyone are cause for alarm. But Dash is a viscount—a viscount, my dear," she said with emphasis. "They do not come along every day."

Lord Carrington visibly cringed at Lady Mowbray's words.

Elena's face felt hot. She drew a deep breath, her fingertips gripping the edge of the table. "No, Lady Mowbray. I say this with all due respect, but I believe you are the one that is confused."

"I disagree," the older woman promptly shot back. "You have come to London to retrieve your father's books. But would it be such a hardship to return to Dorset with a viscount in tow?"

"But only hours ago, you spoke of guarding my well-being," Elena said, clearly bewildered. "I cannot . . . That is to say, I will not . . ."

"Bessie, do have a care," the viscount admonished Lady Mowbray. "Miss Barnes is uncomfortable with the conversation, as am I."

"All right, then." Lady Mowbray squared her shoulders and took up her tea. "I did not mean to offend you, Miss Barnes. I simply want what is best for you. And when I believed there may be a spark—"

"Bessie!" Lord Carrington growled.

"Have I done it again, then?" Lady Mowbray asked, looking apologetically at Elena.

Elena could not be angry with the marchioness. She was too busy fighting back the wave of humiliation caused by the viscount's obvious disdain for the very idea. "It is all right, Lady Mowbray. Do not give it a second thought."

"Thank you, my dear girl. But do not think for a moment that this means the social invitations are forgotten."

"Did you not just agree that the pursuit of eligible bachelors was, as they say, off the table?" Elena responded, gently rubbing her temples with her fingertips.

Lady Mowbray beckoned the footman stationed near the door. He nodded and disappeared, only to reappear a moment later with a silver tray, a number of invitations stacked tidily upon the gleaming surface. He set the tray at Lady Mowbray's elbow and returned to his position.

"Now then," the marchioness continued. "I did not agree to such terms, not in the slightest."

Elena rubbed her temples harder.

"I did not dismiss the idea of your seeking a husband altogether," the woman added. "I agreed to dismiss any designs I may have harbored concerning the viscount."

Elena's head ached. She felt warm all over and completely out of place. And it really did not help matters that the marchioness was correct.

"I cannot argue," she said succinctly, the words leaving a bitter taste in her mouth.

Lady Mowbray nodded in agreement, setting her china teacup onto the matching saucer with a definitive click. "Splendid. Now, do come sit here beside me and we will discuss these," she urged. Her fingertip tapped the stack of thick, creamy paper.

"Of course," Elena replied, hesitating for a moment at the edge of her chair.

"Well, it looks as though I'm no longer needed," the viscount announced, tossing his serviette next to his plate and standing.

Lady Mowbray peered down the length of the table at him somberly. "No, my lord. You are of little use to me now, I'm afraid." She winked at him, then shooed him away with her hand. "Go, then. Off to your club, or wherever it is you men wander off to during the day."

Lord Carrington turned to Elena and nodded. "Miss Barnes."

"Lord Carrington," Elena replied, lowering her chin a touch in farewell.

"Honestly, a quarter of the invitations will be outdated by the time you're through," Lady Mowbray scolded. "Perhaps I'll confirm our attendance at all of the events and be done with it."

"You wouldn't," Elena uttered disbelievingly.

"She would," the viscount replied dryly, then turned and walked from the room.

Lady Mowbray cleared her throat and tapped on the invitations a second time.

"Of course you would," Elena muttered to herself, then went to join the marchioness.

"*This* is where I belong," Elena addressed a delicate shepherdess figurine that stood prettily atop a slender oak table near one of the windows in the Carrington library. "A place for everything, and everything in its place."

Unlike her fevered dreams last night that had found her in the arms of Lord Carrington.

She looked beyond the shepherdess to the window itself, where the shadowed blues and grays of dusk were beginning to darken the mullioned panes. From the looks of it, night was ready to fall, and she was still thinking about the viscount.

Shameful, really, Elena chided herself, wiping haphazardly at the dust smudges on the bodice of her gown. She turned her attention back to the books and sighed.

Normally, the library would have absorbed her attention entirely. The very act of entering one such as Carrington House's was like attending church on Christmas Eve for Elena: holy, a touch mysterious, and completely awe-inspiring. But she'd been distracted.

She reached out and caressed a well-worn copy of *The Lais of Marie de France,* the once-stiff spine now soft and supple in her hands. It was more than mere distraction. She couldn't stop her mind from mulling over last night's interlude, or her heart from cringing at the pain and embarrassment of the viscount's indifference.

Elena returned the volume to its shelf and walked toward the second aisle. *Kinship.* While she'd been overcome by his scent and lost in his piercing stare, Lord Carrington had been thinking of her . . . What? Sisterly qualities? That is, if he'd been thinking of her at all.

She pressed her fingertips against her lips, then covered her face with both hands. She never should have come to London.

Elena clenched her teeth and willed herself not to cry. Yes, she should have stayed home. But she hadn't. There was nothing to be done about that now.

No, now, she would tend to the books and avoid Lord Carrington. She would make the best of her situation, including Lady Mowbray's blasted engagements.

"One in particular," she whispered to herself. Lord Elgin's ball was sure to be a horrific crush. But the marbles on display there? The very thought buoyed Elena's spirit.

Elgin's Marbles. Distracted, she stopped in the middle of the aisle and stared down at the Aubusson carpet, her head full of the most beautiful images. The imposing figure of Iris; the powerful horse of Selene, the Moon Goddess; a noble river-god reclining against a rock. She was not particularly pleased with Lord Elgin's removal of the art from its Greek homeland, but there was little that could be done about that now. The least she could do was offer it homage here in London.

Would she be allowed to touch the cold, ancient marble? Place her fingers upon the finely crafted statues and feel the years of history embedded in their every curve and line?

"Miss Barnes."

The glorious figures faded from Elena's mind's eye until all that remained were two perfectly polished boots. She squeezed her eyes shut tightly and counted to four, then hesitantly opened first one eye, and then the other.

The boots remained.

She inhaled deeply and slowly tipped her head up, taking in the full length of Lord Carrington. Somewhere around his expansive chest, which was covered perfectly in a dark blue silk waistcoat and matching superfine coat, a tickle teased her throat. She swallowed and her gaze continued upward, reaching his strong yet perfectly proportioned chin, then his chiseled cheekbones and nose, and finally his piercing, ice-blue eyes.

Her heart constricted. She could not help but take note of his likeness to Elgin's stolen treasures. Hard, muscular, beautiful, perfectly proportioned.

No more than three seconds had passed since her resolution to avoid the man and put him completely from her mind, and she'd already failed.

The tickle in her throat tormented her and she coughed. Hard.

"Are you all right?" Lord Carrington asked quizzically.

Elena clapped her hand over her mouth and coughed again.

Lord Carrington spun her about and thumped her on the back, his aid so forceful Elena had to brace herself against the polished bookshelf. Two more hacking coughs followed and then the tickle ceased—as did the thumping.

"Miss Barnes." Lord Carrington's hand settled on the small of her back, his voice unsettlingly close to her ear. "Are you all right *now*?"

Elena hadn't the faintest clue how to respond. Her face felt hot, salty tears mixing with perspiration on her skin. Her neat chignon was askew. Her dress was twisted uncomfortably about her waist. Her chest burned. Her pride stung. And her throat ached.

Actually, it wasn't only her throat. The exact expanse of skin where the viscount's hand rested literally pulsed. As did a spot just below her neckline—and just below her waist.

"Stop," she commanded herself.

Lord Carrington quickly withdrew his hand. "I'm sorry."

"Not you," Elena protested, realizing belatedly that the demand *should* have been for the viscount—and she was immediately irritated by the fact that she'd not thought of it first.

She released the shelf and swiped at her hair, tucking the tendrils behind her ears and attempting to repair her face with her handkerchief. It was hopeless, of course, and she resolved not to care.

Elena slowly turned toward the man with all the confidence she could muster. "I apologize, Lord Carrington. And after you came to my aid. It was really quite dreadful of me to . . ."

She couldn't bring herself to say it, so instead Elena pasted a friendly smile upon her lips. "Well, that is, thank you."

She awkwardly stepped around the viscount and continued down the aisle. "What brings you to the library, my lord?"

"You."

Elena stopped abruptly and turned to face the man. She searched his eyes, hopeful for some hint of the depths she'd discovered last night. There was nothing there.

Stupid, delusional woman.

The viscount stared back at her and smiled cheerfully. "You haven't left the library all day, Miss Barnes. It can't be good for a person to concentrate in such a manner. Perhaps a walk in the garden with your maid would do you good."

"My lord, I must focus on the task at hand if I want to return to Dorset—which I do, most fervently," Elena replied, though distractedly.

It wasn't that the volumes sitting on the shelf just past the viscount's right shoulder were out of place. Quite the contrary, they were exactly where one should keep

Froissart's *Chronicles*—that is, if one were at all concerned with a well-ordered and sensible library.

Which Elena knew the late viscount was not. She'd spent a relatively short amount of time in the Carrington library, but one detail had made itself glaringly clear from the start: the man may have valued his books, but he had not valued order.

"Miss Barnes?"

Elena ignored Lord Carrington's voice and squeezed past him, stopping in front of the volumes.

She reached for one of the books and pulled. It remained unmoved. She tried again with both hands, and yet, it continued its stubborn immobility.

She pulled hard at the book a third time, infusing her attempt with every last sensation of humiliation and embarrassment she felt and succeeded in moving it a fraction toward her.

"Miss Barnes?" the viscount said a second time. "May I be of assistance?"

"This book seems to be stuck," she explained, gritting her teeth. Elena knew she shouldn't force the volume. It could damage the binding. Or tear the pages. Even dent the cover. She grimaced at the nightmarish list of possible outcomes.

"So it is," he replied, watching the decidedly unimpressive progress Elena was making.

Elena blew out a frustrated breath. *Ah, that might just help*. She knew it was cruel, but the man's brainless state might in time quiet her heart and mind.

"And would you make an attempt, my lord?" she asked, gesturing toward the bookshelf.

"With what?"

Last night's dreams suddenly faded a touch. "The books, my lord."

The viscount stared at the volumes, his brow creasing. "But why?"

Elena squinted at the man, watching as his soft, sun-kissed hair dulled before her. "Because they're stuck—and in need of unsticking," she answered.

"Oh, yes, of course," he answered, offering her a vacuous smile.

Lord Carrington reached for the book, placing one hand upon the top of the volume and the other around the bottom. And then he pulled. And pulled again.

"Unhand that book!" Elena demanded, suddenly struck by his attempt to force the book from the shelf with no regard for potential damage.

Lord Carrington immediately released the volume and held his hands up in surrender. "But you asked for my help."

"Yes, but there must be another way." Elena couldn't concentrate while he was so near. She closed her eyes and tried to focus. "Let me think . . ."

"Not my area of expertise, I'm afraid," he replied. "Besides, one more attempt and I'm sure we'll have success."

Elena's eyes shot open just in time to see the viscount reach out and grasp the book with both hands. He yanked hard.

She gasped in horror.

And the book moved, only not quite as Elena would have imagined. Instead of the one volume, all six of the books shifted forward in unison, until the entire row sat teetering on the edge of the wooden bookshelf. "How peculiar," Elena muttered, her interest thoroughly piqued.

Lord Carrington lifted the collection out, revealing not books at all, but a carved box.

Elena traced her finger along the carved top, noting an intricate design that marked nearly the entire surface. "Do you recognize this, my lord?"

Lord Carrington studied the box intently, his expression unreadable. "I'm afraid not." He grasped the box in both hands and turned it around, clearly searching for a lid. Though he pulled and pushed, the box remained shut, revealing nothing. He set it back down on the shelf and shrugged his shoulders. "I suppose it belonged to my father."

Elena craned her neck for a better view. "There's no visible keyhole," she said to herself, desperate to try her hand at opening the mysterious box, but loath to move any closer to the viscount.

"Miss Barnes, are you here?" Lady Mowbray's clear voice broke in, the sound of her skirts swishing as she marched toward the two. "If I didn't know better, I would think you were hiding from me."

"She is impossible to avoid," the viscount said. "You might as well give me the box."

"We've still much to discuss," the marchioness continued, the growing power of her voice signaling that she was drawing nearer. "I would like to give my modiste some idea of what we're hoping for in terms of dresses."

Elena eyed the wooden box. She didn't want to talk with Lady Mowbray at the moment. Especially about dresses. She grabbed the box and cradled it tightly, turning in the opposite direction of Lady Mowbray's advancing voice.

"You never saw me, my lord," she whispered to the viscount over her shoulder, and then ran silently from the room.

7

Dash padded silently along the west wing, Carrington House still as a grave in the night. The servants were abed and all was quiet, the faint noise of his bare feet brushing against the Axminster carpet the only sound to be heard.

Why had Miss Barnes taken dinner in her room?

More specifically, *why Miss Barnes*?

The answer to the second question would suffice for the first as well.

Dash slowed his steps, his conscience plaguing him. He'd revealed too much to her last night. And God, but she'd responded to him, her kindness and vulnerability running him through.

And then he'd betrayed her. Turned his back and resumed his role as if her words had all meant nothing.

Dash stopped and leaned his back against the wall. It was *something*. And Dash didn't know how to make it stop.

The talk with Bell had sorted things out. What he'd revealed reminded Dash of the responsibilities he bore to his father's memory. And to his friends. He needed to move forward with finding Lady Afton's killer. And he couldn't do so with Miss Barnes under his roof. She was intensely distracting. But more than that, the longer she stayed, the more danger she was in. If he had any luck at all, each day would bring Dash closer to finding the Bishop—which would only place Miss Barnes within the killer's grasp. The Bishop attacked the wives of

Corinthians. Not that Dash had any plans to marry Miss Barnes; quite the contrary. But his growing feelings for the woman surely wouldn't do her any favors.

Conservatively speaking, it should take no more than a fortnight for her to finish with the books and be gone. Unfortunately, he could not trust himself around the woman for such a length of time.

Last night, he'd been caught off guard by the rush of unfamiliar emotions. He could not afford to make the same mistake again.

Dash pushed off from the wall and continued toward Miss Barnes's chamber. He needed the puzzle and what he hoped were valuable clues inside the box. He could not wait any longer.

The carved wooden container was a burr puzzle. The box was meant to safeguard those things a Corinthian could not entrust to anyone else. Only the owner knew the cipher that allowed him to solve the puzzle and open the box. Dash's earlier searches of the late viscount's study had unearthed nothing nearly as promising as the box.

Why had his father not told him of its existence? There could only be one reason: it contained information about the Afton case.

He reached Miss Barnes's door and pressed his ear to it. Hearing no movement within, he looked down the hall both ways, then placed his hand on the carved brass doorknob. Turning it noiselessly, he gently pushed and the paneled door opened, revealing very little in the darkened boudoir.

Dash slipped silently inside and eased the door closed behind him, taking a moment to get his bearings. It had been some time since he'd been in this particular room, but the faint light from the fireplace embers lit the shadowed space. The wall directly across from him bore a row of high mullioned windows that were heavily draped. A pair of chairs sat near the fireplace, separated by a low table. And to his left was a canopied four-posted bed, where Miss Barnes slept.

The bed curtains were only partially closed. He moved stealthily to the edge of the bed and gently tugged the fringed curtain.

Something swung toward him just to his left and Dash ducked, reaching out and capturing the small fist that had nearly connected with his face.

A shrill scream, followed by an "Ow," sounded in the dark.

Miss Barnes tumbled from the bed, landing in a tangle of nightgown and coverlet at his feet.

"Ow!"

"You repeat yourself, Miss Barnes," Dash commented, pulling her to stand.

She yanked her hand from his as if she'd been burned. "I'm afraid eloquence escapes me at the moment. It often does when I'm set upon in my bed."

Dash didn't respond. He could only stare. Her chin was lifted haughtily, her full, soft lips trembling slightly. Her labored breathing forced her chest to rise and fall unnaturally fast.

"Well, my lord. I assume there's a rational reason for your presence," she ground out, turning away. A moment later, the sudden dim glow of a lone candle illuminated her and little else. A plain white night rail clung to her body, accentuating her lush curves. Dash knew he should look away, but he found it impossible to resist the breathtaking view.

"Oh!" she squeaked, looking down at her night rail and crossing her arms over her breasts. "Turn around!" she commanded, then added "and please, fetch me my wrapper."

Dash did as she asked, crossing the room to where a soft linen wrapper lay folded neatly on the edge of one of the chairs. He picked it up and turned back to Miss Barnes.

"No," she urged, gesturing for him to turn around. "Your presence in my room is highly inappropriate. Do not make the situation any worse than it already is."

"Of course," Dash agreed, immediately turning around and walking backward until he felt her palm flatten between his shoulder blades. He laid the wrapper over his shoulder and waited.

She whisked the garment away and a moment later, tapped efficiently on his arm. "You may turn around, my lord."

Dash slowly shifted to face her. "There is a rational reason."

"I'm sorry?" she questioned, folding her arms tightly across her chest.

He adopted what he hoped was a look of confusion. "For what, Miss Barnes?"

She looked down and fiddled with the tassel at the end of her wrapper's sash, blowing out a frustrated breath as she did so. "Shall we start again, my lord? Why, exactly, are you here?"

"Oh, yes, of course," Dash replied obtusely. "For the puzzle."

"The puzzle?" Miss Barnes parroted, squeezing her upper arms as if for support, then unfolding them and gesturing toward the two chairs. "Now," she began again, walking across the room and sitting down. "You needed the puzzle now?"

"No, I wanted the box earlier," Dash replied, following her and taking the chair opposite. "But you failed to appear for dinner."

"I see," she replied hesitantly, nodding her head at the simple logic. "Well, then. You shall have your puzzle."

Dash sat on the edge of his seat, like the simpleton Miss Barnes believed him to be, and began. "I'm very curious about the box. Can't imagine what my father would have kept inside of it."

"Well, you won't have to wait long, my lord. I've nearly figured it out."

"That's impossible," Dash growled, forgetting his role and drumming his fingers on his knees.

"Really?" Miss Barnes answered, her countenance changing abruptly.

Dash realized his instantaneous rejection of her claim had been too quick. Too sure. He was becoming too comfortable with the woman. She made him forget himself far too easily.

He ceased drumming his fingers and brought his palms together, then spread his hands wide in a pleading gesture. "Well, isn't it? From what I could see, there wasn't even a keyhole."

Of course there hadn't been a keyhole. The Corinthians—and their enemies across the Continent and beyond—made use of numerous tricks to protect their secrets. In the few minutes Dash had been given to examine the box, he'd narrowed the possible opening mechanisms down to three.

"Viscount Carrington, have you ever heard of a burr puzzle?" she asked slowly.

"I'm afraid not," he lied convincingly.

Miss Barnes nodded, and then rose from her chair. "A man of your . . ."

Dash thought to offer aid and suggest that "limited mental capabilities," or, and perhaps more to the point, "stupidity" could be exactly the word or words she was looking for. But decided against it.

"Your station in life," she continued, walking back to her bed, "would hardly have use for such things. It's nothing more than a game, of sorts, really."

She dropped to her knees and nearly disappeared beneath the massive bed. "Smchdoe dlap dop doapleln."

All right, that Dash had truly not understood. "What's that?"

Her head popped out from beneath the bottom of the bed curtains. "The burr puzzle was fairly simple to solve."

Her head disappeared again, and then the box scooted out, followed by Miss Barnes. She rose to her feet and picked up the box.

"But the numerical lock beneath is not," she continued while retracing her steps, her voice rising with excitement. She set the box and six beveled sticks on the table between them and reclaimed her chair.

The top panel hadn't been a solid piece at all, but was instead the burr puzzle; the oak sticks notched and set in so as to appear flat on one side. Beneath was a highly ornate padlock bearing the Carrington crest. A ring encircled the lock, the numbers zero to nine appearing with an ornate slash forged between each.

He examined the puzzle more closely, fingering the sticks. Such puzzles had been a favorite of his father's. One of Dash's earliest memories was completing a similar puzzle while his father had looked on with pride.

"I've only ever read about burr puzzles," Miss Barnes offered, bending down closer and smiling. "And one with a flat side to it? Brilliant."

"That was my father for you," he replied, his fingers moving to glide over the padlock. "Bloody brilliant."

Miss Barnes watched as he tried to force the padlock. "I'm afraid the lock requires a specific combination of numbers—eight in total."

She turned the box toward her and stared hard at the lock. "I've tried prime numbers, combinations in relation to the Greek alphabet. Anything that might appeal to a learned man," Miss Barnes offered, pushing her mass of mahogany brown curls over her shoulder. "But I've yet to discover the answer."

Dash mentally reviewed his father's favorite areas of

scholarly interest, his Corinthian cases, even his most treasured books. They had discussed numbers in relation to patterns, but none that seemed more important than any others.

Miss Barnes worried her ripe lower lip in concentration. Dash found the act mesmerizing.

She was visibly easing, her shoulders relaxing until her wrapper fell open, revealing her gauzy night rail beneath.

Miss Barnes looked up and he realized she'd caught his heated appraisal. A faint rose blush colored her cheeks, but she did not look away. "Well, have you figured it out, Lord Carrington?"

Dash knew it was selfish of him. But he wanted badly to kiss Miss Elena Barnes at that very moment. Not because he needed her gone. But because he wanted her to stay.

❧ ❧

Elena's breath caught when Lord Carrington leaned in until his face was no more than a hairbreadth away. "Not the lock, Miss Barnes," he murmured. "But I have figured out *you*."

Elena felt a trickle of perspiration slide between her breasts. "Whatever do you mean?" she managed to ask, holding his gaze, though she felt it was dangerous to do so.

The viscount knelt, his big frame boxing her in. He placed a hand on the damask seat cushion on either side of her hips, his gaze never leaving hers.

Elena fought the urge to reach out and run her finger along the soft, supple seam of his lips.

"I believe you already know." His deep voice was dark silk over gravel.

He bent his head and his breath grazed her breasts beneath the fine cotton lawn of her nightgown. The heated, inviting brush sent a wave of want coursing through her. "I'm sure I haven't the slightest idea what you're talking about, my lord," she managed to say, her voice quavering.

"Don't lie, Elena," he growled.

She balled her fists at her sides, desperate to hold on. But there was something so raw in his request. Something so like the base need threatening to devour her that Elena could no longer fight him. And in all honesty, she didn't want to.

She tentatively relaxed her hands and reached up, cupping his face in her palms.

He raised his head and captured her with a soul-searing gaze.

Elena's heartbeat pounded in her ears, and she felt buffeted by a crest of emotion, desire, and fear that hammered her.

Lord Carrington slowly closed the space between them and tenderly touched his lips to Elena's.

His hands caught her waist, drawing her closer to him until her breasts pressed against his chest. He deepened the kiss and gently nudged her lips apart, his tongue seeking out hers.

Her first kiss. It was warm and wet, the welcoming heat kindling fires of desire throughout her body. Elena's tongue hesitantly matched the pace of the viscount's with inexperienced yet earnest enthusiasm. One of his hands left her waist and inched lower, until he palmed her derrière. He squeezed with such delicious pressure that Elena gasped. She gripped his waistcoat to pull him closer, then hitched her left leg up and around his waist, eliciting a growl of pleasure from him. He broke the heated kiss and moved down her throat, leaving a trail of white-hot kisses that surely branded her skin. He licked torturously at the sensitive skin just above her neckline, first the top of her left breast and then the right. Elena pulled feverishly at his waistcoat in a vain attempt to press closer and relieve the growing sweet pang of anticipation rising within her.

His teeth tugged at her bodice and she moaned with pleasure, straining at the fabric of her gown to give him more of her. He dropped feverish kisses back up the length of her exposed neck and took her ear with his tongue, lightly sucking the sensitive lobe, then teasing the shell with quick, darting attention.

Elena reveled in the wash of heady, earthy pleasure. Her body responded to his touch with whimpers and moans, her back arching while her hands begged him for more. No longer was she the awkward, undesirable bluestocking. She was wanted. Needed.

And it was a revelation.

"Why," she whispered urgently, passion's flames threatening to engulf her. "Why now?"

Lord Carrington suddenly stilled. "Because I wanted to," he said, his head lowering once again to her breasts.

Knuckles rapped loudly on the door and Elena jerked away from him, instinctively curling down in the chair to hide.

"Miss Barnes," Bell's voice called. "One of the maids thought she heard a scream."

Lord Carrington raised his head and gestured for Elena to remain quiet. "The house is riddled with secret passageways and doors—one of which is connected to your dressing room," he whispered. "Give me thirty seconds, and then see to Bell."

He pressed one last, hard kiss to her lips before grabbing the puzzle box and disappearing into the dark.

"Miss Barnes," Bell called again. "Are you all right?"

"Not in the slightest," Elena replied in a shaken voice, low enough so that she was sure the butler could not hear. "Nor will I ever be again."

✦ ✦

"Beg your pardon, Miss, but didn't we come to town for the books back at Carrington House?" Rowena asked, picking up her step when Elena linked her arm with hers and urged the maid on.

"Lord Carrington's library does not contain the volume I desire," Elena replied simply, dodging to avoid a flower cart as they crossed Crown Street and headed toward Finsbury Square.

Elena hadn't slept last night, and yet she felt oddly energized. She'd remained seated in the peach damask chair for a long time after calling out to Bell and assuring him that she was perfectly fine. She'd run her fingers over every last square inch of skin that Lord Carrington had touched, some with his eyes, others with his hands, and many with his mouth. One moment he'd been caressing her, and the next, he'd disappeared. She'd needed to assure herself that it hadn't been her imagination.

Rowena sighed in understanding. "And the walk doesn't hurt a bit, now does it?"

"A walk never hurts," Elena answered, looking up the cobbled street to where the square opened before them. "Especially on a fine day such as this."

The sky was ominously gray, as though it might turn an angry, deep black at any moment and let loose raindrops the size of spring lambs.

"Not exactly 'fine,' I suppose," Elena amended, steering Rowena toward the address she'd gotten from Bell. "But still, weren't you just complaining about the limited size of the parks? And this gives you an excellent opportunity to see more of the city."

By the time Elena had dressed and made her way downstairs to breakfast, the viscount had already left for his club. She'd been both disappointed and relieved by his absence.

And desperately in need of a walk to clear her mind. So far, she was as hopelessly confused as when she'd awoken. But the day wasn't over, she assured herself. Not yet.

The Temple of the Muses shop front appeared and Elena's step quickened. "Well, the rain will have to wait, as we have reached our destination."

"Right," Rowena said enthusiastically, reaching for the ornate door handle and gently pushing. "You've something on your mind—or should I say, someone?" she added, a knowing smile on her beautiful face.

Elena stepped in and waited for Rowena to follow. "I can't answer such questions *here,* Rowena."

"Of course, Miss," the young woman replied apologetically. "I'm sorry."

Elena instantly regretted the slight reprimand—especially since Rowena had been correct in her assumptions. Even now, hours after her encounter with Lord Carrington and with many city blocks between them, she continued to turn last night's events over and over in her mind.

"No, Rowena, it is I who should be sorry," she corrected herself in a reassuring tone. "I've simply far too much on my mind," she continued, lowering her voice as she beckoned for her friend to follow her. "But do note that I neither said 'something' nor 'someone.' It is too much, and we will leave it at that. Agreed?"

Rowena nodded solemnly, just a hint of mischief in her eyes.

Elena dearly loved Rowena. But she was not about to unburden herself in the middle of a bookshop.

Elena glanced about the interior of the Temple of the Muses bookshop and temporarily forgot all about burdens and the casting off of such things.

Before her, down three wide steps and past rows upon rows of books, stood a circular wooden counter where a number of clerks busily addressed the needs of several customers. Elena took the steps quickly, still staring at the counter—or to be more precise, the ceiling above where the counter stood.

Elena belatedly realized with delight as she drew

nearer to the backs of the customers that it wasn't a ceiling at all. Rather, a massive circular opening revealed what must have been at least two additional floors above, iron railings the only thing standing between Elena and literally thousands more books.

The volumes were housed in what appeared to be curved bookcases that mirrored the circular nature of the top of the building, making Elena feel as though she were surrounded by nothing but books.

"Elysium," she murmured, leaning even more forward and examining the candelabra that was suspended from the center of the tower.

"Miss!" Rowena whispered urgently. "You're talking to yourself again."

Elena rolled her eyes in response, realizing belatedly that a clerk stood just in front of her, a quizzical look on his face.

"May I be of assistance?" he asked, looking entirely too ready to flee at the sight of her.

There were times when Elena wondered whether she bore a badge emblazoned with the letter "B" upon her breast. She straightened and clasped her hands at her waist. "As a matter of fact, yes. I'm looking for a book on burr puzzles."

The clerk leveled a supercilious stare at her. "I'm sorry, but why would *you* need a book such as that?" he asked, his tone suddenly contemptuous.

Rowena took a step forward and squared her shoulders. "That's none of your business, is it? Just fetch my lady's book—or better yet, tell us where we might find it so that you'll not be touching it one whit."

Elena knew she should swiftly step in to rectify the situation, given Rowena's cheeky response.

And yet, she just stared at the clerk for a moment, relishing his discomfort.

Aware her behavior was verging on the impolite, she cleared her throat and took hold of Rowena's arm. But when the man's thin mouth curved into a dismissive smile, she hesitated. "Mr.," she paused, waiting for the man to offer his name.

"Tinyrod," he replied quietly.

Rowena giggled and Elena tightened her grip. "I'm sorry?" she queried, sure that she'd misheard the man.

"Tinyrod," he repeated, his smile disappearing.

Elena bit the inside of her cheek until she feared it would bleed. "Very well, Mr. Tinyrod," she managed to say without laughing. "I do believe I would prefer to fetch the book myself. So, be a good man, and tell us where we might find the volume in question."

Elena could feel Rowena begin to shake from the effort of holding in a second giggle. She squeezed her friend's arm harder. "Now, if you please."

Mr. Tinyrod retrieved a square of pasteboard and a quill. "On the third floor, just beyond drawings and games," he answered, bending down to write out instructions for the women.

"There will be no need for directions," Elena assured him, then tapped her finger upon her temple. "It's all in here."

Elena noticed that his fingers clenched until the quill looked ready to snap. She nodded regally in dismissal and shooed Rowena toward a broad set of stairs near the back of the room.

"You'd think silly men like Mr. Tinyrod would have been warned about you, Miss," Rowena commented, stepping to the side and allowing Elena to ascend the stairs first.

"Perhaps news travels slowly from Dorset. Besides, I never offered the man my name," Elena answered, struggling, albeit weakly, with a smidge of guilt over Tinyrod. After all, his rather rude and forward assumption that a woman could have no interest in a topic such as burr puzzles was, unfortunately, too commonplace. At home in Dorset, she'd even taken to ordering books in her father's name, the bother of doing anything else having quickly grown tiresome.

Rowena's boots clicked on the oaken stairs just behind her, the quick, rhythmic tap soothing to Elena's ears. "Not that Mr. Tinyrod had any right to put up such a stink, but this book . . . Well, it's not even got the tasty bits that those histories of yours do. Just puzzles? Is that right?" Rowena added.

The tapping of Rowena's shoes slowly faded until all Elena could hear was her mind as it circled, again, and again, and again around the real reason for their visit to the bookshop.

Viscount Carrington.

Well, Elena reasoned, in truth, she was simply curious. That was all. He'd denied any knowledge of the burr puzzle, yet his fingers seemed to literally itch when she'd brought out the oak sticks. As though he could solve it with his eyes closed.

But that was impossible, of course. A man of his intellectual limitations couldn't solve a complicated puzzle involving mathematics. Elena frowned. Something about the viscount's reaction to the puzzle bothered her, but she couldn't put her finger on the precise detail.

"Oh, my," Rowena uttered as they reached the landing of the third floor.

Elena noticed the Minerva Press novels to her right. Mrs. Kitty Cuthbertson's latest lurid tale, *The Castle of Prince Roderick,* was prominently displayed on a large mahogany table. As far as Elena was concerned, good for Mrs. Cuthbertson. There were many, many people who enjoyed the adventurous, romantic tales—including Elena. And she was glad to see that the bookshop agreed. And then she discovered what had actually caught

Rowena's attention. To their left, just beyond a second table laden with fiction, were books of more questionable taste. A volume of engravings was propped upright near the front, its pages opened to reveal a suggestive nymph and her shepherd at sport.

"We meet again," a male voice drawled in their direction, interrupting Elena's gawking.

She looked up to find the rude man from the park standing near, a book in his hands.

Elena abandoned her contemplation of the engraving and protectively moved to Rowena's side. "Actually, since we've never been properly introduced, as far as I'm concerned, we've never met."

The man returned the book to one of the cases and made his way toward the women, eliciting a sharp intake of breath from Rowena.

"Stop right there, if you please," Elena ordered, her heartbeat quickening.

But the man refused to obey and drew nearer. "Really, Madam, you act as though I mean you harm. But I assure you, quite the opposite is true."

It wasn't like Elena to be dramatic. And yet, this man and his sinister half-smile made her want to scream. Loudly. Or perhaps push over a bookcase on top of him and make haste for the Continent.

Absolute balderdash. But there it was.

"Mr. Tinyrod," Elena called in a firm voice. "We've need of your assistance."

At the sound of Tinyrod's boots on the treads, the stranger altered his course and made for the stairs. "Such a pity."

"Not in the least," Elena ground out as Tinyrod appeared.

Elena was sure she'd never been, nor would she be ever again, quite so thankful to see a Tinyrod.

8

Dash stared out the study window of Carrington House and watched as the dark sky opened wide with showers. The rain beat against the thick glass and then lightened, settling into a mellow, almost hypnotic pattern.

He traced his finger along the glass, following the path of one, lone drop until it mingled with the others and disappeared into a sea of translucent moisture.

He'd spent the morning at his club, too much of a coward to face Elena over the breakfast table. She'd given of herself in such a beautiful, innocent manner that Dash continued to be affected by her even now. He held out his hand in front of him and watched his fingers tremble at the thought of her cries of pleasure.

If it hadn't been for Bell's arrival? He rested his head on the cool pane and closed his eyes.

The door hinges creaked, followed by the butler's calm voice. "My lord, Mr. Nicholas Bourne."

"Thank you, Bell," Dash replied, opening his eyes to look out once again at the rain.

"Bloody hell, I'd forgotten how wet this island is. You could have waited for a break in the weather to summon me. I nearly drowned out there, Carrington."

Dash turned at the sound of Nicholas's voice and took in the sight of his wet friend. "You're still English, you know," he said dryly. "Rain comes with the territory, I'm afraid."

Nicholas allowed Bell to assist him in removing his sodden greatcoat, thumping the man on the back for his efforts. "Thank you, Bell."

The butler folded the coat over his arm and bowed. "Might I bring you the port, my lord?"

"God, yes, my good man," Nicholas answered for Dash. "Think on my offer, won't you?"

"A fine one, indeed, sir. But I'm afraid the answer is still *no*," he replied, and then stepped from the room, quietly closing the door behind him.

Dash lifted one eyebrow. "Please tell me you're not attempting to hire away my butler."

Nicholas shook his head, the water flying from his dark hair. It reminded Dash of one of his wolfhounds after a romp in the rain-soaked forest on his country estate.

"Of course I am. Bell's the best there is," he replied, giving his black hair one more shake, then raking it back from his face. "And now that I've returned to London, I find myself in need of such things. Well, actually, I find that everyone else finds me in need of such things and I tire of objecting."

Dash gestured for his friend to take one of the Sheraton chairs situated in front of his desk. "Then you will not be returning to India?"

Nicholas dropped into the comfortable seat and settled back, crossing one ankle over the opposite knee. "I don't plan to, not anytime soon anyway. Honestly, I've no idea. Never felt as though I wanted to put down roots—God knows you could have knocked me over with a feather when I realized my . . ." he paused, spearing his fingers through his hair. "Well, my fondness for the place. Except for this blasted rain."

His tone and words were classic Nicholas—so blithe that they couldn't possibly be true.

"You were born here, raised here too," Dash pointed

out gently, picking up the interlocking keys that lay near the one and only item he'd found within the puzzle box.

Nicholas quirked a brow sardonically and leaned in. "If you're not careful, my friend, you'll make me weep."

Yes, Dash thought, classic Nicholas indeed.

Dash separated the two keys easily, and then interlocked them again before settling the puzzle on the desktop. "I see India didn't soften you, then."

"Not in the least," Nicholas answered easily, settling back into the chair once more. "Actually, if anything, I'm even more of a bastard than before I left—which, I know, you'll find hard to believe. No doubt my brother will be thrilled."

Dash tried to smile at his friend's words, because he knew how this visit was meant to go. Wry, ironic talk, followed by amusing banter, and finally the afternoon ending with Nicholas in his cups.

There wasn't meant to be any acknowledgment that something was wrong.

Dash was about to change the rules.

"Is that so?" Dash asked, looking up when Bell knocked gently on the door.

"Oh yes, I'm afraid it is," Nicholas answered ominously. "A right rum duke, I am. No doubt about it. Dangerous—wily, even. I'd go so far as to bandy about words such as 'sinister' and 'calculating.' "

Bell unobtrusively entered, settling the silver tray containing tawny port and two crystal glasses on the sideboard. "May I pour?"

"No, that's all right, Bell. I'll see to it," Dash answered. "That will be all."

The butler bowed his head in understanding and noiselessly left, shutting the door once again.

"Worried he'll under-pour, are we?" Nicholas said with a grin.

Dash stood and walked the short distance to the sideboard. "Come now, Bourne. As you said yourself, Bell is the best." He uncorked the decanter and poured a reasonable amount into the first glass. "No, I've entirely different reasons for requiring absolute privacy."

He handed the glass to Nicholas, then returned to pour his own.

"Well, you've got my attention, now. Don't keep me in suspense." His friend's light words possessed a darker undertone.

Dash didn't answer immediately. Instead, he watched the amber liquid flow into the cut glass, then returned the cork to its rightful place and carried his port to the desk.

He reclaimed his chair and took a drink before speaking. "What would you say if I told you that new evidence has come to light regarding the Afton case?"

Nicholas seemed to stop breathing. The glass of port was suspended halfway to his lips as though frozen in a winter river. "You know better than to joke about that, Carrington," he finally uttered, the words cutting, stark, and cold.

"You're right, I do," Dash replied simply, taking a second drink before setting the glass down.

Nicholas's hand finally moved and he brought the port to his lips, emptying the glass in one swift move.

"Well?" Dash pressed, beginning to question his decision. Perhaps Nicholas wasn't truly ready, or prepared, to finally settle this once and for all. Perhaps, Dash thought with a growing sense of concern, he never would be.

"I'd say it's about bloody time," Nicholas answered, his voice hard, gravelly with grim conviction.

Dash nodded with relief, taking up his glass once again and raising it. "What I'm about to tell you cannot be shared with anyone. Not Stonecliffe, and especially not Sophia. Agreed?"

Nicholas uncrossed his legs and stood, walking to the sideboard. He unstopped the decanter and poured a second glass, turning back toward Dash and raising it. "Goes without saying," he answered.

The two men drank deeply, the only sound in the room that of the rain steadily falling outside.

Nicholas picked up the decanter and returned to his chair, setting the port on the edge of Dash's desk. "Enough cloak-and-dagger, Dash. Out with it."

Dash moved the decanter until it was outside of his friend's reach, then picked up a leather-bound book and handed it across the desk to Nicholas. "My father's diary."

Nicholas set his glass down next to the decanter and took the book. He began to thumb through it slowly, a frown forming on his mouth.

"It was hidden inside a puzzle box. He used my birthdate for the combination, sentimental old fool," Dash explained, secretly touched by the gesture. "From the looks of it, my father only picked up the case again shortly before his death."

"How can you tell anything from this gibberish?" Nicholas answered, his fingers flipping through the pages, obviously frustrated.

"It's in code—one created by Sir Francis Bacon."

Nicholas looked up at Dash and scrubbed at his jaw. "Ah, like father, like son. As you well know, such things are not in my purview, so if you'll skip to the important bits?"

"Of course," Dash answered, leaning forward to prop his elbows on the desk. "A woman by the name of Daisy Melville visited my father a week before his death. She told him she was dying of the pox and needed to unburden herself."

"Of what?"

Dash picked up the puzzle keys again. "Seems Daisy

worked at the Rambling Rose at the time of Lady Afton's death. The madam there had confided in Daisy that she'd blackmailed a customer—a man who'd boasted that he'd slit the throat of a lady of quality. She didn't tell Daisy the man's name, wanting to keep the valuable information for herself. But she did say that he was a member of the ton. The madame died two days after telling Daisy, her own throat slit from ear to ear."

Nicholas's eyes narrowed. "And how did she find your father?"

"The Duke of Ames likes to talk when he's in his cups. After the madam died, Daisy decided to do a bit of poking about. It wasn't long before Father's tie to the Aftons—Lady Afton, in particular—was revealed by her favorite customer, the duke."

"And I suppose Daisy was too frightened to go to the authorities?" Nicholas asked, closing the diary and setting it on the desk.

"Precisely," Dash answered, taking up the diary and turning to his father's account of the meeting with Daisy. "A prostitute would never get their full attention—at least not in the way she required if she were to stay alive. And her madam had been killed. She assumed the man would come after her next."

Nicholas reclaimed his glass and held it in both hands, rolling it this way and that between his palms. "No, she was absolutely right not to talk—bloody authorities." He took a long drink. "And the Rambling Rose? Was your father able to investigate who the customer was?"

"I'm afraid his health didn't allow him to do so," Dash answered, still struggling to come to terms with his father's willful hiding of the vitally important information.

"Well, for my part I'm glad he didn't have the opportunity. Gives us something to do. That is if your Corinthians don't get in the way."

"Ah yes, well, about that," Dash began, carefully choosing his words. "We'll not have any Corinthian help with this. If Carmichael finds out, he'll have my hide. It's just you and I."

"All the better." Nicholas finished his port and reached for the decanter yet again. "You may be good with numbers. But I've talents of my own."

"Such as?" Dash asked, sliding his glass across the desk toward Nicholas.

"Well, we're beginning our search at a brothel. God only knows where that will lead—somewhere equally seedy, I would assume. And eventually to the bastard who killed Lady Afton—a run-in that will require certain skills. Let's just say you've picked the right man for the job."

He topped off Dash's glass, then filled his own, raising the glass and slowly rotating it so that the contents gently swirled within.

"This is not a game, you know," Dash said quietly, watching his friend ruminate. "This 'bastard' has a name: the Bishop. He's killed many since Lady Afton and wouldn't think twice about pursuing our families and close friends—including Sophia."

"No, no, it's not," Nicholas agreed with cold certainty, continuing to turn the glass. "It's our very lives. Now, you've obviously been keeping secrets from me regarding the case. It's time to tell me all about the Bishop."

Madame Celeste, the marchioness's modiste, gestured grandly at the bow festooned with rosettes somewhere in the vicinity of Elena's shoulder blades while Lady Mowbray looked on, a satisfied smile playing across her lips.

Elena wasn't convinced that she was entirely prepared for shopping with the marchioness.

In truth, she didn't know that she was prepared for *anything* after . . . Well, once the viscount had stroked her breasts. Sucked her earlobe. Licked her throat. Kissed her lips.

"My dear, does the capucine meet with your approval?"

Elena realized that the marchioness was talking to her. "Oh, yes. It's fine."

The modiste huffed. "Fine is not what we do, Miss Barnes. If the gown does not delight you, there is no point."

Elena turned and gazed at herself in the full-length looking glass. Somehow, the woman's creation flattered her figure, accentuating her slim waist, while delicately framing her considerable bosom and derrière.

"How did you do this?" Elena asked, dumbfounded, turning to see the bow and rosettes.

Madame Celeste arranged the skirt of the gown and stepped back, eyeing Elena critically. "You did this, Miss Barnes. How could I not create something beautiful when given such inspiration?"

Elena looked up at the woman and quirked an eyebrow, waiting for the cutting remark or titter of amusement. But the modiste simply stood there, pulling at the fabric this way and that until it appeared she was satisfied. *"Parfait."*

Elena turned back around and took in her reflection once more. Could Madame Celeste be right?

She stared hard at herself in the glass, examining her body from head to toe while worrying her bottom lip.

"My dear, you have a charming smile," Lady Mowbray commented, coming to stand next to Elena. "You really should show it more often."

The marchioness reached for Elena's hair and began to efficiently pull pins out. She did not stop until every last lock of hair danced about Elena's shoulders.

"Unruly. Absolutely awful," Elena muttered, moving to twist the mass into a simple plait.

Lady Mowbray batted her hand away. "Hold these," she instructed, pushing all but six of the pins on Elena. She stepped behind and took up several pieces of hair, arranging them this way and that before finally settling on something that pleased her and pinning the style into place. She fluffed the remaining hair about, seemingly willing the curls to do her bidding.

"My dear, you're a very bright girl—about most things."

Elena looked again in the mirror and her breath caught in her chest. She looked . . . She couldn't even think the word without feeling befuddled.

"Beautiful," Lady Mowbray said simply.

"*Mais oui,*" Madame Celeste agreed, nodding her approval.

"But we must continue. Otherwise, we'll have no time to discuss your gown for Lord Elgin's ball—never mind the list of suitors who will be in attendance."

Elena allowed the modiste to undress her, stepping out of the satin fabric and donning an offered wrapper. "List of suitors?"

"Come now, my child. We'll not argue the point. You will be introduced to men at the agreed-upon events. While I respect your wishes, I do think it wise to at least investigate the opportunities here in town."

Elena tied the sash at her waist and followed Lady Mowbray to a plush lavender settee as the modiste left the room. "I don't know that it's necessary."

"And why is that?" the woman asked leadingly, reaching for the tea set situated on a low table and pouring the first cup.

Elena narrowed her eyes at the marchioness. "What do you mean?"

"Why do I feel as though we're speaking in code?" she began, dropping two lumps of sugar then a splash of cream in the cup. "You said that it might not be necessary to look for a husband. I'm merely curious as to why."

She briskly stirred the tea and handed it to Elena, waiting for an answer.

The would-be matchmaker suspected that there was *something* between Dash and Elena; that much was clear. Elena absolutely could not give Lady Mowbray even the merest hint of hope. If she did, the marchioness would surely wheedle the truth from her and the kiss would be revealed.

"I would have thought it was obvious," Elena answered, taking a sip of tea. "I've no intention of allowing a man to distract me from my real work, Lady Mowbray. I'll attend your events with 'marked enthusiasm,' as I agreed. And that is all."

Lady Mowbray prepared her cup, then relaxed back onto the settee and sipped. "I see."

Elena returned her cup to its saucer. "Splendid," she replied, relief settling into her stomach.

"And 'this work' that you speak of, Miss Barnes. Do tell me about it."

Elena placed her cup and saucer on the tray and folded her hands in her lap. "Well, as you know, I've a great interest in the Halcyon Society and the work that they do," she began earnestly.

"Yes," the marchioness confirmed.

"So many women—too many—are forced into prostitution, Lady Mowbray. For a variety of deplorable reasons, they find themselves with no other choice. But what if they were given the support and opportunity that every single human being deserves? What then?" Elena asked, her hands gesturing excitedly. "I believe they could prosper. And more important, I know that they could be happy. A donation is all well and good. But I want to help with my *own* two hands."

Lady Mowbray smoothed a stray lock of hair into place. "You are inspiring, my dear."

"I don't know about that," Elena began, pausing to reclaim her cup. "It is organizations such as the Halcyon Society that are the true inspiration."

"Yes, well," the marchioness countered, plucking a seamstress's thread from her skirt. "Either way, it is a true pity that you've no use for men. Viscount Carrington could do with a cause or two to support, now that he's taken on the title."

Elena leaned in, nearly spilling her tea. "Oh, but I can't imagine he'd have any interest in women's issues."

"Quite to the contrary, my dear," Lady Mowbray replied energetically. "The viscount has always been pragmatic when it comes to such things—and remarkably softhearted. I suppose it has something to do with his intelligence."

Elena stared at the marchioness, unable to formulate a response. She sipped some tea. And then some more. "I'm sorry, Lady Mowbray. His intelligence?"

"Did I stutter, Miss Barnes?"

"No," Elena answered, fearing that she'd insulted the marchioness. "And I meant no offense, truly. It's just that . . ."

Elena took yet another drink of tea.

"You've not spent enough time in the viscount's company to truly discern his intellect?" Lady Mowbray offered helpfully.

"Yes! Precisely," Elena lied.

The marchioness smiled in understanding. "Yes, well, that would make sense. But trust me, Miss Barnes. The viscount is remarkably bright. Rather like you."

"Ladies," Madame Celeste called as she reentered the room. "Let us continue. I've a fetching red silk, just arrived from India today. It's absolutely exquisite, with gold thread interwoven throughout. There's also a lovely emerald green."

Lady Mowbray sat up at the sound of "fetching," and "exquisite." "We'll see the red first," she replied efficiently, rubbing her hands together. "It just might be perfect for the Elgin ball. Then the green, if you please. No need to be confined to missish pastels, my dear."

Elena nodded at the woman's suggestion. *Rather like you.* She drained her cup and set it gently down on the saucer. She was growing fonder of the marchioness with each passing day, which made the fact that the woman was as mad as a March hare that much sadder. Oh, she'd questioned her original estimation of the viscount since first arriving at Carrington House. But Elena worried that she'd been thinking with her heart rather than her head. "Remarkably bright." The viscount would have to be if he were to offer any meaningful support to the Halcyon Society. And even then, he'd still be a man. Elena was not quite as militant as other bluestockings, but she'd been under Lord Carrington's roof long enough to know that he was dangerously distractive.

Madame Celeste returned with the fabrics and gestured for Elena to rise.

Elena pushed the pointless notions from her mind and stood, allowing the modiste to drape the soft silken red material around her.

"Oh," Lady Mowbray said appreciatively. "Well, Miss Barnes, what do you think?"

Elena stepped in front of the glass and examined herself. The woman may have overestimated the viscount, but she did have a way with fashion. "It's lovely. Would you agree?"

"Completely."

Elena slumped slightly, relieved to be done.

Madame Celeste grasped her by the shoulders and pulled her back up. "No slouching, Miss Barnes. Now we must choose a pattern."

"And then we'll look at the green. It may make for a lovely opera dress," Lady Mowbray added, then retrieved a fashion magazine from the low table and began to turn the pages thoughtfully. "What do we think of slashed sleeves, Madame Celeste?"

"For the green?" the modiste asked, eyeing the emerald fabric that she'd tossed upon the settee.

"I think so," the marchioness confirmed. "Come, look at this dress. It's perfectly suited to Miss Barnes's shape, wouldn't you agree?"

Madame Celeste released Elena's shoulder and joined Lady Mowbray. "This is precisely what I had in mind for her. Understated but breathtaking."

Their conversation turned to accessories. "Did you bring many jewels from Dorset, Miss Barnes?" the modiste asked.

"Pearls or diamonds?" Lady Mowbray wondered out loud.

"Diamonds. No question," Madame Celeste answered firmly.

Elena allowed her shoulders to slump again. She hadn't thought to bring any jewelry with her to London. But she didn't want to spoil their fun. So she remained silent, and pondered just what a "slashed sleeve" might be.

It wasn't like Rowena to be late.

Elena stared at the puzzle book in her hands, trying to concentrate. Usually by this time in the morning, Rowena would have been seeing to her hair while regaling Elena with colorful and clever stories from below stairs. Recognizing that her attempts to read were futile,

Elena discarded the book on the night table. Standing from the plush bed, she crossed the room to retrieve her shoes. She'd dressed an hour earlier with the help of Maggie, a chambermaid whom she'd heard walking down the hallway. The maid had promised to find Rowena at once, but Elena had assured Maggie that fetching her friend could wait until she'd completed her morning duties and all the fires were lit. She'd not wanted the maid to get into trouble.

Elena fussed with the lacings on her kidskin shoes, finally finishing the task and rising. Though Carrington House was very large and grand with many, many rooms, Maggie should have found Rowena by now.

Which begged the question: where was her friend? A sense of dread filled Elena's chest and she breathed deeply, forcing the feeling from her as she exhaled.

Elena straightened the skirt of her Pomona green striped morning dress and walked to the door, opening it just as Maggie came running up the hall.

The maid slowed to a walk but her eyes remained fixed on Elena's. She'd been crying, her face flushed from the effort.

Bell rounded the corner just at the end of the hall and moved stealthily toward Elena, which struck her as rather odd.

Butlers never moved stealthily.

Unless something was wrong.

"Beggin' your pardon, Miss," the maid began, curtsying before Elena. "Mr. Bell will have a word with you. 'Tis about Miss Rowena. I promise, I'd no idea she'd gone."

Elena flattened her palm against the wall and looked at the girl. "Maggie, I've no idea what you're talking about."

Bell stopped abruptly next to Maggie and bowed to Elena. "Maggie, quiet, if you please," he said to the girl,

who'd started to cry again. She did as she was told, stepping back and turning her gaze to the Kidderminster
carpet.

"Now, Miss Barnes, I've some distressing news. Would
you prefer to sit down?"

Elena pressed hard against the wall with one hand,
her other coming to clutch at her neck. "No, Bell. Thank
you. Now, if you would please tell me what is going on.
Where is Rowena? And why is Maggie crying?"

Bell looked disappointed with her decision to remain
standing, but pressed on. "It seems that Rowena received a missive late last evening from a certain Mr.
Brock."

"Am I meant to know this 'Mr. Brock'?" Elena asked,
scouring her brain for any hint of association.

"You wouldn't, Miss. He's a nasty one—not the type
the ton would take notice of," Maggie answered, garnering a quelling look from Bell. "It's true enough. I'm
not lying—never would to you, Mr. Bell. Nor you,
Miss."

The butler shushed the girl, then returned his gaze to
Elena and continued. "I've been told by the staff that
this Mr. Brock performs any number of *services* for a
cadre of men—"

"*Dangerous* blokes, Miss," Maggie interrupted a second time. "Or so I've heard. A gang run out of White-
chapel. Controls all of this side of London."

Elena released her neck and shakily placed her hand
on the wall. *The man from the park.* She'd assumed his
appearance in the bookshop had been an unfortunate
coincidence. Oh God, what had she missed? "I'm sorry,
but what, exactly, are you telling me?"

"Among other things, Mr. Brock procures young
women for use as prostitutes," Bell answered, his lips
drawing into a thin line.

"What on earth is going on?"

All three looked to where Lady Mowbray appeared, her skirts swishing violently as she hurried toward them. "My Gemma will not stop crying and carrying on— something to do with Rowena, though I could hardly decipher her words."

Elena's heart was racing. Her head felt dangerously light, and she was suddenly so angry she could not stand still. "It seems that Rowena has been taken by this—this Brock," she said as she pushed open the door to her chamber and stepped quickly inside.

"Brock?" Lady Mowbray parroted, following her. "I'm not acquainted with the man."

Elena retrieved her pelisse and chip hat. "Nor should you be. Apparently he lures young women into . . ." She paused, haphazardly placing the hat on her head. She couldn't finish the sentence. Couldn't even think it through. "I need to find her. Now."

She made to step by Lady Mowbray only to be caught by the woman's surprisingly strong hold.

"Bell, where can we find this Brock?" she asked, staring into Elena's eyes reassuringly.

"I took the liberty of asking the staff. It seems Mr. Brock is associated with the Rambling Rose, my lady," the butler answered. "A house of ill repute, located in Covent Garden. Unfortunately, Lord Carrington is not here to accompany you."

Lady Mowbray wrapped Elena in her pelisse and turned toward Bell and Maggie. "Well, then we'll have to make do with a manservant, won't we?"

"You cannot possibly accompany me," Elena insisted and attempted to loosen the marchioness's grip on her arm. "I will not allow it."

Lady Mowbray only tightened her hold. "You've no choice, Miss Barnes. Either I go with you, or you wait for the viscount to return. I am your chaperone, remember?"

"But I am responsible for Rowena," she ground out angrily.

"No, my child. I am."

The marchioness would not stand down, and Elena could not wait.

"Mr. Bell, have the coach readied," Elena boldly instructed the butler. "There is no time to waste."

9

"Hold for a moment," Dash whispered to Nicholas as he picked the lock on the door of the Rambling Rose. He turned the tool this way and that until the door opened.

Nicholas scanned the alley, then consulted the hastily drawn map in his hands. "You really must visit India, Carrington," he said. Pausing in the doorway, he turned to his friend and grinned. "Your skills would be put to good use."

Dash gestured for his friend to turn back, but not before arching an eyebrow in response. "I'm sure they would. But my Corinthian duties keep me here," he answered sardonically, following Nicholas into the building.

He pushed the door shut, easing it back into place, and waited for his eyes to adjust to the dim morning light. A worn brown runner accompanied by faded wallpaper and painted sconces slowly came into focus. A peculiar smell permeated the area, sour and sickeningly sweet at the same time.

"We only need access to this floor, thankfully," Nicholas whispered, gesturing for Dash to follow him. "According to the map, the madam's office should be the first door on the left, just there," he explained, moving slowly so that his Hessians didn't make a sound.

Dash thought to ask where the map had come from, but decided against it. The more time he spent with

Nicholas, the less he wanted to know about the man's time in India.

"They'll be asleep above stairs, won't they?" he asked, listening for any sign that someone might be afoot.

Nicholas pointed to the door. "In theory, yes—the girls anyway. But there's the madam to consider. And her henchmen—who are quite adept at cracking skulls, according to the information I received." He tried to turn the knob, but it wouldn't budge.

Dash reached for the tool within a concealed waist-coat pocket, knelt down, and set to work.

"Information? Supplied to you?" he asked, despite his concern. He finished with the lock and stood, returning the tool to his pocket.

"Do you want to catch this man?" his friend asked.

"Of course I do. I just don't want you killed in the process," Dash replied, bothered that Nicholas had asked him such a thing.

Nicholas tried the knob and smiled when it turned. "Carrington, I never pegged you for being such a sensitive soul. Really, quite soft, when it comes right down to it."

"Stow it," Dash grumbled, and then walked into the office.

Nicholas followed, closing the door behind them. "Well, someone is tidy."

Dash narrowed his eyes, taking in the small, organized room. He walked to a window along the opposite wall and drew one curtain aside just enough to let a measure of light through. "Yes, quite tidy, indeed."

The beechwood desk was scratched and worn, but every last item upon it was dusted and perfectly ordered. A row of leather-bound books stood up against the back wall, supported by a matching beechwood case. Each book was the same size as the one before it, their spines facing out and perfectly aligned.

"I'll start with the books. You see to the desk," Dash instructed Nicholas. He turned to examine the spines of the books. Each bore a rose and a number, which Dash assumed indicated a year. He moved down the row until he found 1798.

He pulled the volume from its place on the shelf and turned back, gently placing the book on the desk.

"Do you think they'd leave such information out, where anyone could find it?" Nicholas asked, rifling through the contents of a drawer.

Dash opened the volume. "Plain sight is oftentimes the most effective hiding place of all," Dash answered, thumbing through the entries. "Besides, we've no idea what information will tell us which customer we're looking for."

Nicholas walked around the desk and eyed the pages. "Well, it looks to be in alphabetical order."

Dash ran his finger across the top, where six columns were identified. Name, address, date of last "service," preferred girl, money owed the brothel, and money owed the customer.

"Money owed the customer?" Nicholas asked, looking to where Dash's finger had stopped on the page. "What does that mean?"

Dash tapped his finger, and then ran it down the length of the column to where the first amount was noted. "It means said customer must have done something for the Rose. We've a way to track him, Nicholas," Dash replied, reaching for a scrap of foolscap and a quill.

He moved to the left along the columns until landing on the customer's name. "John Trenney."

"Is that him?"

Dash looked at the man's address, and then moved on. "No. Remember, the woman that my father spoke to swore that the man was of quality. We're looking for someone with a title."

He flipped page after page, not finding another notation until reaching the Fs. That too failed to identify a nobleman.

The sudden pounding of footfalls upstairs sent Nicholas toward the door. He opened it just a hair and the noise from above intensified.

He closed the door suddenly and turned to Dash. "Looks as though we may be interrupted."

"I need more time," Dash demanded, quickening his pace and happening upon a notation in the Ks. "Dammit," he swore under his breath when the name was not one that he recognized.

Nicholas walked back to the desk and snapped up the discarded map. "I'll do my best, but you'll need to hurry."

"What the bloody hell are you talking about?" Dash asked, the last of the sentence lost when Nicholas opened the door, stepped out into the hallway, and shut Dash inside.

The pounding of men's footfalls and vicious words followed.

"Catch me if you can, you filthy whore spawn," Nicholas spat out, his maniacal laughter fading as he ran down the hall for the alley.

Dash dove beneath the desk with the book in his hands. The door burst open and Dash held his breath.

"Nottin' in 'ere. Go get 'em, boys."

He waited until the door closed again, then crawled out and stood. He'd left off at the Ks, meaning he still had over half of the book to search. Dash turned to the correct page and began again, racing through each entry with renewed vigor.

No new entries appeared until the surnames starting with S.

"Christ Almighty," Dash growled, his finger landing on Mr. Francis Smeade. The "sums owed" column showed a payment made to the man in July 1798—the month Lady Afton had been murdered. And there were more, the same sum, but in different months, during different years. He'd seen the exact dates before, on a document from the Afton case. There'd been murders of Corinthian family members since Lady Afton's death, and the dates of their deaths were the precise ones he was looking at now.

Smeade was the Bishop. But someone connected to the brothel had paid the man to brutally kill Lady Afton and the others. He'd pointed the knife and committed the murder, but someone other than Smeade had made the decision.

Dash had never cared for Smeade. But now pure, unadulterated hatred flashed in his heart.

He'd put that to good use. He returned the book to its place on the shelf and finished with the remaining volumes, finding no other possible suspect. Walking to the door, he listened for any noise in the hallway. Complete silence filled the basement.

He opened the door, looked both ways before stepping out into the corridor, and then shut the door behind him. Reaching the exit to the alleyway, he crossed the street and began to walk north, turning back only once to look at the front of the brothel.

Where his matching bags and coach stood waiting.

✦ ✦

"I demand that you bring me the girl at once."

Elena swallowed hard. Lady Mowbray's words had been delivered with due severity, but they'd clearly underestimated what awaited them at the Rambling Rose.

She looked to the far corner where James, the manservant sent along to protect them, lay, incapacitated by a single blow.

"And I demand that you shut your potato trap, love," the ringleader replied casually. "Or I'll shut it for ya."

As the coach had dipped and dodged its way across London, Lady Mowbray had assured Elena that they would retrieve Rowena with superior breeding, morals, and intelligence.

Right would win out over might.

Elena had been so intensely gripped by fear for her friend that she'd convinced herself Lady Mowbray spoke the truth. Her misgivings over the woman's presence had abated and she'd allowed her indignation to lift until their success was all but guaranteed.

And then they'd clawed their way into the foyer and it had deteriorated from there.

Elena held tightly to the marchioness's arm as she attempted to slap the offender. "Sir," Elena pleaded, wincing at the sound of her frightened voice. "The girl is my maid. She's been with my family for some time and ultimately, I am responsible for her safety. Please, return Rowena to us. I'll happily pay you a very reasonable sum."

"Maybe Rowena don't want to leave. Maybe she's keen on a new life, ain't that right, Mr. Brock?"

The man from the park and the bookshop came around the corner, his filthy smile sending sparks of anger up Elena's spine. "She appears quite settled in—almost as though she were born for such things."

"Mr. Brock." Elena released Lady Mowbray's arm and walked slowly toward the man. "Should you not do as I've requested, I'll alert Bow Street and your business will be cited—perhaps even closed if I have any say in the matter. And Lady Mowbray's considerable connections and place in society will surely do you no favors. You vile, villainous, bloo—"

"Well, knock me down with a feather," a deep voice spoke out from behind Elena.

Startled, she paused in her advance upon Brock and turned to see just who was speaking.

Lord Carrington stood just inside, leaning lazily against the doorjamb, an expression of baffled confusion written on his handsome face. "There I was, strolling about town and minding my own business, when suddenly I spy my very own coach—parked outside of the infamous Rambling Rose, no less. Funnily, I don't remember leaving it here last night. Of course, I don't remember being here last night, either. So, I would be grateful if someone would be so kind as to explain just what is going on."

"This ain't none of your affair, guv," the ringleader spat out. "So just take your fancy self off, now. Lest you be interested in a fight."

Lady Mowbray pulled a long, sharp pin from her hat and pointed it at the man. "You've no right to speak to Lord Carrington in such an insolent manner. Rowena was living under the viscount's roof when she was taken. Therefore, she is *his* responsibility. And yes, should you refuse to return the girl, he is most assuredly looking for a fight."

Lord Carrington pushed himself off the doorjamb, his demeanor menacing as he slowly walked toward the man. "Trolling for fresh meat for the flats, were we?" he asked, gesturing for Elena and the marchioness to move behind him. "Well, I hate to be the one to tell you this, but the chit's not for sale. And I'll give you my purse, just to prove my point. A very generous offer, wouldn't you agree?"

Elena couldn't see exactly what was taking place, but Lord Carrington pulled something from his waistcoat and tossed it to the man, who looked all too happy to comply.

"Brock, go get the girl," he ordered, then greedily opened the drawstring bag and began to count the coins.

Brock eyed Lord Carrington warily and backed up,

nearly falling on the stairs before turning and running to the floor above.

Lord Carrington walked to where James lay, nudging him with his boot. "Time to wake up."

James rolled to his back and opened his eyes, the sight of Lord Carrington looming over his prostrate body making the young man squeak. "My lord!"

"Are you able to walk?" the viscount asked, offering his arm.

James accepted the man's outstretched hand and managed to stand. "I believe so, my lord."

"Splendid. Take the women to the carriage and wait for me there. I'll be out in a moment."

James bowed, nearly falling over, then righted himself and made haste for Elena and Lady Mowbray.

"Filthy heathens," the marchioness said pointedly to the ringleader, threatening him once again with her hatpin. Then she reached out for Elena's hand and placed it in the crook of her arm.

Elena was both considerably grateful and oddly irritated. Only a moment before, she'd been in danger of joining Rowena above stairs, her ill-considered tirade thankfully interrupted by the viscount.

And now, her dear friend was nearly safe. And Elena had done nothing to help.

"My lord, I'd rather stay until Rowena is brought down. She'll be terrified. The sight of me will calm her. I must insist."

"That won't be necessary." His jaw visibly tensed. "Rowena and I will be right behind you. James," he called out authoritatively. "See to the women."

Lady Mowbray pulled her the length of the foyer. James opened the door and waited as the women crossed the threshold. The manservant closed the door behind them and ushered them down the narrow steps of the Rambling Rose. Elena heard the front door open as she stepped into the coach and looked back to see Lord Carrington, his arm protectively around Rowena's shoulders as he all but carried her toward the conveyance. Relief flooded Elena and she stepped inside, sitting down on the plush, comfortable seat across from Lady Mowbray.

The viscount held Rowena's hand tightly as she climbed into the coach, releasing her only once she'd settled against Elena. Then he climbed in and sat next to the marchioness. "Go," he ordered, thumping the ceiling with his fist.

"Miss, I'm so sorry," Rowena whispered in between sobs.

Elena held her friend tightly and stroked her hair. "You've nothing to apologize for, Rowena. I'm the one who should have seen to your safety."

"But my reputation, Miss. It's all but—"

"Intact," Lord Carrington interrupted firmly. "Do not think otherwise. You were taken against your own will, Rowena. Given no choice by men who would do you harm . . ." He paused, anger simmering just beneath his skin. "I will not allow a man such as Mr. Brock to rob you of your reputation."

Rowena's sobs quieted and she rested her head against Elena's shoulder.

"Thank you," Elena mouthed to the man, sure that he couldn't know just how much his words had meant to her dear friend. And to her.

Elena had insisted that Rowena be brought to her chamber the moment they'd arrived at Carrington House. Lord Carrington had carried her up the marble stairs himself, then left the girl in Elena's care while he spoke with Bell.

Lady Mowbray had offered to help, but Elena had assured her that she could take care of Rowena—and indeed, needed to—on her own. She'd asked the marchioness to see that tea was prepared and told her she'd join her soon in the drawing room.

She'd called for a bath to be drawn and seen to her friend's needs, gently scrubbing the dirt and blood from Rowena's skin and hair and sluicing the warm, steaming water over her dear friend's exhausted body.

"Burn these," she told Molly firmly, handing Rowena's filthy dress and underpinnings to the maid. "And let me know the moment the doctor arrives, will you?"

Molly took the clothing in hand and dipped a polite curtsy, her eyes wide with horror as she stared at Rowena. "Of course, Miss," she answered, managing nothing more than a whisper and turning to go.

"Rowena, can you stand for me?" Elena asked softly, reaching for the length of linen that Molly had supplied earlier. She held out her hand and her friend took it in hers, allowing herself to be pulled to her feet.

"They gave me something, Miss," Rowena said, her voice hoarse. "It made me sleepy."

Elena held tightly to her friend's hand as she coaxed her to step from the tub. "I know, dear. Don't worry. You'll sleep soon."

Rowena had informed Elena of this very fact several times since their return to the viscount's home. She prayed that the haze had taken control some hours before and left Rowena with very little memory of her ordeal.

Rowena drew one foot out and placed it on the carpet, and then the other.

Elena wrapped the linen around her friend, the sight of her battered body stealing the air from her lungs. The skin on both Rowena's wrists was raw and bleeding where she'd clearly been tied up with rope. An angry purple mark in the shape of a large hand was a darkening shadow where the base of her neck had been seized more than once. And small, red scratches marred her forearms and feet, blood oozing from a broken toenail.

Rowena held tightly as Elena carefully dried her, wincing with pain when her injuries were touched.

Elena bit the inside of her cheek to keep from crying, finishing with the linen and laying it over the side of the tub. She retrieved the night rail from the sideboard and urged Rowena to lift her arms.

"I'm tired, Miss. They gave me something. I tried to spit it out. But they just gave me more."

Elena dropped the gown over her friend's head and carefully placed each arm into its respective sleeve, before catching the hem in her hands and drawing it the rest of the way down Rowena's body.

Her throat ached with unspent tears. She looped one arm about Rowena's waist and guided her out of the dressing room and across the chamber to the bed.

Molly had already seen to turning down the bed. Elena released Rowena and slowly swung her about, holding her shoulders as her friend slumped to a sitting position, raised her legs, then lay down. She drew the coverlet up and delicately tucked it under Rowena's arms, noting how fragile her friend looked. Her wet hair was spread out upon the pillow, the blond curls haphazardly spinning this way and that, so unlike her usual neat knot. There were blue smudges of exhaustion beneath her eyes, and her lips were ashen.

It wasn't Rowena. At least not the Rowena she'd been only the day before. And Elena couldn't stop her mind from wondering if she'd ever be the same again.

Her friend shifted slightly and grimaced. "I'm sorry, Miss. I thought it would be a lark. He was so handsome, so refined. I never should have gone. I know that now," Rowena confessed, her eyes fluttering closed. "You told me he was dangerous and I didn't listen."

Elena knelt next to the bed and took Rowena's hand

in hers. "Do not apologize, my dear, dear friend. It is my fault, and mine alone," she assured Rowena. Sharp, stinging tears forced their way past Elena's will and down her cheeks. "Those men will not go unpunished. I promise you."

"Excuse me, Miss, but the doctor's here."

Elena wiped at her face before meeting Molly's gaze. "Of course. Send him in."

She turned back to Rowena and caressed her dear friend's gaunt cheek. "Rest now. Everything will be all right. I'll make sure of it."

10

Dash stood behind his desk in the study. He watched as the afternoon sunlight collided with the crystal decanter on the sideboard and sent sparkling shards of light dancing upon the wall. Three days had passed since the Rambling Rose incident. Brock had roughly shoved the girl down the stairs and watched with amusement as she'd lost her balance on the last step and landed in a heap at Dash's feet. She'd cried out at the sight of him and gratefully accepted his protective arm about her shoulders, hiding beneath his coat until he'd delivered her safely to Miss Barnes.

Dash stopped to consider why he was standing. He'd wandered through the last few days in a constant state of confusion, or so it seemed. He walked around his desk and stepped out into the hall, hesitating as he decided where to go.

The interior of the coach had been eerily calm. The marchioness was clearly shaken, but quietly proud. Rowena had settled against her mistress's side, weeping silently as Elena whispered reassuringly to her maid, holding tightly to the woman the entire ride back to Carrington House.

He began to walk down the hallway aimlessly, his fingers reaching out to skim the wall.

Dash would never forget the look upon Miss Barnes's face. Her milky skin had gone ashen and her lips had drawn into a tight, grim line. But it was her eyes that had chilled him, the deep brown glistening with pain and regret.

He'd hardly seen the woman since their return. Rowena had been sent back to Dorset two days after her rescue, the doctor assuring them she would convalesce best at home. And Miss Barnes had retreated to her room, Lady Mowbray visiting often in the hopes of lifting her spirits, or so the marchioness had told him.

Dash had willed himself to keep his distance, but he knew what must be done. Their kiss in her chamber was nothing more than the means to an end—or so he had told himself whenever he thought on it. She trusted him. And now, he had to break that trust. It was cruel to be sure, but she had to leave London. He needed her safe.

He curled his fingers into a fist and struck the wall, failing to notice whether it hurt. He didn't deserve to feel, physically or emotionally. Before Miss Barnes, it wouldn't have mattered. But now, it was all that did.

Once they'd returned from the Rambling Rose, the doctor had no more than closed his kit when Bell had informed Dash that a visitor awaited him in his study. It was Nicholas. He'd evaded the brothel's men, and then doubled back, making sure that Dash had escaped, too.

When Dash had told Nicholas of Smeade, his friend had gladly accepted a snifter of brandy and drank deeply, closing his eyes as he did so. "We'll have to wait," he'd told Dash, his eyes opening once again. "We'll need proof. Give me time. I've a man in the Rose. He should be able to tell us more."

Dash reached the front of the house and turned into the library. And so he'd waited a day. And another. And now a third, he thought begrudgingly, stepping across the threshold.

He reached out and stole a lilac blossom from an arrangement that sat upon a table. Smeade's place in society, though questionable, secured a certain privacy that

Dash would find difficult to penetrate. And there were no Corinthians to speak to on the matter, not even Carmichael.

Especially not Carmichael.

No, there was nothing to be done but wait for news from Nicholas. It was bloody torture, and Dash was nearing the end of his rope.

"Lord Carrington?"

Dash looked up to see Miss Barnes coming toward him, a pair of odd-looking gloves in her hand. "Miss Barnes, what a surprise to find you here."

"Is that so?" she asked quizzically. "I was going to make the same observation about you."

She offered him a small smile, though it was tinged with sadness. "I'd grown restless in my chamber and needed to do *something*."

Dash understood all too well. "Of course. I feel precisely the same way."

"Ah," she replied, looking at the flower in his hand. "We all do, I think."

He looked down at the bloom contemplatively. Miss Barnes possessed much in common with the flower, both beautiful, hardy in an English rain, yet intensely fragile in certain ways.

Breakable, really.

He held the lilac out to her. "It's one of my favorites."

"It's lovely," she replied, bringing the bloom to her nose and delicately sniffing.

"And yours?"

Miss Barnes lowered the lilac and twirled it between her fingers. "My what, Lord Carrington?"

Dash winced at the awkward quality of their conversation. He knew what to do with ledgers and financial sleight of hand, ciphers, and secret letters. But Miss Barnes had a way of undoing his senses, even when he'd made up his mind that she wouldn't.

"Your favorite flower," he answered, adding "and do call me Dash, won't you?" in the hope that a less formal address would help ease their stilted back-and-forth.

"Hmmm . . ." she replied, biting her lip. "I suppose the use of your Christian name would not be too untoward at this point in our friendship." A faint blush appeared on her cheeks. "Oh, and my favorite flower is the wild dog rose. It absolutely covers Dorset in the springtime."

She'd flinched the moment the word "rose" had come out of her mouth.

"And these gloves," Dash asked, suddenly desperate to distract her from such thoughts. "What do you plan to do with them?"

She looked at the paper-thin gloves in her hand as if she'd forgotten them altogether. "Oh, yes, of course. It's something rather exciting. I'm going to pack the Paolini. Would you care to join me?"

He knew he should say no. But her enthusiasm was infectious. Dash couldn't care less about the book on Greek mythology, but all at once, he needed to see it prepared for travel.

"I would like nothing more, Miss Barnes." He offered his arm to her.

She smiled softly and looped her arm through his. "Splendid. And you must call me Elena."

Dash guided Elena to the case where the Paolini was kept.

Elena released his arm and returned the flower to Dash. "Giacomo Paolini's *Abecedary Illustrations of Greek Mythology*," she said reverently, donning first one glove and then the other.

"And why is this book so special to you?"

"Well, as I explained before, it's very rare—"

"Yes," Dash interrupted, watching as she opened the glass case and gently reached inside. "I remember why it's special to the world. But that's not what I asked. I want to know why it's special to you."

He shouldn't be asking such questions. But he had to know more of her before she disappeared from his life.

Elena slid her fingers beneath the lower right corner of the leather-bound book and slowly opened it, supporting the cover with her left hand. "Many call it the Grotesque Alphabet," she began, carefully turning the title page to reveal Atheonis artistically twisted into a capital A with Diana in the background. "But I think it's beautiful. All of the power and intelligence—the very mystique of the Greek gods—distilled down into twenty-six engravings. Most miss how truly special the book is because they're too busy expecting it to be something else."

Like you. Dash stared at the book as she gingerly turned the pages, each letter revealing Paolini's talent and imagination. He saw it, the beauty and truth beneath the paper and pencil.

Just as he saw the same in Elena.

"And you, Dash. What is your favorite book?"

"Sun Tzu's *The Art of War,*" Dash answered distractedly. "Fascinating stuff, really. Subduing one's enemy without fighting . . ."

Elena had stopped turning the pages and was instead staring intently at Dash. "My lord, what an *interesting* choice."

Ciphers and secret letters never suspected Dash of being anyone other than his Corinthian cover. Nor did ledgers or questionable finances.

He smiled at her, groping for the most vapid thoughts he could summon. "It's Dash, remember," he teased. "And I was only having a bit of fun with you. I overheard two gentlemen discussing the book at my club. Thought it might make me look intelligent."

She closed the book and turned to face him, her eyes

narrowing as she inspected his face. "Are you quite sure? Because both author and title rolled off your tongue most naturally."

"Elena, are you suggesting that I forgot about reading this Tzu chap's book?" Dash asked skeptically. "Because that would truly make me a dimwit, wouldn't it?"

"My lord," Bell interrupted as he walked toward the two.

"Lady Mowbray wishes to remind you that you're expected at the opera this evening."

"Miss Barnes, you mean?" Dash sought to confirm.

"Both of you, actually," Bell answered and bowed.

"Oh," Elena replied hesitantly. "I should go. The marchioness will be anxious to see my new dress."

She turned back to the Paolini and secured its case once again. "And if not Tzu's *Art of War,* then what?"

"*Mother Goose,*" Dash answered, his tone humorless.

Elena pivoted about, nodding somberly at Dash, a small smile appearing. "*Mother Goose,*" she repeated quietly, then followed after Bell.

Dash brought the lilac bloom to his lips and closed his eyes.

※

"Did you enjoy the first two acts?"

"Not in the slightest," Dash answered, steering Lady Mowbray and Elena through the throng that had abandoned their boxes in favor of champagne and conversation during the opera's interval.

Lady Mowbray glared at him. "I wasn't asking you—as you well know," she said pointedly, taking Elena's arm in hers. "Well, my dear? Is the opera to your liking? I must say that I rather enjoyed Madame Catalani—such power, such presence. Really quite exceptional."

Elena pasted a smile on her lips and nodded enthusiastically. The truth was, she'd never been much for the theater, the mad crush of bodies only serving to remind her why she loved the open country best.

"My dear, you look positively frightened," the older woman observed worriedly. "Are you quite all right? Perhaps this was too much, too soon. I'd hoped to take your mind off of poor Rowena with a bit of entertainment, but it appears I've only aggravated the situation."

Elena couldn't think on Rowena. She wouldn't. Late at night, in her bed, with the coverlet over her head, then she thought of her dear friend and wept. And wrestled with the guilt she suffered over allowing such a thing to happen. And plotted her revenge.

And wept some more.

But she would not allow the mere mention of the girl's name to toss her into histrionics. "I am fine, Lady Mowbray; only a bit overwhelmed by the evening. Perhaps I'll return to Carrington House now. But do stay for the rest of the performance," she urged the woman, readying to make her escape through the endless sea of nattering nobility.

"Lady Mowbray," a booming voice called, the man attached to it coming forward and stopping next to Dash.

Lady Mowbray curtsied and allowed the man to kiss her hand. "Lord Finesmith."

A young woman followed after Lord Finesmith. She was clearly uninterested in Elena, a frown of irritation clouding her beautiful face. And then she caught sight of Dash, and it was as if she'd been smiled on by the gods themselves.

"Lady Meeks, delightful to see you out again," Lady Mowbray said to the woman, though her enthusiasm was clearly for Lord Finesmith.

The woman curtsied. Her slim form, encased in sapphire-blue silk, elegantly folded and then returned to its noble line. "Lady Mowbray, it is indeed a pleasure to be back in society where I belong. And what a lucky girl I am to chance upon you and Lord Carrington. It has been too long."

Elena fidgeted with the slashed sleeve of the green silk dress Lady Mowbray's modiste had sent over. She hated the fact that the mere presence of a fashionable lady of the ton could make her feel nervous.

"May I introduce you to Miss Elena Barnes?" the marchioness replied, gesturing to Elena. "She's just up from Dorset."

The woman offered Elena a polite smile, her eyes taking in the length of her. "How do you do, Miss Barnes."

Elena couldn't decide if it would have been worse to have been ignored altogether by the duo. She smiled in return and curtsied, rather suspecting that she would have preferred the latter.

Lord Finesmith took Elena's hand and kissed it gently. "Welcome, Miss Barnes. Glad to have you in town. And during the season, no less. Perfect timing on your part. Plenty of people to meet, parties to attend, so on and so forth."

"Yes, it's always lovely to see new faces—especially one from the country," Lady Meeks agreed, her gaze now turned back to Dash. "Such colorful stories you people have of life on the farm. Wouldn't you agree, Lord Carrington?"

Elena swiftly realized that she did not like Lady Meeks. Actually, she'd already figured that out before the woman accused her of being a shepherdess. But now, she really did quite loathe her.

"Oh, yes," Dash agreed, winking at Lady Meeks in a conspiratorial manner and smiling. "Colorful indeed."

Elena ceased fidgeting with the slashed sleeve and grasped one gloved hand in the other behind her back, locking both elbows. "Yes, well, we rustics do adore our color," she replied sarcastically.

The entire party laughed out loud, save Lady Mow-bray and Elena.

"Nonsense. Without such 'rustics,' as you delicately referred to them, England would not be the great nation that it is today," Lady Mowbray stated, glaring at Dash, then Lord Finesmith and Lady Meeks in turn. "Besides, Miss Barnes is, by far, the most charming girl I've had the honor to chaperone—and the smartest. I would go so far as to say she's the brightest woman I've ever had the pleasure to know. You'd do well, Lady Meeks, to have such friends."

Elena wanted to kiss the woman, but knew such a breach in etiquette would only prove the others correct in their assumption that she was nothing more than a country bumpkin.

"Ah, a bluestocking then?" Lord Finesmith said, wag-gling his eyebrows. "It's all right, Miss Barnes. I don't mind an intelligent woman—as long as she's not overly so. Deuced unattractive though, when she is."

Lady Meeks's hand came to cover a small, delicate giggle that had escaped from her heart-shaped mouth.

Elena's heart began to race and she could feel the heat forming in bright, red spots on her cheeks. Fear stuck in the base of her throat, thickening as it wound its way about her neck and squeezed every last sensible word from her.

She instinctively looked at Dash for something. Anything. She didn't know what, precisely, and didn't really care. But she needed him to respond.

"I've no idea what color Miss Barnes's stockings are, Finesmith, and it's rather indelicate that you would make reference to such a thing," he jokingly replied, garnering a second giggle from Lady Meeks for his ef-forts and a thwack on the arm from the marchioness's fan.

Elena grasped her hands together so tightly she feared

losing a finger. "Not to put too fine a point on it, my lord," she began, jutting her chest out and standing as straight as she could. "But yes, I am, by far, the most intelligent one within our friendly circle, here, with the exception of Lady Mowbray."

The marchioness rapped Dash on the shoulder a second time, and then pointed the fan at Lord Finesmith. "You've hardly half your wits left, thanks to your hunting accident ten years back," she began sternly. "But you, Lady Meeks, should know better."

Lady Meeks's damnably perfect mouth formed an "O" of surprise, but she said nothing.

"And you, my boy," Lady Mowbray pressed on, giving Dash a stern look of disapproval. "Your father would have never stood for such behavior. I dare say he'd have been rather disappointed in you this evening."

Dash swallowed hard, though the insipid smile remained. "Come now, my lady, we were only playing."

With my heart, Elena couldn't help but think, her hands nearly numb.

She wanted to strike him. Needed to make him understand what it was to feel trapped like an animal, completely at the mercy of a stranger with nowhere to turn. She wanted to hide, far away from the deplorable pain that was threatening to overtake her.

But she wouldn't give the man the satisfaction—nor Lady Meeks. She couldn't.

"Well, as much as I enjoy a bit of banter, I'm afraid I have a headache. Lady Meeks, Lord Finesmith," Elena said, biting her tongue while curtsying to the two.

"Do take the coach, my dear," the marchioness replied gently. "Dash will see that it's brought round."

"No," Elena protested instantly, rising and straightening her skirts. "That is, I'll ask a footman to call for the coach. I would not want to ruin the viscount's evening."

"I believe he's managed to do that on his own," Lady

Mowbray said. "Besides, it is the least he can do. Now go, you two. Miss Barnes requires rest."

Elena turned to the crowd and waded in, hoping against hope that she would lose the man among the sea of faces—and never clap eyes on him again.

꙰

"You were not meant to accompany me."

Dash tapped the roof of the landau coach and it rolled into motion, the matching bags expertly steered into traffic before turning down Pall Mall Street. "I know that," he bit out, instantly regretting his response.

Elena folded her hands in her lap and stared out the window.

"I would like to apologize," Dash began, harnessing his temper.

"Apologize?" Elena repeated in a lethal tone. "For what, my lord?"

Dash didn't want to play this game. In truth, he was tired of games. Tired of pretending to be someone he wasn't. Exhausted by the need to push Elena away at every turn.

God, he'd made a mess of things. He wanted her, but knew that he shouldn't need her. Her safety was threatened by Smeade if she stayed and continued to work her way into his heart, and yet he was desperate for her not to go. She'd challenged his credibility until he'd been forced to prove his stupidity, his worthlessness to her that evening in the only way he knew how.

"You know very well, Elena," he answered quietly, staring at her.

Her lips trembled as she fought hard to maintain her composure. "That horrid woman tortured me for her own pleasure and you did nothing. How could you? I thought that . . ."

"God dammit, Elena," Dash spat out, leaning forward until his hands rested on the velvet cushion on each side of her. "Finish the bloody sentence. You thought what? That you knew me? Don't you see, that's the problem. You do—better than anyone else ever has. It terrifies me that I've allowed you so close."

"Yes, it's true. I thought you'd revealed yourself to me—tiny glimpses here and there," Elena replied angrily, averting her eyes toward the window. "In the library alcove and standing before your mother's portrait. And your obvious interest in the burr puzzle—the mention of Sun Tzu's book? These things found me contriving all sorts of fanciful realities about you. But tonight you proved me wrong. The man I thought you were would not have acted so cruelly."

Dash swore under his breath. "You're too insightful for your own good. Do you know why I hide my intelligence? To keep people away. And it's worked up until this point. But there's something about you, Elena. I couldn't help myself. Still can't."

She made to push him away. "If you truly cared for me, you'd never have allowed Lady Meeks to treat me in such a way. What do you think drove me from London all those years ago? It was women such as Lady Meeks. Beautiful on the outside, but harpies within."

Dash wouldn't move, no matter how Elena pressed. "You're wrong. I do know everything about you—that's why I let that shrew attack you. I need you gone—away from me. Out of my life."

It was nearly the truth. And that was everything that he could give.

"Is that what you want?" she asked, her hands slipping from his chest and landing softly in her lap.

She would comply, he thought bleakly. She was strong—the strongest woman he'd ever met. But his actions had cut her to the core. Elena would leave that very night, with as many books as possible stuffed into her baggage, and disappear forever. All Dash had to do was say one simple word.

He looked hard into her eyes, willing his mouth to open and "yes" to tumble out. But he saw her soul in his reflection, and it undid him completely. He was utterly lost in her depths, and it felt so right.

"Don't be such a gudgeon," Dash demanded, taking hold of her upper arms and shaking her. "I want you. More than anything."

Suddenly, the only thing that made sense in Dash's disorganized and chaotic world was Elena. She was everything that was wrong, yet everything that could be right.

And he didn't want to fight her anymore.

He pressed his lips to hers and took her mouth in a savage kiss, the feel of her breath on his as she reacted to his bold move only feeding the fire of desire growing in him.

She shoved him hard, and he released her reluctantly.

"Please," he uttered, desperate for the feel of her once again.

Elena touched her lips with one hand, gently caressing where Dash's lips had been but a moment before.

And then she slapped him hard across the cheek. "I will choose when I give myself completely, do you understand?"

"Of course," Dash whispered, guilt and regret beginning to flood his senses.

"And I choose now."

Elena grabbed his lapels and pulled him against her, crushing her lips to his.

Dash reached for the curtains and yanked them shut, repeating the process on the opposite side. "Circle the park," he yelled to the coachman.

Bracing himself on his knees, he wrapped his arms about Elena's waist and surrendered to the kiss, his tongue seeking hers as his hands grabbed at the buttons on her dress.

Elena's tongue touched his and she gasped, her breasts pressing against his chest as she sought to close what little space there was between them.

She brought her hands to his cravat and untied the knot, deftly pulling at the ends until it was released. She broke their kiss and started on his linen shirt. "I need to feel you against me."

Dash's cock throbbed at the sound of her words, his desire to be inside Elena matched by her hunger. He shrugged out of his coat and swiftly set to work on the buttons of his waistcoat, deftly releasing each one. Then he finished the work Elena had started on his shirt, yanking first one sleeve and then the other from his torso.

Elena tugged at his breeches, but they held. "Hmmmm . . ." she uttered breathlessly, continuing to pull at the fabric.

"It's your turn, Elena," Dash instructed, gesturing for her to turn around. "Once we've lightened you of your dress, I'll show you."

She hesitantly obeyed, carefully standing in the small space and turning as he'd told her to do. Elena braced herself with both hands splayed out against the walls of the coach while Dash finished with the remaining buttons. He reached for her right shoulder, slowly pulling the gown down her slim arm before turning his attention to the other.

Once the fabric bunched at her waist, he untied her laced corset, and then pushed the dress to the floor of the coach. His hands came around to cup both of her breasts and she leaned her head back against him.

He kneaded the heavy, deliciously soft orbs, and then rolled the tips in his fingers, lightly pinching until Elena moaned with pleasure. Dash reached for her stockings, but Elena stopped him, her hand holding on to his.

"I believe the breeches are next."

Elena desperately wanted to face him—to discover his body and all that he offered to her. She glanced down the length of herself, relieved that her corset and stockings continued to cover at least a portion of her abundant flesh.

"Elena," Dash crooned, his hand coming to rest gently on her shoulder.

She steadied herself against the window while turning around, taking in the sight of Lord Carrington's sculpted chest. It was far more spectacular than any work of art she'd seen in person—and, she'd ventured to guess, any she would encounter ever again.

She wished that simply staring at the man would satisfy the cravings that threatened to overtake her entire being. But she needed to see more—touch more. And feel more.

"You are the most beautiful woman I've ever seen," he said in a reverent tone, drawing Elena's eyes up to meet his.

And he meant it. His worshipful gaze told her so.

"I don't know what to say," she admitted, feeling shy once the admission had left her mouth.

He took her face in his hands and held it, looking at her as though he were memorizing every last measure of space, from the top of her forehead to her chin. "Say nothing. Only believe that I speak the truth."

Elena began to cry. "Please, don't . . ."

"Don't what?" he asked softly, concern clouding his eyes.

"Don't make me cry," she whispered, biting her lip.

He leaned in and kissed her. "I promise you, there's

nothing I wouldn't do to dry your tears. Simply say the word."

"This," she uttered, grabbing the curve of her hips, "and this," she continued, lifting her breasts as though they were bags of flour. "They're not beautiful. They're ample. Robust. Generous. But not beautiful."

Dash quieted her mouth with his finger, emitting a shushing sound from his lips. "Those are words of your choosing, not mine. To me, you are perfect."

He reached for his boots, pulling the right one off and leaving it on the floor of the carriage before removing the second. Then he unbuttoned his breeches and tugged them down, bringing his smalls with them. "I'll show you how beautiful you are, Elena, with my body."

He stepped out of the garment and kicked it aside, reaching for his stockings and yanking them off.

He knelt before her, his head bowed as though he were a slave at the feet of mighty Aphrodite. Elena looked down at the man, his muscular shoulders and back, his perfectly formed buttocks and strong thighs. She wanted him. But it was more than that. She wanted to see herself as he did—wanted to know what it was to join with someone until you didn't know where you ended and the other began.

"Please, show me what you see," she whispered, her hands coming to rest on his capable shoulders.

Dash lifted his head and nodded, then began to slowly roll one stocking down Elena's leg, his mouth placing delicate, wet kisses on the inside of her thigh, then her calf, and finally the arch of her foot. He started on the second stocking and Elena closed her eyes, the sensation of his lips and tongue on her intoxicating. She gripped his shoulders tightly, the sway of the carriage adding to the heady spell he cast.

"Sit," he murmured, gently taking her hands and helping her back onto the velvet bench.

Elena allowed him to guide her and dazedly relaxed against the tufted seat. She made to cross her legs, but Dash took her knee in his hand and opened her legs wide, settling himself between.

He rested his hands on each side of her head against the wall of the coach and kissed her, tenderly at first, the pressure and heat growing slowly.

Elena felt him lean in farther until their skin touched, the hair of his chest teasing her nipples. She pressed her breasts against him and rubbed, savoring the sensation as it traveled from her chest to her core, where it throbbed headily.

He broke the kiss and looked into her eyes. "You're no longer crying," he breathed. "Good." His tongue took in the shell of her ear and began to draw a tortuous path down her body, touching her right breast with such skillful, sensuous strokes that Elena cried out.

"I'm sorry," she said, embarrassed by her reaction.

He paused, kneading the left breast with his fingers until Elena felt the tension beginning to wind tightly in her belly. "I'm not."

He released her and his tongue began again, dipping lower until he reached the vee between her thighs.

Elena had seen such things in a book, though she couldn't place which one. Her back arched when his tongue found her folds and he gently sucked, his hands pushing her legs farther apart. Her hands reached out for something, anything to secure her, his mouth sending her soaring until she feared she would fly through the very ceiling of the coach.

She wound her fingers in his hair and held tightly as the sensation stole away all rational thought. She began to pant, short, hot breaths that seem to rise in her throat of their own accord. "Please, Dash," she begged, tugging at his hair in an effort to hold on. "Please."

His tongue slowed and he raised his head, an almost

feral look in his eyes that only increased Elena's need. He rose up on his knees, and then reached out for Elena's hips, scooting her toward the edge of the seat. Then he hooked one of her legs about his waist and then the other, his finger finding her clitoris and rubbing smoothly until Elena moaned.

"As one, truly?" Dash asked breathlessly, guiding his cock into her slick skin, then settling his hands on each side of her, his buttocks moving as he rhythmically coaxed Elena's need.

"Yes," Elena heard herself say, as though through a pane of glass. The world was slowly distilling down to this one, single moment that she sensed was about to overtake her.

Dash nuzzled her breasts, biting at the nipples. "I don't want to hurt you, Elena."

"Please," she begged, her nails scoring the velvet seat on each side of her. "I need you. Now."

Dash acquiesced and quickened his pace, his member seductively sliding into Elena until she was sure she'd splinter into a million pieces. She closed her eyes and dropped her head back, the sensation growing until she could no longer bear it.

"God, Elena," Dash uttered, his hands grabbing her hips. "Oh, God." His entire body shook with the force of his orgasm, and Elena held on tight, riding the wave of her own pleasure until it claimed her body and soul.

Elena tilted her head up and opened her eyes, her gaze meeting Dash's as they became one, the fire of their mutual satisfaction ripping a silent scream from her throat. She fell back on the velvet seat and pulled Dash with her, resting her head on his shoulder.

"Elena," he murmured, wrapping his arms about her and holding tight.

She closed her eyes and smiled against his skin. "Dash."

11

"You're distracted."

Dash narrowly missed stepping on a dead rat on the stairs of the Plymouth Building, skipping the tread at the last moment to avoid it. "It's hard not to be distracted here, Bourne."

The two men continued to climb the rickety steps toward the fourth floor, the eerie silence of the ancient Wharf Street building amplifying the sound of their progress even more than the warped wood already had.

"Yes, well," Nicholas continued, reaching the landing of the third floor and stopping. "You didn't expect to find a moneylender in Mayfair, did you?"

Dash joined him, scanning the dark hall ahead. "No, I suppose not. You're sure you can trust the individual who gave you the location of this . . ." He couldn't remember the man's name.

Actually, he couldn't remember anything. And he wondered if he ever would again.

Nothing held in his mind but the feel of Elena in his arms.

"Belville," Nicholas finished for him, gesturing for Dash to follow him up the next flight of stairs. "Implicitly. I would trust May with my life."

Dash scrubbed his hand across his jaw and tried to focus. "I'm sorry, but May? Please, tell me that's a surname, Bourne. Please tell me we're not on a wild goose chase all because the fair May felt like toying with you."

"If by fair you mean no more than, oh, ninety years old, more hair on her chin than her head, and a goiter that, in truth, makes even the most impervious of men blanch—"

"Enough," Dash interrupted, eyeing a large hole in the third tread from the bottom.

Nicholas reached the final landing and turned to look at Dash. "As for toying with me, well, I don't know that such a term exists in her vocabulary. The woman owns one of the largest opium houses in all of London—keeps her rather busy, I would imagine. Plenty of money to be made from supplying her customers, from what I understand."

"Don't tell me that you've fallen into such pursuits."

Nicholas feigned insult. "Really, Carrington. I can't believe you would think such things."

Dash only arched an eyebrow in response, his friend knowing very well that such assumptions would not be beyond the realm of possibility.

"When I began asking around about Smeade, a number of people suggested that I contact May. Apparently, the man enjoys his opium—and May was more than willing to tell me what she knew, including the man's connection to Belville. She despises Smeade—said he treats her like a servant."

"'More than willing' meaning you paid her off?" Dash asked, looking down the dingy hall.

Nicholas dug inside his waistcoat pocket, producing a slip of foolscap. "Of course. Have you ever known anyone to willingly cooperate without money being involved? Speaking of which, Belville awaits."

He peered at the paper and pointed to the end of the hall. "Office number 444, an even number. How apropos for a cent percenter."

Dash and Nicholas walked down the hall in search of 444. Two burly men stood on each side of a door

toward the end of the corridor. They stared straight
ahead, their eyes fixed on the wall in front of them.

"I assume you'll coax Belville with a similar offer?"
Dash murmured, sizing up the two.

Nicholas grinned. "Of course. And if that doesn't
work, I'll beat it out of him. And you'll be responsible
for looking after those two," he said under his breath.

The men turned as one and faced Dash, their com-
bined size blocking out the light from the wall sconces.
"Of course I will," he muttered, elbowing Nicholas in
the ribs. "Wipe that ridiculous smile off your face. You
look as though you're enjoying this."

"There's no need to be rude," his friend whispered,
then stepped in front of the men. "Gentlemen, we're
here to see Mr. Belville, if you please."

"Appointment?" the one on the right asked, cocking
his head and cracking his knuckles as he spoke.

Nicholas retained his friendly manner, speaking as if
they'd been chums all their lives. "I'm afraid not. But
May assured me we would be welcome."

"Her with the opium house—the one who makes her
money off the likes of you?" the other asked, chuckling
to himself.

"That's the one, my good sir."

"Well," the first one said, opening the door to reveal a
small, well-appointed room. "You'd hardly be the first
to need Mr. Belville's help after May got her hooks into
ya. Go on then. Ring the bell and he'll be out for ya
quick-like."

Nicholas dutifully stepped over the threshold, assuming an air of apologetic defeat.

Dash followed, barely inside the room before the men
shut the door.

He looked around, noting the Axminster carpet and
Chippendale chairs. A landscape by Richard Wilson
hung on the wall and a rosewood table stood to the side,

supporting a crystal decanter and four glasses neatly displayed on a gleaming sterling Paul Storr tray.

"The Plymouth Building cleans up well," Dash said dryly, wondering if Belville had purchased the items in the room or accepted them as payment from his desperate clients. "Makes one wonder why he keeps an office here."

"Gentry coves at *point non plus* are not fond of airing their affairs in public," Nicholas answered, picking up a chased silver bell. "It's one thing to sneak away to the Plymouth Building where an anonymous hackney and a servant's clothing will hide your identity. Quite another issue entirely to do such questionable business surrounded by your peers."

He rang the bell, the light tinkling sound almost too delicate for such a place.

A door on the opposite side of the room opened and a man appeared. "Gentlemen, do come in."

Dash didn't know what he thought a moneylender would look like, but Mr. Belville was not it.

As the men moved toward their host, Dash couldn't help but compare the man to a kindly great-uncle he'd had. Close to eighty, with a wisp of snow-white hair that wound about his head and spectacles so thick he was surely blind without them, the diminutive moneylender didn't look threatening in the least.

Dash was beginning to wonder at Nicholas's contacts. Surely the entire underbelly of London could not be run by aged individuals such as Belville and May, could it? Or perhaps that's exactly what kept them from being apprehended. After all, who would ever think to accuse Belville of wrongdoing?

The man walked behind a modest walnut desk, then gestured for the two to take their seats. He waited until they'd settled before taking his own, opening a fresh ledger and dipping his quill into a crystal inkpot.

"Now, gentlemen, if you don't mind, please tell me how you came to find me?"

Nicholas crossed his legs and began. "May Fletcher suggested that we speak with you."

Belville made note of something in the ledger, his head nodding as he did so. "I see. And what is the figure that you owe Mrs. Fletcher?"

"Oh, no, you misunderstand. We do not owe Mrs. Fletcher anything," Nicholas answered simply.

Belville returned the quill to its holder and looked up at the two. "Yes, I'm afraid I don't understand at all. Perhaps you're not aware of the nature of my business?"

Nicholas shook his head. "We're completely aware, Mr. Belville, but it's not money we're in need of. It's information."

The small man closed the ledger and sat back in his chair, pausing to fold his fingers together before resting his chin on them. "Gentlemen, discretion is more important to my clients than anything else. I'm afraid I cannot be of help to you."

"Not even for this?" Nicholas asked, fishing a black leather pouch from a hidden pocket within his tailcoat. He tossed the pouch toward Belville, the sound of numerous coins clanking against each other drawing the man's attention.

"Tell me this first: who is it that you wish to know more of?" The older man picked up the pouch, testing the weight of it in his narrow hands.

"Six pounds. Am I correct?"

Nicholas eyed Belville with appreciation. "You are. And there's more where that came from if you answer our questions concerning Mr. Francis Smeade."

"Oh, well, you hardly needed to offer me coin for information on Smeade," Belville answered, opening the center drawer of his desk. "But I'll take it all the same."

"Not very fond of the man?" Dash asked.

Belville tossed the pouch inside, closed the drawer, and settled back once again. "No one is. My clientele are men of noble birth—such as you. Smeade bought his way into polite society and now he's holding on for dear life. There's nothing noble about that man—of course, there's nothing noble about me, either. But I don't go about pretending to be someone I'm not."

Interesting, Dash thought to himself. It seemed that no one could stomach Smeade, which could work to their advantage. A person without connections was vulnerable—and Dash planned on finding out just how vulnerable Smeade was.

"Mr. Belville, I assume that, in your line of work, you're careful to gather information on your clients?"

Belville nodded in agreement. "And Smeade's is an interesting story. The man wastes money more than any other I know—and that, gentlemen, is saying something. Opium, drink, business ventures that fail time and again. He's either incredibly stupid or ridiculously optimistic."

Nicholas laughed out loud. "Perhaps the two are not mutually exclusive?"

Belville smiled, reminding Dash of his kindly great-uncle yet again. "Perhaps. But there is money that cannot be explained. I keep track of my clients. There's competition among my type, you see, and it pays to know who is borrowing from whom. But Smeade doesn't do business with any of my competitors. And yet, there are funds beyond what I lend."

Dash experienced the oddest sense of guilt over his growing admiration for the man. Surely no Corinthian was meant to ever side with a moneylender?

God, his desk at the Corinthian Club with endless paperwork would be a welcome sight after all of this, he thought.

"There's no trail," Belville continued. "The money simply appears, Smeade spends it faster than the crown can make it, and once his pockets are empty, he finds his way to my door."

Dash considered the man's words, his gut tensing. "It's just as we suspected. He's working for someone, then."

"I still find it hard to believe," Nicholas muttered. "Who would employ a fool such as Smeade?"

"Have you been able to establish a connection between the man and our concern?" Dash asked, careful to remain cryptic in front of Belville.

Nicholas begrudgingly shook his head in response.

"Nor have I. This scenario makes much more sense."

Dash uncrossed his legs and sat forward in his chair. "Where does Smeade keep his money?"

"James and Mulroy Merchant Bank," Belville replied. "We've witnessed the man making deposits—even relieved him of his deposit record a time or two. But there's never been a source mentioned."

Dash frowned at the man's words. "With all due respect, Mr. Belville, is forcing your way into a merchant bank after hours really beyond your purview?"

Belville smiled again and winked. "Strictly speaking? No. But James and Mulroy make it their business to know anyone who might profit from doing such a thing. It would be too risky for my men. And though I'm curious, there's really no reason for me to do so. Smeade continues to need my services, and that's good enough for me."

"Unfortunately," Dash replied grimly, "it's not good enough for us."

The Carrington carriage rolled to a stop in front of 317 Tavistock Place, one of a tidy row of brick townhomes. Two large bird cherry trees flanked the walkway. "Rather serene, isn't it?" Lady Mowbray asked as she took the groomsman's hand and stepped to the ground.

"Yes, quite so," Elena agreed, following the marchioness. The ground was covered in soft, white cherry-blossom petals that drifted up and around her ankles as she walked. "I must admit that I'm surprised."

Lady Mowbray lifted her skirts and ascended the steep stairs. "As was I when I first visited the Halcyon Society. It seems peculiar to find a charity with such a serious undertaking in Bloomsbury. But I suppose it's important for the women who come here to see the possibilities beyond their current lives. Inspiration, if you will."

Elena minded the hem of her cream patterned muslin dress. "Yes, that makes perfect sense."

Lady Mowbray reached the landing and waited for Elena. "You see, Miss Barnes, I can be quite clever too," she said with a wink.

The black lacquered door opened wide with an audible whoosh. A girl no more than twelve stood in the entryway, a frightened expression on her thin face.

"Ladies," she said in greeting, dipping a curtsy. "Please, come in, won't you."

Elena allowed Lady Mowbray to enter first, then crossed the threshold herself, looking kindly at the girl. "Thank you . . . May I know your name?"

"I'm sorry. My name is Abigail. I was meant to meet you at the coach. And now I've cocked up my name as well," the girl replied, her eyes welling with tears.

"Come now, my child, you've not 'cocked up' anything." Lady Mowbray patted the girl gently on the head. "Miss Barnes and I are perfectly able to find our way from the street to your door. And as for your name, we know it now. I am Lady Mowbray and this is Miss Barnes."

Abigail dipped again, holding each side of her gray cotton dress wide as she curtsied. "A pleasure to make your acquaintance Lady Mowbray, Miss Barnes."

"That was lovely, Abigail," Elena remarked, taking

the girl's hand in hers. "I don't believe I could perform a more perfectly executed curtsy if I tried."

Abigail managed a small smile at Elena's words. "Thank you, Miss Barnes. May I take your wraps and bonnets?"

"That would be most welcome, Abigail." Lady Mowbray released the silver clasp on her burgundy cape and handed it to the girl, then untied the silken ribbons of her poke bonnet and did the same.

Elena unbuttoned her own quilted lilac spencer and took it off. "Thank you," she said, carefully laying the garment in Abigail's outstretched arms. She removed her bonnet and allowed the girl to take it as well.

"Now, my child, would you fetch Mrs. Mason for us, please?" Lady Mowbray asked politely.

"I'm to put you in the front room, my lady. There will be tea and shortbread for you there," she said proudly. "I'll go fetch Mrs. Mason once you're settled."

Abigail turned to the left and gestured for the women to follow her to where a door stood open just off the entry. "Please be seated. Mrs. Mason will be with you in a moment."

The girl waited while Lady Mowbray and Elena situated themselves on a faded puce settee, then dipped her third curtsy of the day and disappeared out the door.

A maid bustled in almost immediately, carrying the tray of promised refreshments. She settled the tea and shortbread on a low oak table, bobbed in recognition, and left as quickly as she'd arrived.

"May I?" Elena asked, reaching for the teapot. Lady Mowbray nodded and she prepared the cup, taking the liberty of adding two squares of shortbread to the saucer before passing it to the marchioness.

Too tense to drink tea, Elena paused and took in her surroundings. The entire room looked washed out, as though the furnishings, carpet, and wallpaper had been exposed to the sun for far too long. Despite the shabby aspect, however, it was rather pleasant, with a cheerful fire in the fireplace and ample light from the large windows. A vase full of bright yellow and red tulips sat on a sideboard with a large leather-bound Bible next to it.

A man and woman walked into the hall; their appearance pulled Elena's attention away from the room and she discreetly studied them. They were deep in conversation, the tall, thin man making occasional notations on a card with a stubby pencil as they spoke. The woman offered him thanks and showed him to the door, closing it firmly behind him. A moment or two passed before she appeared in the sitting room, a subdued smile on her lips.

"I'm sorry to keep you waiting, Lady Mowbray," she apologized, walking to a damask chair opposite Elena.

"Quite all right, Mrs. Mason," the marchioness answered, then gestured to Elena. "I've brought a friend with me, Miss Barnes from Dorset."

Elena stood as the older woman curtsied.

"It's a pleasure, Miss Barnes."

Elena nodded and smiled warmly. "Thank you, Mrs. Mason. I've long admired the Halcyon Society's work. I hope to one day help the women in my community by offering such services as those you provide here."

Mrs. Mason waited for Elena to reclaim her seat, then she settled her petite frame into the damask chair. "I am very glad to hear it. The sad fact of the matter is that there will never be a shortage of women in need, Miss Barnes. Without ladies such as the marchioness, I do not know what we would do."

A rumbling emanated from the hall, the sound of quick footfalls on the steps soon followed by the noise of someone running toward the back of the house.

"Mrs. Mason, I'd rather hoped that Miss Barnes might see your classrooms and meet some of the women.

But I wonder, is there something afoot?" Lady Mowbray asked, peering out into the hall.

Mrs. Mason tucked a stray lock of brown hair back into her severe chignon, then pushed her round gold-rimmed glasses farther up her nose. "In a manner of speaking, yes."

Lady Mowbray returned her cup and saucer to the tray, as did Elena.

"A woman, Mary Fields, was brought here today. Not long before you arrived." Mrs. Mason folded her hands in her lap, her eyes worried. "She was discovered unconscious in her room when the landlady came to collect the rent. She contacted the society, bless her soul. I don't think Mary would have survived much longer."

"And why is that?" Elena pressed.

Mrs. Mason appeared uncomfortable with the question. She wrung her hands and cleared her throat twice before answering. "She'd been beaten. And worse, Miss Barnes."

Lady Mowbray's hand covered her mouth in shock.

"Everything is being seen to. A Bow Street Runner just left after speaking with Mary. The doctor has been called and my maids are tending to her," Mrs. Mason assured the two. "Now, I think we should give Miss Barnes a tour of the premises. Lady Mowbray, you mentioned the classrooms?"

"I want to meet Mary."

Mrs. Mason's mouth opened, but no words came forth.

"Do you think that's a good idea?" Lady Mowbray asked, taking Elena's hand in hers.

"Do you, Mrs. Mason?" Elena asked the woman simply, her voice devoid of emotion.

Mrs. Mason clamped her lips together and tapped her forefinger thoughtfully on her chin. "Well, Miss Barnes. I'm not sure."

"I do not mean to be rude, Mrs. Mason. But to my way of thinking, if I cannot take the sight of Miss Fields, I'll be of no use to others in her unfortunate position. Wouldn't you agree?"

Mrs. Mason continued to tap her chin as she considered the question. "Yes," she said finally. "Completely. I'm simply surprised at your request."

"Well, I've discovered recently that sometimes, surprises can be good," Elena said resolutely, releasing Lady Mowbray's hand and standing.

"I will stay here, my dear," the marchioness announced, settling more deeply into the soft settee.

Mrs. Mason nodded, then walked to the doorway. "Come, Miss Barnes. Follow me."

Elena looked at Lady Mowbray. "I'll return shortly."

"Do be careful, Miss Barnes," she replied tenderly. "Your Rowena still weighs heavily on your mind. I can see it in your eyes."

"I will," Elena murmured, touched by her sympathetic concern.

Elena turned back and joined Mrs. Mason in the entryway.

"Just up here, on the second floor," the small woman said, walking to the stairs at the end of the hall. She ascended the treads at a quick clip, the fabric of her dun-colored dress swishing about her ankles.

The two reached the landing and Mrs. Mason paused just outside the first closed door. "Are you ready, Miss Barnes?"

Elena took a deep breath, exhaling slowly. "Yes."

Mrs. Mason put her hand on the dull metal knob and turned it, then pushed the painted door open. The pungent smell of spirits hit Elena hard and she cupped her hand over her nose. "For the cuts and scrapes," Mrs. Mason explained, ushering Elena into the room.

The maid who'd delivered the tea earlier stood in

front of a sideboard rinsing a rag in a porcelain basin of water. Another maid sat on the edge of a scarred slatted bed. The bed linens were pushed nearly to the end. A pair of ghostly white legs sprawled inelegantly atop the coverlet, red, angry scratches and cuts marring most of the exposed skin.

Elena slowly moved across the sparse room, the shape of Mary Fields revealing itself with each step forward. The woman wore a white cotton night rail that bunched about her knees, a bloom of hateful green and purple bruising rising from the neckline and continuing on to her shoulders. Her matted hair was plastered to the pillow, forming an unearthly halo. And her face.

Dear God. Her face.

Elena clapped a hand across her mouth to keep from crying out in shock and protest. Mary's face was hardly recognizable as a woman. Her eyes were swollen shut and her nose bent at an impossible angle. The planes of her cheeks bore blunt, black bruising. And her mouth was blistered as though something hot had been used to burn her lips. Elena neared the bed and leaned over. The blistering appeared on her neck and chest as well. All of the burns were the same shape; a crude circular pattern.

She'd seen burn marks like those before, on wood. But what had caused them? She frowned, trying to remember—and then gasped in horror.

"A cigar," Elena choked out, sliding her hand down to rest at the base of her neck.

"Yes, ma'am," the maid whispered. "Covers her back as well." The woman nimbly retrieved a damp cloth from Mary's forehead, then stood, gesturing for Elena to take her place.

Elena lowered herself to the bed carefully, not wanting to disturb Mary's sleep. She stared at her for some time, intensely struck by how fragile the woman looked. She'd been found all alone, broken and torn. But alive. Despite everything, Mary lived. "Does she have family?"

"Bow Street is attempting to locate them now," Mrs. Mason replied. She stood quietly next to the footboard, compassion and worry written on her features as she looked at the battered woman in the bed. "Though quite often, these women have families that would rather they stayed gone."

"And the man who did this?" Elena asked, resting her hand next to Mary's on the wrinkled linens.

Mrs. Mason sighed deeply. "It is hard to predict, Miss Barnes. Very few of those responsible for such violence are ever caught. Bow Street will do what they can. But we are Mary's only real hope now."

Elena moved her hand ever so slightly until she barely touched Mary's fingers. "Yes, Mrs. Mason. I believe you're right."

❧

The letter arrived while Elena was with Lady Mowbray in Bloomsbury, but Bell made sure it was delivered to her the moment she returned.

"From your maid, Miss Barnes. A rider brought it from their first stop in Farnborough," he said by way of explanation, adding, "perhaps tea in the library?"

Elena could see why Dash relied on the man. He was efficient, true enough. But more than that, he was perceptive and sensitive to others' needs. And kind.

"Yes, I believe I will. Thank you, Bell," she said gratefully.

The butler nodded in acknowledgment, then disappeared.

Elena held the missive in both hands as she walked to the library, closing the door behind her to assure absolute privacy.

She chose a chaise lounge near the trunk that held the Paolini and sat down.

"Please, let Rowena be all right," she prayed to the putti cavorting on the carved ceiling. She fumbled with the letter, breaking the seal and unfolding the thick sheet of foolscap.

May 19, 1813

Dear Miss Elena,

Thank you for the letter that you sent along in my trunk. It cheers my heart to read your words, truly.

I dreamed of Mr. Brock last night and woke screaming. The Doctor tells me that such nightmares will go away, much like the bruises and cuts.

Miss, we weren't able to speak privately before I left. There's so much I wanted to tell you. You'd get after me for writing such a thing, but you need to know that those men did not take my honor. I could tell from their talk that such a thing was coming, but I crossed my legs tight and didn't let go until I was safe in Lord Carrington's arms. They touched me in places that no one but a woman's husband should, and hit me, as my bruises show. But I left there a virgin, I promise you.

I hope you'll still have me for your maid when you return. I know it would be hard, and if I remind you too much of that horrid place, I'll understand. But I don't want to leave you, Miss.

I pray that you return to Harcourt House soon and safely.

Respectfully yours,
Rowena

Elena laid the letter beside her on the chaise lounge, then dropped her head into her hands and began to cry.

"My sweet, innocent Rowena," she whispered, covering her eyes completely, sealing out the light. "How can you ask such a thing?"

Elena wept, forgetting everything else and completely surrendering to the chaotic storm of emotions that buffeted her. Relief that Rowena's virginity had not been taken from her. Anger and hatred for the men who'd tortured her dear friend. Grief for the loss of innocence that Rowena had most assuredly suffered, her life never to be the same again.

And guilt. Guilt that she'd not been able to protect her loyal friend. Even worse, that Rowena clearly did not in any way blame her—but, in fact, seemed to blame herself.

Men such as Mr. Brock ruined the lives of women every single day. It was a crime. And Elena needed to make him pay.

She looked up at the sound of a knock on the door, swiping at her tearstained face and managing a serene demeanor just as Molly brought in the tea tray.

"May I pour, Miss?" Molly asked as she set the heavy silver tray down.

Elena smiled weakly. "Thank you, Molly."

The maid busied herself with the tea, doing so with supreme efficiency and skill. "Might I ask after Rowena, Miss? Or would that be rude?"

Elena wiped again at her eyes, and sniffled quietly, crumpling her damp, lace-edged handkerchief in her clasped hands. "It's never improper to care, Molly," she assured the maid. "And as it happens, I've a letter from her—though I suspect you already knew that."

"News has a way of making the rounds here," she said guiltily, handing her the teacup and saucer. "Please don't tell Mr. Bell."

Elena sipped, the warm, sweet liquid bracing her spirits. "I wouldn't dream of it, Molly. And as for Rowena, she's going to be just fine. I promise."

12

Elena stood completely alone in Dash's study, her heart thudding with fear. She had no one to blame but herself. Her own selfish desires had brought her to this point.

"Honestly," Elena said out loud, growing more impatient by the moment with her cowardice. She quietly shut the door behind her and leaned against it. The scent of sandalwood that she associated with Dash subtly teased her senses and she braced herself against the emotions it stirred inside of her.

Making love with Dash mere days before had been magical. Mythological, even, Elena thought with a stab of sadness. Much like Icarus, she'd soared on wings made of wax and feathers and experienced what was surely the purest form of pleasure known to mankind. She'd been giddy with the heights they'd reached, so taken with the way he'd made her feel, she'd failed to notice how close she'd ventured near the sun.

Her wings were melted now, and she realized how much her distracted mind had been a factor in Rowena's kidnapping. Elena had placed her own fascination with Dash before the needs of the very people she was meant to protect.

She noticed an iron key puzzle tossed haphazardly upon the polished broad desk. Elena walked around and settled herself into Dash's large Windsor chair, then reached for the keys.

She could not take away what had happened to Rowena, she thought with a deep pang of remorse. No matter how hard she wished it to be so, there would be no going back and obliterating Mr. Brock from her history.

Elena studied the first key in relation to the second, absently calculating possible outcomes depending on the move. It ate at her, the idea that she'd allowed something so desperately awful to happen to her dear friend.

She slid the first key to the right, realizing her mistake instantly. She needed to move forward with seeking justice for her friend and do what she could to atone for her failure.

And moving forward meant leaving Dash behind.

The keys remained entwined and suddenly, Elena felt too tired to go on. She returned the puzzle to the very spot where she'd found it.

She combed her fingers through her hair until the tugging sensation made her scalp tingle. A pin fell from her tidy chignon, but she hardly noticed. Mrs. Mason had said in no uncertain terms that women such as Elena were vital to the Halcyon Society's work.

She dropped her head to the desk and closed her eyes. Elena needed Dash. She wanted him. Craved him with everything that she was. But she could not turn her back and ignore Rowena and the revelations at the Halcyon Society.

The deep timbre of male voices made Elena lurch upright in a sudden wave of panic. Telling Dash that she could not be with him was the right thing to do. But it would be the hardest thing she'd ever done in her life.

Wait. *Men's* voices. Not a man, but men's.

Oh. God.

Elena jumped up, nearly falling back in her haste to do so. It had never occurred to her that Dash would not be alone. There'd been no gentlemen calling on him while she'd been in residence at Carrington House. At least none that she'd known about.

The voices drew closer. Elena didn't recognize a deep male laugh.

She was shaking and perspiration dampened her upper lip. She couldn't do this. Not now. Her gaze darted about the room, searching for an answer to her dilemma. A tall ebony cabinet stood in the far corner. The rumble of voices sounded right outside the door. Elena ran for the cabinet and hauled herself up and in, reaching out to close the door behind her. Kneeling, she settled her backside against her heels and held her breath.

※ ❦

Dash approached his study, surprised to find the door closed, but gave it no more than a passing thought.

"Come in," he said to Nicholas, opening the door and crossing the threshold.

"I don't know about you," Nicholas followed, closing the door behind them. "But the more time I spend on the seedy side of London, the more I like it."

Dash chuckled and sat down in his desk chair. "Why does that not surprise me?"

"I've no idea," Nicholas answered with aplomb as he settled into one of the chairs facing Dash and his desk.

"Hmmm . . ." Dash replied, the sound making him think on Elena. Where was she now? What was she thinking? Was she regretting their lovemaking? Was she missing him as much as he did her?

"Yes?" Nicholas prodded, waiting for Dash to explain himself.

"Oh, a stray thought is all," he answered, nowhere near ready to talk about Elena. "What do we think of Belville's information?"

Nicholas ran both hands through his dark hair, and then folded them behind his head. "I think it's all we've got to go on. That, and Smeade's connection to the Rambling Rose."

"Of course," Dash nodded in agreement. "And did you get any sense of the man while we were speaking? Is he trustworthy?"

A wry smile broke across Nicholas's face. "Well, no, but he is a moneylender."

It had been a stupid question. Dammit, Dash was having a difficult time keeping his mind on the case. He swore that he could smell Elena's perfume. She'd dabbed it on her wrists, and between her breasts. And behind each knee.

He picked up a handful of letters from his desk and fanned himself, noting a hairpin just beside the envelopes.

It could belong to one of the maids, he reasoned, picking it up to examine it.

Delicate diamond flowers ran the length of it. He could hear the marchioness's voice in his head as she'd presented Elena with the pin just yesterday. There'd been four in all. *They're perfect for you, my dear. And I refuse to take no for an answer.*

"Well, well, Carrington," Nicholas drawled, his eyes amused as he looked at the pin. "I must say, I'm proud of you. And in your study, no less? Who is she? Anyone I know?"

Dash raised his finger to his mouth and silently urged Nicholas to stop talking. He looked around the room, his eyes narrowing over the tall ebony cabinet.

He returned the pin to the desktop and rose from his chair. He strode to the piece of furniture. He gripped the knob and pulled the door open. Elena sat within, crouched down low in the small space.

"Elena?" Dash stared at her, supremely confused. "What in God's name are you doing in my cabinet?"

"I'm so sorry," she said. "I was waiting for you . . . Then I heard another man's voice and panicked."

"Well, let the woman out, Carrington. She can't possibly be comfortable. And besides," Nicholas paused, his grin growing, "I would very much like to make her acquaintance."

Dash couldn't begin to imagine why Elena was hiding in the cabinet. But he did know for certain that he'd rather not have an audience while attempting to sort things out with her.

"Bourne, if you wouldn't mind leaving," he asked his friend, pointing to the door when Nicholas remained still.

"Before you go, Mr. Bourne," Elena said around Dash's bulk. "You mentioned the Rambling Rose and a 'Smeade.' I would be very interested to hear more of this."

"Holy Hell," Nicholas said, his smile disappearing.

"Yes, that," Dash agreed grimly.

The cabinet door gently hit him in the back. "Dash?"

He continued to block her escape, utterly determined that Elena not be involved in the dangerous case.

"You'll have to let her out eventually," Nicholas advised, standing. "There's no way around it."

The door hit Dash again. "Dash, are you there?"

There was a part of Dash that damned his decision to ever allow Elena close. That regretted his inability to keep the woman at arm's length.

He closed his eyes and swallowed hard, then turned back to the cabinet and opened the door. "Let me help you."

Elena accepted his hand and stepped out, pausing next to Dash to stare at Nicholas.

"The Honorable Nicholas Bourne, may I present Miss Elena Barnes."

Elena executed a small curtsy and Nicholas approached, took her hand in his, and placed a chaste kiss on her fingers.

"It is a pleasure to make your acquaintance, Miss Barnes. Now tell me, do you make a habit of hiding in cabinets and listening in on private conversations?"

"And if I did?" Elena countered boldly.

Nicholas released her hand and looked at Dash, his eyes narrowing. "The bluestocking, I take it," he said dryly.

"Sit," Dash ordered, then pulled out the opposite chair for Elena and waited until she was comfortably settled.

"I must apologize to both of you," Elena began, looking first at Dash, then turning to take in Nicholas. "I didn't mean to eavesdrop, but it was rather hard not to hear you with only a single slab of wood separating us."

"Do not think on it, Miss Barnes," Nicholas answered gruffly.

"You're most kind, Mr. Bourne," Elena replied caustically. "Now, if you would, please tell me what you know of the Rambling Rose."

Nicholas muttered an oath under his breath. "I don't suppose you'd agree to forget what you heard?"

"No," Elena replied, simply. "And I can't imagine why I would want to. I have a particular interest in seeing anyone with ties to the brothel being brought to justice."

"Would money help?"

"She's the daughter of a wealthy peer, Bourne," Dash pointed out.

Nicholas shrugged his shoulders. "That hardly means anything these days," he replied.

Elena looked pleadingly at Dash. "Surely *you* understand my interest in any information that would avenge Rowena."

"The maid?" Nicholas asked.

"Well, yes," Elena said defensively. "She's my maid. But she's more than a servant to me, Mr. Bourne."

Dash picked up the interlocking keys and rubbed the pad of his thumb over the cool metal. He did understand what avenging Rowena's kidnapping meant to her; that was precisely the problem. Elena craved justice just as he did. And Dash had the means to satisfy that craving.

"Is that all?" Nicholas asked incredulously.

Elena squared her shoulders. "I would think it would be quite enough, sir."

"Then you would be wrong, Miss—"

"Bourne," Dash interrupted, setting the puzzle down.

Nicholas raked his hands through his hair. "You cannot be seriously considering her request?"

"Perhaps Lady Mowbray could secure the aid of the Halcyon Society," Elena offered, a faint blush of agitated color pinkening her cheeks.

Nicholas abruptly stood and made for the sideboard. "Oh, yes, that's right," he said with sarcasm. "You're the one who brought an elderly marchioness to the Rose. Tell me, did she amaze you with her diplomatic skills? Or was it her raw, brute power that got the job done?"

"She gave me no other choice," Elena bit out, the flush turning to a blaze. "Besides, if there's proof of this Smeade's involvement with the brothel, surely 'diplomatic skills' and 'raw, brute power' will not be required."

Dash flexed his fingers and folded his hands together, reaching for calm. "It's not that simple, Elena."

Nicholas unstopped the crystal decanter and poured a glass for himself, tossing it down in one long swallow. "You naïve, innocent girl. You've absolutely no idea what you're getting yourself into."

"Bourne, I must insist that you stop speaking to Miss

Barnes in this fashion," Dash growled, his fingers curling into fists.

Nicholas returned his glass to the silver tray and walked to the door. He reached for the knob and turned it, pausing to look back at Dash. "It's your decision. But if she gets in the way and Smeade goes free, it will be on your head."

He turned back and opened the paneled door wide, stepping over the threshold and disappearing down the hallway.

❧ ❧

"Dare I say, you're in need of a woman's touch," Dash commented, looking about the dark, unkempt rooms that comprised Nicholas's bachelor quarters at the Albany.

"Would you be referring to my home—or me?" his friend replied, lifting an eyebrow in lazy inquiry as he waved Dash to a seat on the soft couch.

Dash could vaguely recall the last time he'd set foot inside the apartment in Piccadilly. At that time, Langdon had been in residence, his father still alive and in command of the familial home in Mayfair. The quarters had been kept in pristine condition, just as Langdon liked it. The pale yellow walls had perfectly accented the Turkish carpets, which in turn had perfectly matched the various shades of gold in the furnishings. The furniture had probably even perfectly matched Langdon's eyes, Dash imagined.

So very different from what presented itself to Dash now.

The air was stale and hinted at cigars and neglect, as though the rooms hadn't been aired in years. The furniture and walls were faded, as were the carpets. A thick layer of dust covered everything—save for the low table in front of him where a mess of documents and maps was spread open, one on top of the other, edges sticking out here and there.

"Both, actually," Dash finally answered, swiping his hand along the French walnut table to his right, and then showing his grime-covered finger to Nicholas. "As you know, I am a complete domestic slouch compared to Stonecliffe's high standards—which makes what I am about to say even more disconcerting: Bourne, you really ought to do something about this."

Nicholas handed Dash a cut crystal tumbler of brandy, then took up his own. "I've just arrived. Give a man some time to sort things out."

"It's been nearly a month, my friend—which in most parts of the world, does not qualify as 'just arrived.' And drinking at two o'clock in the afternoon?" Dash pressed, setting his own glass down. "Is that the custom in India, then?"

Nicholas swallowed the contents of his glass whole, and then eyed Dash warningly. "And what if it is? What if I choose to drink at two o'clock and three o'clock? Hell, let's make it an even twenty-four hours, shall we? Do you want to make something of that, too?"

Dash knew better than to cross the line when it came to Nicholas. He loved the man like a brother, but the demons that kept Nicholas awake at night were far more sinister and numerous than Dash's. Furthermore, they'd not be slain in a day. Nor even a week or a month, Dash feared. And he couldn't afford to lose the man's help now.

Dash carefully chose each word. "You know why I ask. We're all concerned for you."

Nicholas balanced the glass on his palm, staring into its emptiness as he spoke. "I do know, Dash. But I cannot consider myself. Not now—not when we're so close to catching the killer. I cannot allow myself to think on anything else but Smeade. Let us leave it at that."

"Of course," Dash answered, giving in with a shrug of acceptance before sitting forward and examining the documents piled on the table. He had no choice but to respect his friend's wishes, aware that even if he pressed, Nicholas would likely continue to drink too much. "Now, shall we discuss Miss Barnes?"

Nicholas set the glass out of reach and turned his attention to the mess before him. "Must we?"

"You know the answer to that, Bourne," Dash replied, readying himself for an argument.

"God, Carrington," Nicholas began, blowing out a breath before continuing. "I don't have the patience to waste any more time on Miss Barnes. As I said before, it is your decision."

Dash stared at his friend. "Then she'll aid us in the investigation," he replied, surprised that his friend wasn't putting up more of a fight.

"Very well."

Dash continued to stare at Nicholas. "Then it's decided?"

"You're beginning to irritate me," Nicholas growled. "If you truly believe that you're making the right choice, then I'll trust you. Now, may we move on?"

Dash nodded, dumbfounded but thankful.

"Look here," his friend began, rummaging through a stack of documents and pulling a page from the unruly stack. "My inquiries into Smeade revealed much that you would expect, which is why I didn't dwell on most of the information. But look here, a record of a mistress on Berkeley Street. And here," he paused, grabbing for a smaller stack of what looked to be shop receipts. "Bills from Weston for tailoring, record of sale from Tattersalls. And an additional footman brought on just last month. Yet, according to Belville, the man has pockets to let. And he still continues to spend. From what I could tell, not once did the man consider altering his spending habits—he's addicted to his existence as it is—no matter that it's empty and a complete sham. What do you think Smeade would do if something threatened to take it all away?"

Dash considered all that Nicholas had told him, leafing through the documents and reading the expenditures for himself. "Would he do anything to preserve his life, including giving up who he works for?"

"It's a possibility," Nicholas answered, reaching for his glass and standing. "And, unfortunately, the only option we have left. Though your Miss Barnes should come in handy. We've need of Smeade's bank records. And she might be the perfect woman for the job."

Elena had read Penelope's story so many times over the years that she'd lost count. The tale of the clever and steadfast wife of Odysseus never failed to fascinate her. The cousin of Helen of Troy was truly one of the most important female figures in Greek mythology, at least as far as Elena was concerned.

The late viscount's book containing the woman's story was not precisely like Elena's. She'd realized the disparity the moment she'd fetched it from a shelf in the library and sat down to read. In his copy, her favorite passages were not underlined. Her name was not to be found inside the front cover, written in bold, flowery script as only a twelve-year-old girl could do. And his pages were clean and crisp, not worn and loved.

But Elena knew it wasn't the book's fault that she couldn't settle and enjoy the well-loved tale. She closed the volume and stared at the candelabra, watching the flames flicker and twist. She'd waited seven hours for Dash to return from speaking with Mr. Bourne. And she was waiting still.

"There you are."

Dash's voice startled Elena and she jumped, looking over her shoulder. "You frightened me half to death."

He strode forward, emerging from the darkened aisle to claim a chair next to hers. "I'm sorry. That was rather the last thing I wanted to do."

He bent forward and glanced at the book in Elena's lap. "Penelope, eh? Always thought she had a tougher time of it than Odysseus. Twenty years spent weaving a shroud, then unraveling it each night. And all those suitors, pestering her to remarry."

Elena smiled faintly. "I agree completely. But I didn't wait hours for you to return so that we could argue the merits of Penelope."

Dash settled back against the chair cushions, resting his elbows on the padded arms. "I know."

"Then tell me," she urged. "Tell me what Mr. Bourne had to say."

"Oh, quite a lot—most of it unfit for your ears." Dash rested his chin on the palm of one hand and studied her. "But he stands by what he said this afternoon. The decision is up to me."

Elena instinctively made to rise and go to him in order to show her thanks with a kiss. But she gripped the arms of her chair and forced herself to remain seated. "Thank you, Dash. Truly."

"Do not thank me yet, Elena" he replied, sighing deeply. "First, I will tell you of Mr. Francis Smeade and his importance. Agreed?"

"It will make no difference to me," Elena assured him. "I will not be denied—"

"Agreed?" he interrupted, then waited for her to respond.

"Agreed."

"Good. Now, Mr. Francis Smeade is a distant relation of mine on my mother's side. The man came from very limited means and managed to work his way into polite society through various and assorted ventures. This much is public knowledge," Dash began, settling deeper into his seat. "And the rest is not. Do you remember in the alcove when I made mention of a family tragedy?"

Elena nodded immediately, the image of Dash's grief-stricken face as he'd told the story flashing in her mind. "Yes, of course."

"The woman was Lady Afton, the mother of Sophia, a dear friend to Nicholas, his brother Langdon, and myself. Her death was, for obvious reasons, devastating to her daughter. As it was for us boys. The killer was never caught—not even a possible suspect identified. Until now."

"How?" Elena asked, eager to hear more.

Dash sat up and stretched both arms above his head before resting them on the chair arms again. "That is not important," he said, his expression grim. "Nor are the steps that led us to Smeade. But I can tell you we know for certain Mr. Francis Smeade is the man who murdered Lady Afton."

Elena considered the facts as Dash had presented them. "But why would Mr. Smeade be connected to the Rambling Rose?"

"We've uncovered information at the Rose that ties Smeade to the brothel—records of payment and dates that correspond to not only Lady Afton's death, but others. This proves that he didn't act alone. We don't know who he works for, but we can assume that he's not unlike others of his ilk within the London underworld. These men manage a web of businesses and illegal endeavors, making vast sums of money in the process."

"And the Rose is one of those businesses," Elena said.

"Yes," Dash confirmed.

Elena nodded in understanding. "Then it's Mr. Smeade's boss you want. But you'll have to go through Smeade to capture him."

Dash crossed his arms over his chest. "Right again. Smeade may have held the knife to Lady Afton's throat, but there's a puppet master pulling his strings."

Dash's voice was even and pragmatic. But Elena could see in his eyes what she'd understood in the alcove: there was much more to the story than he was revealing.

"Tell me this: revenge in Lady Afton's name—what does it mean to you?"

"She was like a mother to me, Elena," Dash replied, propping his elbows on his knees. "To all of us, really. When she died, our lives seemed to stop. Oh, we grew older. But our hearts simply no longer possessed the capacity for true happiness. We were frozen in time—still are. Revenge is the only way I can think of to at least give us all a fighting chance to live, truly live, not walk through the world disengaged from everything—and everyone. Do you understand?"

He reached for her, but Elena folded her hands in her lap and squeezed her fingers tightly, her heart breaking at his words. "I do."

"And can you see the inherent danger in something of this sort?" he pressed, resting his elbow on his knee once more. "Smeade has killed before. And would do so again."

Elena nodded and bit the inside of her cheek to keep from crying.

"How can you ask me to let you risk your life, Elena? How?"

One lone tear fell down her face and Dash leaned forward to gently wipe it away. Elena turned her head to avoid his touch. "How can you ask me not to?"

Dash bowed his head and gripped his knees with both hands, staying that way for some time.

Elena longed to comfort him with her touch, but she couldn't risk the feel of his skin on her fingertips.

Finally, he looked up, his expression bleak but resigned. "All right, Elena. I will not fight you."

Elena automatically reached out to cup his face, instantly realizing her mistake. She dropped her hands and pressed her back against the cushion. "Thank you."

Dash's face clouded with confusion. "Elena, are you all right?"

"I'm overwhelmed, that is all," she answered him, offering a reassuring smile. "Now, tell me what you and Nicholas spoke of this afternoon." Elena watched the shadow of doubt disappear from his eyes and waited for him to speak.

"First," he began, "you must understand that Smeade is a man who values his life, and the possessions and privileges contained within it, above all else. Without money, Smeade loses his place in society. And without his place in society—"

"Smeade is nothing," Elena interjected.

Dash nodded. "So if logic follows, take Smeade's money away and he'd be willing to do anything to get it back."

"Brilliant," Elena murmured, struck by the simple yet perfect logic. "But how will you go about it? Short of robbing him, there's very little I can think of to part the money from the man."

"Precisely."

Elena furrowed her brow at his statement, sure that she'd misheard him. "I'm sorry. What was that?"

"We're going to rob the man of his money—in so many words," Dash began. "First, Nicholas will forge banknotes so that they appear to be written by Smeade to other parties in payment for his debts. Those notes will be cashed at his bank over a short period of time, quickly depleting his savings until there's nothing left. We'll let slip that Smeade has had the unfortunate luck to invest in a number of unsuccessful ventures. This

news will be most upsetting to those Smeade relies upon
to keep his lifestyle at an acceptable level: his tailor and
jeweler, the finest restaurants in the city, even his mistress. He'll be refused service soon enough."

"And then we'll send Smeade a letter from his boss,
stating that his work has been poor of late and he's
taken the liberty of lightening the man's bank account.
When Smeade confirms this, he'll have no choice but to
arrange a meeting with the man."

"And we'll follow." Elena finished.

"Something like that, yes," Dash confirmed, reaching
for Elena's hand.

She let him twine his fingers with hers. "It's a good
plan, Dash," she said, wanting nothing more than for
him to hold her. "Do you think it will work?"

"It has to."

13

Nicholas knocked three times, then opened the passageway's hidden door to Elena's dressing room. He stepped in and noiselessly shut it behind him.

"Mr. Bourne." Elena stood before a looking glass, dressed in a stunning coquelicot colored gown that expertly hugged each and every one of her delicious curves.

Nicholas took a seat on a shockingly small caned beechwood chair opposite her. "Miss Barnes," he replied, his tone no more amiable than hers.

She glared at him in the glass. "Well, your missive insisted that I don the dress you sent over, which I've done, at precisely the time you requested. I believe it's your turn, Mr. Bourne. What, exactly, is going on?"

Nicholas cast a critical eye over her form, noting the snug, low-cut bodice with satisfaction. "As you already know, I strongly advised Carrington against allowing you to participate in Smeade's capture."

"Yes, if you'll remember, I was standing in the room," Elena said sternly, turning around and facing him. "Can I assume your presence here this evening means you've reconsidered?"

"Not in the slightest," he replied gruffly. "I still believe Carrington is thinking with his heart rather than his brain, but he won't see reason. At least not when it comes to you."

"Why do you dislike me, Mr. Bourne?" Elena asked, fidgeting with the skirt of her gown.

Nicholas raked both hands through his hair. "It's not that I don't like you, Miss Barnes," Nicholas replied impatiently. "Tell me, did Carrington explain *everything* to you—including Lady Afton's death?"

"Yes, he did," Elena answered.

Nicholas nodded. "Then you know how important Smeade's capture is? And not only to the two of us, but to my brother and Lady Afton's daughter as well?"

"You may find this hard to believe, but yes, I understand." Elena stepped closer and folded her hands in front of her, her fingers clasped tightly. "My Rowena wasn't killed, but her life was irrevocably changed, Mr. Bourne. And it's my fault."

"That's ridiculous," Nicholas replied impatiently, waving off her statement with a raised hand. "She's a grown woman, Miss Barnes, surely capable—"

"It matters not," Elena interrupted, her mouth set in a tight line. "She is like a sister to me, Mr. Bourne. And though I know she was not a blood relative, was Lady Afton not like a mother to you?"

Nicholas didn't want to understand Elena. But he did. "Bloody hell, Miss Barnes."

"You didn't answer my question."

"You already know the answer," Nicholas growled. "But it's a completely different thing altogether."

Elena planted her fists, arms akimbo, on her hips. "I don't see how."

Nicholas's blood heated with frustration. "You've not spent the majority of your life desperate for revenge, Miss Barnes. You can't know what it feels like to wake every morning, hopeful something will change and you'll finally have the chance to make the man pay. It's a living hell, and one you cannot begin to imagine."

"I believe *that* is why Dash allowed me to participate in this, Mr. Bourne. To spare me the pain you've all lived with for far too many years," she answered quietly.

Nicholas propped his elbows on his knees, his head bowing as he absorbed the weight of her words.

"Yes, well, enough arguing," Nicholas said, breaking the tense, heavy silence. "I see now that you're far too obstinate to stand down, so let us discuss the gown."

"Then you're surrendering?" Elena said disbelievingly.

"If you insist on courting danger," Nicholas began, straightening up and standing, "far be it from me to get in your way.

"Carrington did warn you of the danger, yes?" he added, hopeful that her courage was less robust than her obstinacy.

Elena folded her arms across her bodice and raised her eyebrows sardonically. "The gown, Mr. Bourne, if you please."

Foolish, insufferable woman.

"Very well, the gown." He gestured for her to turn and face the looking glass before standing behind her. "The James and Mulroy bank is where Smeade keeps an account. As Carrington has already told you, our plan is to drain the man's money away until he's left with nothing. Your assignment is to steal his account number."

Elena stared quizzically at him in the reflective glass. "And how am I meant to do this?"

"With this gown, Miss Barnes," Nicholas answered dryly. "And your breasts."

Her hands flew to her bodice, fingers splaying over the silk, and her eyes widened with alarm. "Mr. Bourne, I'm sure that I misheard you."

Nicholas came round to face her. "No, you did not, Miss Barnes. And that is precisely why I am here without Carrington's knowledge."

He stepped aside and turned to look at her in the glass. "James and Mulroy's head clerk is a Mr. Devon.

And I have it on good authority that our Mr. Devon is a breast man."

"What on earth do you mean, a breast man?" she asked incredulously.

Nicholas suspected his patience was nearly at an end, but he pressed on. "Men, Miss Barnes, are partial to different parts of the female anatomy. I myself am a leg man. Give me a long leg with a well-turned ankle and—"

"That's quite enough, Mr. Bourne," Elena snapped. "I believe I understand now. This Mr. Devon prefers the upper regions of a woman's form, yes?"

"Precisely," Nicholas replied. "And yours, Miss Barnes? Well, yours are spectacular."

Nicholas could not tell from the woman's expression if she was about to slap him or preparing to faint.

"Thank you?" she muttered, looking at her bodice in the glass.

"That is," Nicholas continued, "in this dress. It more dramatically emphasizes your assets, if you will, than your other gowns."

She continued to stare at her breasts, then suddenly shifted her weight so that one knee was slightly bent, forcing her hip to jut out seductively. She leaned in ever so slightly and a pale expanse of skin was suddenly revealed.

"God," Nicholas said, admiring her instinctive response to his words. "There's not a man in the merchant bank who stands a chance."

"Now," he continued, returning to the beechwood chair. "I assume you have some knowledge of flirtatious intercourse?"

Elena blushed and Nicholas didn't know if it was "flirtatious" or "intercourse" that had embarrassed her.

"Well, it's rather simple really," he went on. "Allow Mr. Devon to believe that he's the only man who could possibly help you. He'll eat it up like a Christmas pudding."

"That's it, then?" Elena said, returning to her normal stance. "A flash of ample skin, made to feel the hero, and you men are rendered useless?"

"Your words, Miss Barnes. Not mine."

※ ※

"Elena, my dear girl, please do try and look as though you're enjoying yourself," Lady Mowbray exclaimed, allowing Dash to assist her out of the carriage.

Elena took a deep breath and prepared to disembark from the landau. "And who says that I'm not looking forward to the garden party?" She took Dash's hand and carefully stepped onto the gravel drive of Tointon House, savoring the spark of awareness that heightened her senses.

"Your face," Lady Mowbray answered flatly, shaking out her skirts, then turning her attention back to Elena. "And your demeanor. Really all of you, though the dress is quite cheerful."

Elena looked down at the deep rose silk gown, still surprised that she'd never seen how well such a color complemented her skin. "Thank you, Lady Mowbray. And I will try to do something about the rest."

"A smile, my dear, start there," the marchioness replied, gesturing for Dash to take her arm. "Now, my lord, compliment the girl. Though you've both turned up your noses at my attempts to throw you together, you're still a man. A nice word here and there will not kill you."

"Your dress is quite fetching, Miss Barnes," Dash said dutifully, looking back at her and winking. "And your shoes match. How clever."

"Is that the best you can do?" the marchioness asked with a long-suffering huff of disappointment, allowing

Dash to lead her up the broad marble stairs. "Really, young man. No wonder you've not married yet. Once I've found a husband for Elena, I promise to turn all my attention on you. Poor, poor boy."

The liveried servant standing at the top of the stairs opened the front door and stood aside, allowing Lady Mowbray and Elena to enter, with Dash following behind. Another servant assisted the women in removing their pelisses, then disappeared, while yet another appeared as if on cue to lead them down the hallway.

It was all so organized. So calm and dignified, Elena noted to herself. And so very different from what she was feeling at that very moment.

Lady Mowbray murmured, briefing Elena on the eligible men who were rumored to be in attendance, her military style both alarming and admirable.

Elena tried her best to concentrate, not wanting the woman to think her rude. But she found her mind drawn inexorably to the man walking directly behind her.

They reached the French windows and stepped across the threshold. Before them stretched a broad manicured lawn, thronged with guests gathered in groups or strolling in couples, trios, or foursomes. The large garden party hardly helped Elena's strained nerves.

Elena curtsied as the marchioness introduced her to the hosts. Dash bowed and thanked them for the invitation, then steered the women toward the center of the garden where most of the partygoers stood, chatting and enjoying refreshment.

His hand rested briefly against the small of Elena's back as he gestured toward the location, his touch so very, very right. She steeled herself against the sensation and casually shifted so that he no longer touched her.

"My dear, do pay attention. Mr. Smeade approaches," the marchioness murmured quietly. "A most unlikable sort, but a relation of Dash's. There's a certain duty, if you understand my meaning."

Elena startled at the sound of Smeade's name. Anticipation turned to simmering anger and hate. And fear. She was loath to admit it, but she was afraid.

"Smeade?" Elena repeated, looking about for Dash.

"Unfortunate name, I'll admit," Lady Mowbray answered, preparing to receive Smeade. "But it rather fits him. There he is now."

Smeade came into view. Not a monster, as Elena had prepared herself for, but an ordinary, older man. He possessed wispy, ginger-colored hair and was of impressive stature and build. His head was a bit out of proportion to the rest of him, and his ruddy face bore the markings of far too many years of strong drink.

There was nothing in the man's bearing that hinted at who he really was.

Which made Elena shiver.

The man approached, stepping into a sweeping bow in front of the marchioness. "My dear Lady Mowbray," he said in a lilting tenor voice, rising to reveal a sparkling smile.

"Mr. Smeade," the marchioness replied, offering her hand to the man, her face remaining emotionless as he placed a lingering kiss on her knuckles.

He released her hand and turned to Elena, his lips curving into the practiced, rather too dazzling smile once more. "And who might this be?"

Elena looked into his unusual pale gray eyes and forced herself to smile, a chill skipping across the back of her neck as she did so.

Lady Mowbray drew Elena's arm through hers in a possessive gesture. "Miss Elena Barnes, daughter of Baron Harcourt. In town from Dorset for the season."

The man repeated his overblown bow and waited for Elena to offer her hand, which she did reluctantly.

He took her fingers in his and pressed his too soft lips to her gloved hand, releasing her and rising once more. "Now, Miss Barnes, what brings you to London?"

"Mr. Smeade," Elena said politely, her voice weaker than she would have preferred. "To be precise, books."

The man looked quizzically at Elena, her answer clearly confusing him. "Books? Are there no lending libraries in Dorset?"

"Don't be ridiculous, Mr. Smeade," Lady Mowbray admonished impatiently.

"These are not just any old books, my lord," Elena explained, her words clipped. "They belonged to the late Lord Carrington."

"Oh, I see," the man replied, his interest piqued. His eyes sharpened with speculation. "Rather worth a fortune, I would think, given Lord Carrington's tastes and interests. Has the viscount had the books appraised?"

The simmering anger and hate in Elena's belly started to boil.

"I suppose so, though that's hardly my concern," Elena answered simply, hardly able to endure Smeade's calculating assessment. "They hold some sentimental value for my father, never mind the wealth of information to be found between their covers. They'll be treated with the utmost care while in our possession, and then more than likely, will be donated to the Bodleian."

Smeade drummed his fingers impatiently on his thigh, stopping only when Elena finished speaking. "I see. Though I do find it somewhat odd that the books would be given to someone *outside* the family. Usually, such treasures would be passed on to relations, you see. Wouldn't you agree, Lady Mowbray?"

"I can hardly speak to such things, Mr. Smeade," the marchioness answered, clearly uncomfortable. "Seeing as I am not a member of the family by blood. But I'm sure Lord Carrington would be most eager to address your question."

"Ladies," Dash called as he approached from behind the man, a cup of punch in each hand.

He stopped just to the right of Mr. Smeade's elbow and handed the drinks to Elena and the marchioness. "I'm afraid I've only fetched two, Smeade. You'll have to see to your own refreshment," he offered jovially, thumping the man on the back.

Mr. Smeade laughed good-naturedly, adjusting the sleeves of his coat. "Carrington, it's been some time since I last had the pleasure of your company."

Dash tapped his chin as though deep in thought. "Yes, it has been, hasn't it? The Young Corinthians' club, I daresay?"

"I believe you're right," Mr. Smeade confirmed. "Your memory is far superior to mine, Carrington. Why, my recall of today's events will be forgotten by the middle of next week, I fear."

Elena fought the urge to ask the man if he knew of Rowena's kidnapping.

Lady Mowbray sipped her punch and swallowed. "It seems Mr. Smeade has a keen interest in your father's books," she announced. "Isn't that right, Mr. Smeade?"

Dash's expression was one of thorough confusion. "What's that about books?"

"The issue of your father's library arose while Lady Mowbray made the introductions. Nothing to concern yourself with, I assure you," Smeade answered smoothly, nervously tugging at his earlobe. "Merely making conversation, you see."

Elena could not hold her tongue. "Really? I rather thought it was something of importance to you. Or did I misinterpret your interest entirely?"

"I'm a bit thirsty myself, old boy," Dash interrupted

Elena. "Would you mind very much? A cup of punch would be just the thing."

Mr. Smeade swallowed hard, his Adam's apple bobbing from the effort. "Of course, Carrington. I'll only be but a moment. Ladies. Until we meet again." He bowed perfunctorily and turned away.

The trio watched him wander off in the general direction of the punch bowl, Lady Mowbray sighing with relief when he insinuated himself between Admiral Harvey and his wife and began to chatter incessantly.

"I know that he's family, Dash," the marchioness said, her eyes narrowing as she continued to watch Mr. Smeade. "But he's . . ."

"Insufferable?" Elena offered, garnering a look of surprise—then a rather satisfied smile from Lady Mowbray.

"I do admire a nicely sharpened pair of claws, my dear Elena," the older woman replied, "Especially when it is warranted. Oh," she paused, her eyes now focused on the back of a woman standing near the quartet. "It appears that Lady Cumberbatch has managed to sit in something. Poor thing—the embarrassment would kill her. I'll only be but a moment." She gracefully strolled off to rescue her friend.

Elena turned her attention to Smeade, the very sight of him sending a chill up her spine. "How did you keep yourself from throttling the man?"

"I hardly have a choice," Dash muttered in a low tone, waving amiably at a passing couple. "We need information from him, and he's not going to give it to us if I choke the life from him in the middle of a garden party. You must have patience, Elena. Otherwise, all of our efforts will have been for naught. And he'll never be forced to pay for Lady Afton's death. Is that what you want?"

"Of course not. How could you ask such a thing?"

"I'm sorry," he growled, pulling at his cravat as if it choked him. "I saw you with Smeade and I . . ."

Elena didn't ask him to finish the sentence. She clasped her hands together tightly behind her back and held her tongue. It no longer mattered. It couldn't.

 ※ ※

Dash watched Elena walk down Threadneedle Street toward the James and Mulroy Merchant Bank. She wore a coquelicot crepe dress and a poke bonnet; her hair curled about her face, and a small smile curved her lips. To the casual observer, it surely must have looked as though she was enjoying a stroll in the waning sun, much like those around her. But Dash knew the truth of it. "What have I done?"

"What on earth are you talking about?" Nicholas countered, crossing one booted foot over the other as he leaned casually against a lamppost, his gaze intent on Elena.

Dash ground his teeth together until his jaw ached. "You know precisely what I mean. In fact, it was you who told me that I'd regret allowing Miss Barnes anywhere near the Afton case."

Nicholas punched Dash lightly on the arm. "Do not choose this moment to grow a conscience, Carrington. The last thing we need is for you to go crashing into the bank, set on rescuing Miss Barnes."

"I've always had a conscience, Bourne," Dash snarled. "Never more so than when it came to Elena's involvement. That was the problem, you see. I knew too well what she was feeling after Rowena's kidnapping. I couldn't allow her to suffer from the pain for the rest of her life. That would leave her no better off than we are."

Nicholas grimaced at his words. "You and your feelings, Carrington," he muttered, punching Dash again. "I'll admit, she's far too intelligent and irritatingly easy to admire. And for the love of God, could Miss Barnes find it in her heart to disguise her affection for you? Honestly, it's in poor taste, I tell you. But her breasts almost make up for it."

"Well, Bourne. I believe that's as close as I'll ever come to hearing you open your cold, dormant heart. I'm honored," Dash replied, his anger cooling as reason returned. "But I cannot let the breast comment go without mention. It simply isn't done."

His friend turned, his voice completely lacking his earlier sardonic inflection. "Yes, of course I mentioned her breasts. Really, Carrington. You didn't think that we would use Miss Barnes for her brains, did you? Look at her. She's beautiful, which is rather the point. Besides, the bank clerk is a breast man."

Dash's gaze followed Nicholas's to where Elena continued on toward the merchant bank. Men on the street turned to watch as she walked by, casting appreciative glances in her wake. And the ladies on their arms were responding as well—Dash was suddenly very thankful that looks could not kill.

"God," Dash murmured, a revelation hitting him square between the eyes. "She's beautiful." It was more than her hair or her dress. Much more. It was a confidence that he'd seen only when she'd talked of books—a firm belief in herself that had always shone through despite the most unattractive of gowns. She was beginning to understand all that she was, all that she could be.

"I've need of a new pocket watch," Nicholas said, turning to walk down Threadneedle Street.

Dash followed dutifully, his gaze never leaving Elena until she disappeared inside. "You see it then, too?" he asked his friend, still piecing his scrambled thoughts together.

"Miss Barnes? Of course," Nicholas answered, setting a leisurely pace. "I am in possession of two fully functional eyeballs, Carrington."

"What do you mean?"

Nicholas stepped aside to allow an elderly gentleman to pass. "What do you mean, 'what do I mean'? Good God man, I believe your fondness for the chit has addled your brain."

"Were we not discussing Miss Barnes's beauty?" Dash demanded, his frustration with Bourne blooming anew.

Nicholas stopped three doors from the jewelers and waited, dusk threatening to envelop them at any moment. "Carrington, I don't mean to be obtuse, but what, exactly, is troubling you?"

"I'm not quite sure, to be honest," Dash answered distractedly.

"God, man, just spit it out. Not everything in life is a puzzle," Nicholas growled, punching Dash on the arm.

"Blast it, we're not twelve. No more punching, do you hear me?"

"Spit. It. Out."

"I've made a terrible mistake. And Elena will pay for it with her life—a life that she's just now beginning to live," Dash roared, then punched Nicholas in the arm with all of his might. "There. Are you happy now?"

Nicholas looked at his arm, then at Dash, his mouth agape. "Not in the slightest. And you do realize that, at some point in the near future, I'll have to give you a sound thrashing for that barbarous jab, yes?"

Dash arched a brow in response, though he did rather suspect that Nicholas would eventually deliver on the thrashing.

"If you would be so kind, answer this question: do you hear what you're saying?"

"What a ridiculous thing to ask. Of course I can hear myself," Dash replied, mentally reviewing his words. "She's in danger and I'm the one who put her there."

"And?" Nicholas pressed, gesturing for Dash to continue.

Dash paused, his brow furrowing as he reviewed the situation once again. "No, I think that is all."

"God Almighty, for a man of exceptional intelligence, you really can be quite dim," Nicholas said, rubbing his temples. "You allowed Miss Barnes to aid in our task so that she'd be spared the lack of the very thing we've needed our entire lives. Justice, Carrington. A clear and concise line drawn between right and wrong. And responsibility taken on the part of the wrongdoer. How could that ever be seen as a mistake?"

Dash widened his stance and shook off a sudden attack of dizziness. "Do you truly believe that?"

"Yes, I do," Nicholas answered gruffly. "God, but you try my patience."

Damn, but the man made sense. Perfect, bloody sense. Dash nudged his friend with his shoulder. "When did you become so wise?"

"I always have been—you've just been too busy admiring your own intelligence to notice," Nicholas retorted. "Now come along. We'll have information to review soon. Thanks to your buxom Miss Barnes."

"Would you do me one favor?" Dash asked.

"What's that?"

"Do not think about her breasts. Ever again," Dash said seriously.

"When you say think, do you mean I can't speak of them?" Nicholas asked. "Or does this include mental consideration as well?"

"Spoken reference only," Dash agreed begrudgingly.

"Done."

14

Mr. Peter Devon, head clerk at James and Mulroy Merchant Bank, was, as Mr. Bourne had announced three days prior, a bosom man. Elena had balked at the idea, insisting that his sex surely possessed enough intelligence to resist something so practical. "They're no more than mammary glands," she'd stated pragmatically, looking down at hers with dismissal.

Mr. Bourne, in turn, had laughed in Elena's face and told her to wait and see, of all things. He'd gone on to create a fantastical story that she was meant to deliver to Mr. Devon should her breasts fail to brain the man into complete submission.

Elena leaned in over Mr. Devon's high desk inside the bank on Threadneedle Street and saw his eyes dilate with each additional bit of creamy, bergamot-scented skin that edged above her neckline. He seemed transfixed, the hazel irises disappearing at an alarming rate.

Quite awful, actually. Yet useful. Blast. Mr. Bourne had been right.

"It's terribly tragic, really," Elena began, lifting a lace-trimmed handkerchief to her nose and delicately patting. "Uncle Reginald was never a favorite of the family. The man was always impatient, extremely rude with everyone—even his very own wife," she paused, dabbing at her eyes. "I can imagine you, yourself, have relatives of the same sort, Mr. Devon. Even my uncle's dog wasn't spared from his truly detestable nature. The man couldn't be bothered to pat his own dog on the head."

While his eyes continued staring at her bodice, his mouth turned down in an expression of sympathetic dismay, as though she'd just told him something of heartbreaking proportion.

She sniffed again and began to cry crocodile tears into the slim wisp of lace-edged linen. "Poor little Oliver," she continued between sobs. "He died from a broken heart, we're sure of it. That dog loved my uncle despite the terrible abuse he suffered."

"Poor little Oliver," Mr. Devon repeated.

Elena braced herself dramatically against the desk with one arm and rolled her shoulders back. The crepe fabric of her dress tightened suggestively across the expanse of her bosom. "So you can imagine our surprise when, upon the passing of Uncle Reginald, a certain mistress arrived on our doorstep! And do you know what she said?"

Peter Devon couldn't help himself. He was staring at her breasts, all but licking his lips. "What?" he asked, distractedly. "Do tell me, Miss."

Elena had him entirely in her hands now. It had almost been too easy. And she realized that she felt sorry for the man—and a touch guilty. After all, Mr. Devon did not work for Mr. Smeade, nor for anyone else connected to the Rambling Rose. He'd only had the misfortune of being employed by the bank that Smeade used. That, and his fondness for the female anatomy, was the reason he was currently being manipulated by a pair of breasts.

But Elena didn't have the time to argue morality. Peter Devon was captured on the end of her fishing pole like a tasty trout, with nothing left to do but reel him in.

"Well, this mistress expected to be compensated. She

claimed that Uncle Reginald had made provisions for her—a secret account of some sort. Can you imagine?"

Peter Devon shook his head. "No, my lady, I cannot."

"Precisely," Elena agreed, bringing her hand to rest just above her heart—Peter Devon's eyes following dutifully. "But she will not relent. Which is why I'm here. You see, Aunt Agatha cannot bring herself to investigate the matter. And quite understandably so, which is exactly what I told her. She's far too busy dealing with the funeral arrangements. But it must be sorted out. Otherwise, this woman is threatening to bring her 'relationship' with my uncle to light—which, you can understand, would destroy my aunt."

"Of course," Mr. Devon agreed quickly. "What can I do to help?"

Elena beamed at the clerk—a true, genuine smile of gratitude. "Oh, Mr. Devon, I'm so glad to hear you say that. It is simple enough. The mistress claims that the secret account is with your bank—all of his other money resides at Hoare's Bank, you see. All I ask is that you confirm the existence of the account. If the mistress is telling the truth, then we'll need to get our solicitors involved. But I'd rather not make mention of something so tawdry until I know for sure that the money is there."

Peter Devon looked down at the top of his desk and picked up his quill, running the feather along the seam of his lips. "The rules state that only the account holder is privy to any information regarding the funds."

Oh, God, she was losing him. The hook had torn free from his mouth and he threatened to return to the lake! Desperate times called for desperate measures.

Elena reached out and placed her hand gently on his shoulder, then sighed a rather large, breathy sigh. The effect was exactly what she'd hoped for. The sudden forced release of air caused her breasts to strain dangerously against the crepe fabric of her dress until they threatened to burst forth in all their firm, pale glory.

The quill stopped in midair and remained aloft. Mr. Devon didn't seem to notice, as if his intent study of the exercise continued to require all of his energy.

"Normally I would not be so bold as to ask such a favor, Mr. Devon. But with Uncle Reginald's unfortunate and rather sudden death—a horrifying encounter with a wild boar on his estate in Wales," Elena explained, pausing to bring the handkerchief to her mouth as she pretended to silently mourn for a moment, then rallying and moving on. "Well, it's impossible for the account holder to request any information as pertains to the funds. And Aunt Agatha is quite desperate to put the matter behind the family quickly and with as little notice as we can manage. Is there anything that can be done?"

She threatened to cry again, taking small, panting breaths that forced her breasts to keep pace.

Mr. Devon was transfixed, his head nodding in time to Elena's breasts as they bobbed up and down. "Yes, of course," he replied, adding, "I'm sure that my superior, were he here, would agree that it's a matter meriting special consideration."

"Exactly," Elena agreed in a soothing tone, careful not to break the spell the man seemed to be under. "Now, whatever may I do to help?"

Mr. Devon's head stopped suddenly as Elena's breath normalized. "Oh, yes. Well, your uncle's full name. And the year the account was opened—or at the very least, an educated guess as to the year."

"Of course. His full name is—that is, was," she replied, letting her lip tremble. "Reginald Xavier Whitcomb. As for the year, give me a moment to think, won't you?"

Mr. Devon began to write the imaginary uncle's name

down on a scrap of foolscap. "Take all the time that you need."

Elena brought the handkerchief to her mouth and looked about the bank.

"I do recall Aunt Agatha mentioning something having to do with Uncle Reginald's particular lack of interest in her some ten years back. I wonder if that could be when he formed a connection with this woman."

Mr. Devon wrote something down on the foolscap, and then rose from his chair. "Possibly. I'll have to look downstairs, anything beyond the current year having been sent down to the storerooms, you see."

"Of course," Elena agreed, moving to the side. "And the current year?" she inquired, worrying her lower lip. "I would hope that such valuable information would be kept safe as well."

Mr. Devon bent the foolscap in his hands back and forth. "Yes, this year's accounts are quite safe, I assure you. They're locked away in the room, just back there," he replied, gesturing toward a door in the back left corner. "I hold the key myself."

"Oh, quite a responsibility, Mr. Devon," Elena said in awe.

He stood up tall and puffed out his chest with pride. "Yes, well. It's one of four official keys I look after. I am the head clerk, after all. They're just over there, on my desk. Would you like to see?"

"Perhaps when you return from the storeroom?" Elena suggested gently. "I'll just wait here, then."

Mr. Devon nodded, then walked past her and made for the stairs at the back of the large room.

Elena waited until she could no longer hear him, and then walked quickly to Mr. Devon's desk. She tucked the hanky into the neckline of her dress and reached for the ring of keys, carefully placing it in her palm and closing her hand tightly.

She scurried to the back of the room and advanced on the door, grabbing the knob with one hand while she tried the first key in the lock. The lock refused to give and she moved on to the second, turning it this way and that, with no better luck. "Blast," she hissed, pulling the second key out and inserting the third. It turned smoothly and the lock released. Elena pushed the door open wide enough to allow entry and walked across the threshold.

Stacks of ledgers stood in neat order, no discernable mark on any of their spines. Elena tamped down her irritation and chose one of the volumes toward the middle, pulling it awkwardly from a stack and carrying it to a table near the door. She flipped the leather-bound volume open and noted the surnames—all beginning with the letter D.

She snapped the book shut and returned it to the stacks. Then she went nearly to the end. Grabbing for the top volume, she brought it quickly back to the desk and laid it flat, opening it and noting that she'd managed to find the names beginning with S. Her finger flew through the pages as she looked for Smeade's name, finding it nearly three-fourths of the way into the volume.

She looked about for a pencil, the sound of Mr. Devon's footfalls on the stairs making her jump. She abandoned the search and instead ripped the page from the ledger and sent up a prayer for forgiveness before folding and stuffing the sheet into her tiny satin reticule, and quickly returning the book to its stack.

She hurried to the door, crossing the threshold and turning to lock up. She ran for Mr. Devon's desk and tossed the keys onto it, pulling the hanky from her dress at the last moment.

"I'm afraid I didn't find anything, Miss," Mr. Devon announced as he walked toward her, a look of genuine disappointment on his face. "And I took the liberty to search five years back as well. There's nothing. Perhaps the woman just wanted to see what she could get out of your family?"

Elena sighed, allowing the man one last look at her breasts—and, while not exactly enjoying it, somehow she couldn't quite hate him for it, either. "I'm sure you're right, Mr. Devon. I do so appreciate your help, though—as does my family."

The clerk bowed. "It was my pleasure. But if you wouldn't mind, please don't tell anyone what I did. As I mentioned, it's against the rules."

Elena nodded in understanding, and then curtsied. "Of course, Mr. Devon. It will remain just between the two of us, I assure you."

※ ♪

"Is it possible to perish from listening to something so horrendous, so heinous, that one would not believe the true atrocious nature of the sound unless they'd heard it for themselves?"

Lady Mowbray's question was one Dash had asked himself a number of times before. "And if I said it was?"

Elena admonished him with a deep furrowing of her brow. "Hush, both of you. Surely no woman would allow herself to be featured, in front of a roomful of her peers, no less—if she was not talented. It's simply not logical."

"Too often I forget that you had but one season, my dear," Lady Mowbray replied, reaching out and patting Elena's hand. "Logic has no place here."

The marchioness turned her attention to Dash. "I would ask that you sit in the end chair, my dear boy, so that when I do die and list one way or the other, I'll not fall into the aisle, but rather into you."

Dash grinned. "Lady Mowbray, the musicale has yet to begin. How can you make such assumptions? Why, this might just be the most accomplished gathering of musicians that the city has ever had the pleasure to hear."

The marchioness nodded an acknowledgment at a couple who passed by, smiling serenely before answering Dash's question with her own. "That, my lord, is impossible. Do you know who is performing this evening?"

"Haven't a clue," Dash answered honestly, his program having disappeared somewhere between the door and their seats as they'd negotiated the crowd.

"Lady Haven's grandchildren. Now, I adore the woman—she's one of my closest friends, actually," she whispered conspiratorially, "but she hasn't a musical bone in her body. Cannot even manage a passable hymn in church—sings like a cat in heat, you know."

Dash thought he saw Elena stifle a laugh.

"Can I assume Lady Haven passed on her lack of musicality to her children—"

"And grandchildren," Lady Mowbray interrupted Dash, gripping Elena's arm. "Except for one. A girl—Millicent, I think. Plays the violin wonderfully. But the rest of them?" She let out a long-suffering sigh. "I really should feel bad about bringing you two here—to die, most likely."

"Then why are we here?" Elena asked honestly.

The marchioness recovered from the dramatic pause and sat up straighter, stiffening her spine with apparent resolve. "Oh, well, I had to come—Lady Haven being a dear friend. And I couldn't be expected to suffer alone, now could I?"

"But you feel bad for doing so?" Elena pressed.

Lady Mowbray looked at her with a bland expression. "Oh, I do, my dear. That's not to say I would have made a different choice, though. Again, logic has no place here, Miss Barnes."

"You are quite crafty, Lady Mowbray," Elena muttered.

"Without a doubt," Dash said, standing up. "Now, if I'm meant to suffer through such a dreadful performance, I would like to at least know the musicians' names. I'm off to claim a program."

Lady Mowbray and Elena rose, clearing the way for Dash.

"I would use the term 'musicians' loosely, viscount," the marchioness warned, gesturing for Elena to claim Dash's vacant seat. "Perfect. Now, when you return, my lord, I'll have Miss Barnes on one side of me, and you, Carrington, on the other. A dignified death, just as I'd hoped it would be."

"Really, Bessie," Dash replied with amused exasperation as she sat down.

"Do try and make her behave while I'm gone," he asked Elena, smiling when she looked to the ceiling and her lips moved as if she offered a silent prayer.

Dash walked down the aisle toward the back of the room and approached the servant holding the programs. "I'll take one of those, if you don't mind."

"Of course, my lord," the footman politely replied, handing him one.

Dash nodded in thanks and walked on, noticing Lord Pembroke propped against the wall in the corner.

"Planning an escape, Pembroke?" Dash said as he drew near.

Pembroke gave Dash a friendly smile. "Well, something has to be done, wouldn't you agree?"

Dash didn't know Pembroke well. They'd not gone to school together, nor did they belong to the same clubs. But the man had married one of Dash's cousins and so they'd fallen into an easy, if infrequent, acquaintance.

The one detail about the man that Dash could attest

to was his intense affection for gossip. Rather like a woman. With sideburns.

"Quite so," Dash answered, leaning a shoulder against the wall next to Pembroke and looking at the audience gathered. "It looks as if nearly every man of our standing is here this evening, which should prove useful when it comes time to beat down the door and run for our very lives."

Pembroke chuckled, his gaze turning to the audience as well. "I say, do you know who appears to be absent?"

"Who's that?"

"Our very own distant relative, Mr. Smeade."

Dash could have kissed the man. "Is that so? Seems rather odd for Smeade. He adores musicales."

Pembroke looked at Dash and moved in a hair closer. "Perhaps it has something to do with his recent financial woes."

"Then you've heard?" Dash replied, his tone low.

"Well, not the particulars, mind you. Why? What do you know?"

Pembroke's eagerness for information left a stale taste in Dash's mouth. But he was making himself useful, Dash would give him that. "He's pockets to let," Dash began. "From what I've been told, all of his accounts have turned the man away."

"All of them?" Pembroke pressed, his eyes going round with interest.

Dash nodded somberly. "His tailor, Tattersalls—hell, the man can't even afford snuff."

Pembroke appeared speechless at the news.

"Be a good chap and keep it to yourself, would you?" Dash asked, turning his attention to the program. "Wouldn't want to make things worse for the poor bastard."

"Mum's the word," Pembroke assured him. "Mum's the word."

Elena cast a surreptitious glance across the room. Dash stood with another man, casually conversing. She wondered if he was spreading the rumor concerning Smeade's financial difficulties.

"Tell me, Miss Barnes. Have you reconsidered your position on the issue of Lord Carrington?"

"I wasn't aware there was an issue," Elena replied with what she hoped was the right mix of surprise and innocence.

Lady Mowbray perused her program casually. "Come now, do you think me a fool?"

"Just a moment ago, I accused you of being crafty—which, by my way of thinking, is very far from being foolish. Though the Middle English origin for both words—"

"I couldn't care less about the Middle English origin of anything," the marchioness interrupted, looking up from the list of performers.

Elena took a deep breath, and then allowed the air to slowly leave her body. She rather wished the dreadful music would begin. "We've discussed this, Lady Mowbray."

"Well, yes, we have. But I'd hoped that perhaps you'd reconsidered."

Elena took a second deep breath hoping to calm herself, her lungs filling until she felt a bit light-headed from the surge of oxygen.

"Oh, do release that bothersome air before you faint," Lady Mowbray said with a sigh, folding the program and laying it neatly on her lap. "Shall I tell you of my niece?"

"Yes, if it means that we'll stop discussing Lord Carrington," Elena replied sarcastically.

"Cheeky girl. Never mind. Now, my niece, not so long ago, made the acquaintance of a man here in town. No one, especially my niece, thought this man was an appropriate suitor—too wild. Too dangerous. And far too devilish for such an irreproachable lady. He was quite persistent, though, in his desire to court her, despite all indications that theirs would be a disastrous match."

Elena nodded, following the story halfheartedly while pretending to concentrate on her program. "He was the wrong man for her, then?"

"Oh, not at all. He was exactly the *right* man," Lady Mowbray answered with complete certainty. "Of course, it took everyone some time to accept this— except for me. I saw the spark right away—much as I did between you and Dash. I've quite a natural talent for such things."

Elena looked up when a group of young women, evidently the evening's performers, entered and took their seats in the front row. "But this man, he sounds as though he's nothing like Dash." It was difficult to focus on both the entertainment and Lady Mowbray's seemingly random story, she thought with a silent sigh.

"You've missed my point entirely, Elena," the marchioness chided. "He was all of those things that I mentioned—and exactly the man for my niece. No matter the differences, the assumptions we've made, or the difficulties we've encountered, if a match is meant to be, you pursue it at all costs. Otherwise, you're simply cheating yourself out of the life that you should have."

Elena's heart suddenly felt unbearably heavy, Lady Mowbray's words having settled squarely in the center, sinking deep.

"At all costs?" Elena repeated the marchioness's words, skepticism lacing her tone. "Surely there are considerations that are more important than one's own selfish needs."

"Love is not a 'selfish need,' " she replied simply, taking Elena's hand in hers. "It gives you purpose, understanding, fortitude—well, everything required to address these 'considerations' that you mentioned."

The woman couldn't know how hard it had been for Elena to deny herself. She wanted all of those things that love brought. But most of all, she wanted them with Dash.

I had wanted, Elena mentally corrected herself. She'd made a decision—a sound decision. Logic may not have much to do with the ton's world. But in hers, it was everything.

"Oh, merciful heavens, they're starting with Prudence, the worst of the lot," Lady Mowbray whispered urgently, squeezing Elena's hand tightly. "I'll leave you alone—for now. We'll continue our conversation later."

15

The following morning dawned sunny and clear. Fortunately for Elena, Lady Mowbray hadn't kept her promise to return to their conversation about Dash. Still, Elena felt as if she were escaping a pending lecture when she set off for the park on horseback, accompanied by Dash and Mr. Bourne.

Scores of the ton surrounded them on Rotten Row, the mild, pleasant weather having coaxed the haut ton out for a bit of seeing and being seen.

"Ah, there's Lady Mowbray," Mr. Bourne commented dryly, tipping his hat at the woman as she rolled slowly by in an elegant landau. "Always was quite the sport."

The marchioness narrowed her eyes at Elena, Dash, and Mr. Bourne. "Gentlemen, I expect you to be on your best behavior. Particularly you, Mr. Bourne," she called.

Mr. Bourne returned her instruction with a beatific smile, as though to assure her there was no reason for concern.

Dash's horse flicked his tail impatiently, the wiry, dark hair swishing against the flank of Elena's mare. "Let us move on before she thinks better of it and insists that Elena ride in the carriage with her."

The three clucked their mounts into motion and started out at a gentle walk.

For her part, Elena was glad for the chance to be out of doors, especially on the back of a horse.

"You see, it is just as Lady Mowbray said it would be," Elena offered, nodding hesitantly at a group of men as they greeted Dash and Nicholas. "Brimming with the best of polite society."

"If you count the horses, I suppose," Mr. Bourne remarked.

"Well, of course I count the horses," Elena muttered. "They're far more civilized than most of their owners. Therefore, it would seem wrong to exclude them."

Elena looked over her shoulder. Lady Mowbray's carriage had stopped and she sat amid a group of matrons, no doubt discussing the latest *on-dits*.

She turned around and faced forward, certain that there was enough distance between them and the marchioness. "Now, gentlemen, please tell me, was the information I stole from James and Mulroy of use?"

"Yes, quite useful," Dash replied. "We needed Smeade's account number in order to forge the banknotes."

Elena settled back in her saddle, relieved to know that she'd been helpful. "Anything else?"

"The moneylender's story was accurate; he told us the truth. Smeade does receive regular large payments from a company called Burlington Shipping," Mr. Bourne answered, patting his bay Thoroughbred on the neck. "Unfortunately, Burlington Shipping does not actually exist."

Confused, Elena looked at him. "What do you mean it doesn't exist?"

"There isn't an actual, functioning entity. More than likely, whoever Smeade works for has a network of businesses—some real, some not—that provide cover, if you will, for the main body of the operation," Dash explained, easily controlling his high-spirited mount when the horse shied at a branch on the path.

Elena nodded in understanding. "Oh, quite like the Hydra, then?"

"Precisely. It makes it nearly impossible to trace any path back to the men responsible," Dash confirmed. "And I would be willing to bet that the similarities do not end there. I'm certain that when the authorities discover and close one dishonest business, two more grow in its place."

Mr. Bourne let out an exasperated sigh. "All right, then. Are we quite done with the mythology lesson?"

"There's much to learn from mythology, Mr. Bourne," Elena countered with asperity. To her dismay, his callous remark stung.

Dash cleared his throat loudly, claiming their attention. "We've enough to think on without you two bickering. Wouldn't you agree?"

Elena knew he was right, although she still felt the urge to strike Mr. Bourne. "I apologize."

"Right," he answered brusquely. "And I to you. Now, may we return to the plan?"

Dash nodded. "We've the account number. I'll secure a likeness of his signature from the Corinthians Club, then Nicholas can move forward with forging the banknotes. The two of us will continue to feed the ton's insatiable appetite for rumors with stories of Smeade's financial woes."

Elena's horse tossed her head and danced. "And what am I to do?" she asked, before murmuring reassuringly to her mare.

"Protect your pretty little head and stay out of the way?" Mr. Bourne suggested acerbically.

Elena continued to coo softly to the mare, refusing to react to the man's words.

"You don't know Smeade, therefore it would appear suspicious if you began whispering about his money problems at every event you attended," Dash pointed out reasonably, his leg brushing up against hers as his horse nudged her mare. "I know this is hard for you.

But right now, your involvement would only jeopardize all that we've done so far."

"I see," Elena replied. The heat from where he touched her only made the situation worse. "And do you anticipate needing my help at some point?"

Mr. Bourne scoffed at her words. "Not if I have anything to say about it." He gestured toward the bend in the track farther ahead. "First one to Hyde Park Corner wins five quid." He lifted his horse into a trot and took off.

Elena and Dash watched as his horse picked up speed and moved from a trot to a canter, the dust rising from his hooves nearly obscuring the two altogether.

"The man would take a bet for five quid?" Elena asked lightly, needing Dash to believe she'd accepted the situation.

Dash continued to watch his friend. "He'd take a bet simply to take a bet—no money need be involved."

"Oh, that will require very little suspension of disbelief on my part," Elena replied, urging her mare into a trot. "I do loathe losing, though."

Dash caught up instantly, his gelding prancing, eager to follow Bourne. "As do I," he replied, loosening the reins and giving the horse his head.

Elena watched for a moment. Reins taut, she patted the mare's neck as the horse danced, anxious for her turn. Then, she promptly wheeled the horse toward Lady Mowbray, leaning forward to whisper to the mare, "I'll simply tell the marchioness that those dastardly men attempted to engage me in a wager. They'll never hear the end of it. Serves them right."

She trotted off back down the row, waving to Lady Mowbray as she drew near. "Protect my pretty little head?" she said out loud. "We'll see about that, Mr. Bourne."

Elena's fingers curved around the brass knocker on the door of the Halcyon Society's brick townhome and rapped it soundly against the wood panel. Waiting for a response, she looked over her shoulder at the hackney she'd hired to bring her to the Bloomsbury location. The driver had jumped down from his seat and was watering his horse, the large bay draft's greedy gulps sending the bucket swinging back and forth.

She glanced past the pair, searching the street beyond. Elena didn't really suspect that Dash had followed her. But she did wonder whether the very thought meant that she shouldn't be here. A full day had passed since he'd made it clear that her part in Smeade's capture was done. Twenty-four long hours and yet the bitter taste left in her mouth by his words lingered still.

"Good day, Miss Barnes."

Elena turned quickly around to find the door opened wide and Abigail standing in the entryway. "Hello, Abigail. Is Mrs. Mason in?"

The girl ushered Elena into the foyer and closed the door behind them. "She is, Miss. Let me see to your things, then I'll fetch her straightaway."

Elena removed her pelisse and bonnet and gave them to Abigail, smiling at the girl's obvious pride in her work. "Thank you."

"Of course, Miss," she replied, bobbing a curtsy. "Please take a seat in the front sitting room. Mrs. Mason will be but a moment."

Elena watched the girl disappear down the hall, her shiny black boots making clicking noises on the floor as she hurried away to fetch her mistress.

Turning toward the front room, Elena crossed the threshold and took a seat on the faded settee. The room looked much the same as it had before, with the exception of the vase of flowers. There were now creamy white and pale pink tulips in place of the red and yellow.

The colors complemented the dull puce fabric of the couch, she thought idly, much more so than the others.

"Miss Barnes," Mrs. Mason greeted her, sweeping into the room with quick efficient movements. "I do not believe that we have an appointment scheduled for today, do we?"

Elena smiled in apology. "No, we do not, Mrs. Mason. I do hope my presence is not an inconvenience."

Mrs. Mason sat down in the chair opposite Elena. "It's quite all right, though I am rather pressed for time today, I'm afraid."

"Of course," Elena replied, appreciating the woman's candor. "Let me get to the reason for my visit, then. Nearly a fortnight past, my maid, Rowena, was taken against her will by a Mr. Brock of the Rambling Rose."

Mrs. Mason scooted to the edge of her seat, concern clouding her face. "Miss Barnes, I am dreadfully sorry to hear this. We are familiar with Mr. Brock and the establishment. Was she . . ." The woman's voice faded as if the question was simply too terrible for words.

"She was rescued from the Rose no more than a handful of hours after the kidnapping," Elena answered reassuringly. "There were cuts and bruises, but her honor remains intact today."

Mrs. Mason's shoulders slumped with relief and she smoothed out the skirt of her gray dress. "Thank the Lord, Miss Barnes."

"Yes, quite," Elena replied, her gaze turning to the Bible on the sideboard. "I cannot begin to tell you just how thankful I am for Rowena's safe return," she continued, facing Mrs. Mason once again. "But I need more, you see. I need justice."

The woman folded her hands in her lap and looked pointedly at Elena. "I do understand, Miss Barnes," she said. "But do you recall our conversation concerning Mary Fields? Justice is hard to come by in such cases."

"Yes, I remember. But I must do all that I can, for Rowena's sake—and mine, to be completely honest. Can you understand that?"

Elena hadn't done all she could, not yet anyway. She'd leave Smeade to Dash and Mr. Bourne. But retribution and justice for Mr. Brock was hers.

Mrs. Mason looked out the large front windows as she considered Elena's explanation. "Do you have time to wait while I send for a Bow Street runner, Miss Barnes?"

"Yes," Elena replied eagerly. "And thank you."

"Do not thank me yet," the woman warned, standing. "I cannot stay, I'm afraid. You'll have to speak with the man yourself. And it will not be easy, Miss Barnes. You'll be required to provide every last detail, no matter how painful the telling."

Elena nodded her head resolutely. "I am prepared."

"No, you're not," Mrs. Mason answered, a compassionate tone to her voice. "But you're strong, and that should help."

She turned to the door and prepared to leave.

"Mrs. Mason, if I may ask after Mary Fields? How does she fare?"

The woman looked back and shook her head slowly. "I'm sorry to tell you this, but Mary died, Miss Barnes. The very night you were here. But she did not die alone. There is that."

Elena focused her eyes on Mrs. Mason's retreating form, a painful ache settling into her heart. "Yes, there is that, Mrs. Mason. There is that."

❧ ❦

Two days after Elena's interview with the Bow Street runner, she received word from the man that Mr. Brock had been forcibly removed from the Rambling Rose and now sat in a cell awaiting further action.

She lay in bed, staring at the heavy damask fabric that

formed the canopy. Lifting both arms above her head, Elena winced with pain. Perhaps she should not have been quite so industrious in her efforts. But the interview with the Bow Street Runner had played heavily on her mind and she'd needed something to throw herself into—something that required physical as well as mental attention.

Elena couldn't move. Her body ached from two days spent in the library, cataloging books, listing them in her ledger, then carefully packing them away in the custom wooden boxes that she'd ordered from Marsh and Tatham. She was quite happy with the progress being made. Her father would be thrilled when he saw all the volumes, a veritable treasure trove for a man who valued the written word above all else.

Lady Mowbray had commented on Elena's fervor at dinner, suggesting that a lovely evening out might be just the thing after such an exhausting day. Elena had politely declined.

And done so again following the fish course, when the marchioness had wondered aloud whether dancing wouldn't ease her aching muscles.

And one more time, for good measure, just as Elena was about to take a bite of strawberry tart. Lady Mowbray's reasoning was sound—the rumor being that the Roxburghe Club possessed one of the largest libraries in all of London—but Elena refused. Again. And less politely so, though admirably, considering her fatigue.

She lowered her arms to the bedcovers, unable to hold back a moan as she did so. Lady Mowbray probably was correct—a ball would have required all of Elena's attention, thereby making it nearly impossible for her to think about Brock.

But it also would have demanded patience and good humor, which Elena couldn't quite muster at the moment. She'd bid good evening to the marchioness, spent two more hours laboring in the library, then retired to her room.

Elena would sleep. Soundly. She needed the rest.

She rolled slowly onto her side, carefully tucking one hand under her pillow.

She wanted Dash. Needed to feel his body molded against hers, his arm around her waist and his breath in her ear.

She closed her eyes and breathed deeply, exhaling with renewed commitment to the task at hand. Elena was a firm believer in the idea that a person could accomplish anything if she set her mind to it.

She *would* sleep. Now.

One eye popped open and she contemplated the curtain in front of her.

She willed her eye to shut. Recitation was just the thing. She pictured her beloved copy of Homer's *The Odyssey* in her mind, and then slowly began to silently recite the words from book XII.

> So I spake, and quickly they [the men] hearkened to my words. But of Scylla I told them nothing more, a bane none might deal with, lest haply my company should cease from rowing for fear, and hide them in the hold. In that same hour I suffered myself to forget the hard behest of Circe, in that she bade me in nowise be armed; but I did put on my glorious harness and caught up two long lances in my hands, and went on the decking of the prow, for thence me thought that Scylla of the rock would first be seen, who was to bring woe on my company. Yet could I not spy her anywhere, and my eyes waxed weary for gazing all about toward the darkness of the rock.

Elena had never quite figured out why it was that the most exciting bits of poems and books lulled her to sleep at such times, but the explanation hardly mattered now. She felt her entire body relax, her limbs now dead weight, her head pressing more deeply into the pillow as her breath slowed.

Somewhere, in the far reaches of her mind, Elena supposed that Homer would be perturbed to know his work lulled her into the arms of Morpheus when sleep eluded her. If she were a writer, the mere fact that someone bothered to read her work at all would make her happy. So really, Homer had very little to complain about, she thought drowsily.

Of course, not having actually known the man, it was entirely possible that he would, in fact, feel this way without any prompting at all.

It was a difficult thing to pin down, really.

And then, a sound reached her ears. Elena wanted to fight responding, her body already sliding into slumber. But her brain did not.

And, as usual, her brain won out.

She opened her eyes and listened again. The sound had stopped. She slowly sat up and looped her hair behind her ears, concentrating on the quiet. Elena knew she hadn't imagined the slight noise.

She crawled on all fours across the bed and reached for the curtains, pulling them to one side and peering out into the relative darkness of her room. Sharp pain slammed into her jaw and Elena instantly saw stars. She lost her balance and fell from the bed, landing hard on her left shoulder and hip.

She instinctively rolled back toward the bed and grabbed at the carpet with her fingers, scuttling under the massive frame as fast as she could.

But it wasn't fast enough.

A hand grasped her ankle in a hard grip and savagely yanked. Elena threw her arms around one of the bedposts and dug into the carpet with her knees, her skin burning as the hand pulled harder.

"Let go of me," she cried out, kicking at the hand holding her.

He only jerked harder, succeeding in pulling one of Elena's hands free from the post.

She tried to dig her nails into the wood, but it was of no use. Her other hand slipped from the post. She clawed at the carpet and kicked again, writhing back and forth while being pulled free from the bed.

The attacker bent closer, his grip punishing as he rolled her over and covered her mouth with his hand, silencing her cries.

Elena fought the urge to beat her fists against his threatening bulk, looking up at the man.

His clothing was black, from his shoulders to his boots, revealing very little beyond a broad form. He wore a dark patterned domino mask. The moonlight, shining through the opened window where he must have entered, cast a low glow across his covered face and Elena stared into the assailant's eyes. They were pale and gray. A shiver captured her entire body and she convulsed with terror. It was Smeade.

He pressed harder with his hand and Elena whimpered, afraid he would smother her. Desperate, she pulled her knees in toward her stomach and kicked up with all of her strength, delivering a sharp blow to the man's testicles. He grunted and doubled over, his hand slipping from Elena's mouth as he fell against the bed.

She seized the opportunity and rolled over, scrambling to her knees, then her feet, screaming and running for the door.

But despite her disabling kick, Smeade's hands were suddenly in her hair, dragging her backward. Her scalp stung as she struggled to regain her footing, and she raked her nails across the man's face, loosening his mask.

He shoved her hands away, took her by the arms, and swung her up onto the bed. He yanked her arms above her head and held them there while he tied her wrists to the bedpost with a rough cloth, then bound her feet together in one swift move. Elena screamed again, her teeth biting down as he stuffed a cloth into her mouth.

Elena flopped about as though she were a fish, hauled up onto the deck of a boat and ready to be gutted.

Smeade stood over her, breathing hard as he watched her frantic movements—her fear. And enjoying it.

He straightened his mask, carefully retying the ribbons at the back of his head before adjusting his coat. His movements were precise, as though he required his appearance to be impeccable before he killed. Elena couldn't know what the mind of a murderer held, but she was suddenly chilled to the bone—so cold that she shivered violently again.

Elena tried to scream, but the fabric muffled the sound, pressing against her tongue and making her gag. He drew a knife from his pocket and methodically wiped it back and forth on his sleeve.

Elena told herself to stop shaking. If she could keep herself from trembling, then perhaps she could focus enough to figure out a way to escape.

He held the knife up and examined it, then ran it along a tasseled pillow, ripping the silk with one clean slice.

The soft feathers, released from their ticking, floated gently down against her skin. Tears of frustration and fear slipped down Elena's cheeks. She choked and gagged again, twisting violently, but only succeeded in stirring the feathers into a storm of downy rain.

"Elena?"

Smeade turned wildly toward the voice.

Elena's heart surged with hope when she saw Dash in the doorway, his figure illuminated by the sconce in the hall.

Smeade was a blur of speed as he ran toward the other side of the room and disappeared around the far side of the canopied bed.

Elena tried to scream for Dash, but her cries were a guttural jumble of bound consonants and choked gags.

"Elena." Dash ran to the bed. "What in God's name is happening?" He quickly pulled the fabric from her mouth and yanked her bound arms and legs free.

Elena coughed hard and tried to speak, her throat ragged from her screams. "Go. The window," she choked out, urging Dash to follow after the man. "He ran off as soon as you entered the room. Go!"

His expression fierce, he moved, swiftly disappearing.

"Dammit."

The thud of a fist connecting with the wall in frustration was loud, followed by the snick of the window sliding back into place and finally the rasp of the lock being engaged.

"What in the bloody hell just happened?" Dash demanded, returning to sit next to her on the bed. He quickly took her in his arms, wrapping her possessively against his chest. "If I'd not thought to visit you tonight, you would have been killed."

She buried her face against the fine linen of his shirt, allowing the scent of him to fill her senses. "It is my fault. Retribution for Mr. Brock. I'm sure of it."

"What do you mean, retribution, Elena?"

She turned her head and looked up at him, afraid. "I couldn't stand by and do nothing, you see. I sought help from Mrs. Mason of the Halcyon Society, who in turn introduced me to a Bow Street Runner. I never made mention of Mr. Smeade, I promise you."

"So that is why Brock is in Newgate awaiting trial, then?" Dash asked angrily.

"Yes," she confirmed quietly. "Justice will be served. But I never dreamed that . . ."

"That they would try to kill you?" he finished for her, his voice raw. "I did."

Elena dropped her chin and wept, pressing closer as fear and regret coursed through her trembling body. "It was Smeade. I recognized his eyes. I'm sure of it."

He kissed her brow gently and tightened his hold on her. "Enough, Elena. You are alive. And that is all that matters."

16

"I shouldn't have allowed you to come."

Dash and Nicholas stood outside the Rambling Rose, watching and waiting for Smeade to appear. Dash didn't know if he would be able to control himself. He was fairly sure that he would not.

"He almost killed her," Dash growled, tired of standing in the door of a pawnshop. He needed to move. Needed to *do* something. "But you are right. I'm not in the right frame of mind today."

Nicholas unfolded his arms and tilted his head toward the walkway. "Let's walk."

Dash followed, but his mind remained fixed on Elena and the Rambling Rose. Their forged letter from Smeade's boss had been delivered that very morning. Stating only that he would exact revenge for the great disservice Smeade had done him, the letter had sent the bastard into hysterics, according to Nicholas, who'd been following him all day long.

Smeade had spent every waking hour since receiving the letter traversing the city from the unsavory East End to the elegant west, each visit the same as the one before it. The man would stay no more than twenty minutes inside, and then Smeade would reappear, his look of worry having grown fivefold in intensity during the short period of time he'd been indoors.

Nicholas had taken note of each location. He believed Smeade was contacting others within the organization in an attempt to secure allies. Their letter had done its job.

They approached a pie cart and Nicholas stopped. "Are you hungry?"

"No," Dash answered impatiently, not even sure when he'd last eaten.

And not caring either.

"Two, please," Nicholas told the street vendor, then poked about in his waistcoat pocket for coins. "You can't give up eating altogether, Carrington. You'll risk losing your godlike physique."

"I'm in no mood, Bourne."

His friend handed a few coins to the man, and then accepted the fish pies.

They turned back toward the pawnshop. "Which is exactly why you need to eat," Nicholas advised. "There is no point in playing the broody type, my man. It's simply not in your nature. And remember, it wasn't you who nearly got the chit killed. Miss Barnes found herself at the wrong end of a blade because of her actions. Not yours.".

"He nearly killed her, you fool!" Dash snarled, wanting desperately to hit something. Or someone. It did not matter to him.

Nicholas took a bite of the pie and chewed. "I have not forgotten the facts. But you seem to have forgotten your strength. Cool, calm intelligence. That is what you're good at—and what I need from you right now. Don't fly up into the boughs now. We could still lose this race."

Dash scrubbed a hand across his unshaven jaw, angry that his friend chose now, of all times, to be insightful. "God dammit, Bourne."

"I know. Believe me, I know," Nicholas replied, then popped a greasy potato into his mouth and chewed. "You want the situation to change immediately. But you cannot have your revenge just now, my friend. This takes time. And patience."

Nicholas held out the second pie to Dash. "Go on."

Dash reluctantly accepted, taking a small bite and chewing automatically. "I used to be a patient man. But now . . ." he paused. Beyond rage and the powerful desire to hit something, he didn't understand what he was feeling enough to explain any of it.

They arrived back at the door to the pawnshop and resumed their positions, Dash leaning his back against the rough half-timbered wall. "And the banknotes?" he asked, needing to stop thinking, for once.

"All I need is his signature."

Once Dash secured Smeade's signature from the Corinthians Club, Nicholas's forged banknotes would be cashed in by a group of men his friend would only identify as "qualified for the task."

Smeade's account would be empty. And when he next visited James and Mulroy, he'd discover the truth of it.

And then he'd be theirs.

Nicholas tapped Dash on the arm and gestured across the street, where Smeade had suddenly appeared.

Unable to stop himself, Dash pushed off from the wall and took a step forward, but Nicholas held on to his shoulder.

"Carrington, old man, patience, now. Eat a real meal. Drink some good wine. Sleep soundly, if you can manage. And tell Miss Barnes to stay put. This will all be over soon."

Not soon enough, Dash thought with cold fury, but he kept it to himself.

🌙

Elena wanted to run.

The warm weight of Dash's hand at the small of her back as they walked down the hall of de Bohun House made her yearn to lean into his side and rest there. Forever.

"They'll be in the drawing room, taking their afternoon tea," Lady Mowbray explained. "And gossiping too, I would hope," she added, tapping Dash on the arm with her ivory fan. "Do unhand Miss Barnes, my boy. Such outré behavior within the walls of de Bohun House will have you married in no time at all. And we wouldn't want that, now would we?"

Dash's hand fell away and Elena immediately felt the loss, as though it was his hand alone that kept her standing upright. She steadied herself against the emotion, realizing again that her resolve had been sorely shaken by the late-night attack only two days past. Her reaction made perfect sense, she told herself once again. As she'd done, over and over, since that night.

"I don't mean to be ungrateful, Lady Mowbray," Elena began, hoping that there was still some way to avoid this social call. "But why, exactly, are we here? It is neither a ball nor a musicale."

The marchioness looked sternly at Elena. "Oh, my dear. The Furies are far more important than anyone you'll meet in a ballroom. Why, one word from Victoria or Charlotte, and you'll find yourself engaged to a duke. Perhaps, even a prince," she finished, nodding her head solemnly.

"My lady, do not lie. I understand it wrinkles the skin," Dash teased the marchioness.

Lady Mowbray turned her attention back to the butler walking ahead of them. "Oh, all right. My sisters are in town for an important sale at Tattersalls. And while I do love them so, they can be quite vexing from time to time. *That* is why you're here. Should I become too bothered I'll simply slip out the door and leave you to the wolves—women," she corrected hastily. "Leave you to the women."

One more minute. Had her attacker been given one more minute, all of sixty seconds, he would have killed her. Elena pictured the knife in his hand, meant for piercing her heart, she supposed, or slitting her throat.

Her cheeks heated and she touched her gloved hand to her forehead, lightly dabbing at a bead of perspiration.

"Oh, come now, my dear," Lady Mowbray said with misplaced reassurance. "My sisters are not that bad. Well, not all the time, anyway."

The butler stopped in front of a door, opening it noiselessly, and then clearing his throat. "Lady Mowbray, Miss Barnes, and Viscount Carrington," he said in rolling, deep tones.

"Really, Stanford, there's no need to announce us," the marchioness chided the man, and then entered the room.

"One hour. That is all. Then we'll make our excuses and leave. Will you be all right?" Dash whispered in Elena's ear, tucking her hand through the bend of his elbow to escort her inside.

Elena pasted a congenial smile on her lips and rolled her shoulders back. "Of course I will," she replied, "but thank you for your concern."

"Dash, do stand aside so that the poor woman might enter," a sharp, authoritative voice rang out.

"Victoria," Dash explained, nearly whispering to Elena. "Watch out for her."

His warning did not put Elena at ease. Still, her only other option was to run for the carriage. She looked down the long hall behind them, judging the distance and determining it would take too long to reach freedom. She'd never personally witnessed Lady Mowbray run. But she was fairly sure the woman would be fast if the situation called for speed.

"One hour," Elena whispered to Dash, and then walked into the drawing room, prepared for the worst.

If she'd found gargoyles or fairy-tale dragons awaiting her, Elena would not have been surprised. But before her sat two very prim, quite attractive older women—though one did appear to be a tad severe.

"Come in, then. Don't be shy."

Ah, you must be Victoria, Elena thought to herself, and then did as she was told.

"Don't tell the girl what to do," the marchioness said crossly. "Elena, sit next to me."

The third woman set her needlepoint down on the striped satin chaise lounge and sighed. "Lord Carrington, if you would be so kind as to make the introductions, please."

"Of course, Her Grace, the Duchess of Highbury. Lady Charlotte Grey, may I introduce—"

"Young man, you are aware that I'm a woman of advanced years?" Victoria asked flatly.

"Yes, of course, Your Grace—"

"Then don't waste my time."

Dash nodded at the woman, his smile genuine and affectionate. "Of course. Your Grace, Lady Charlotte, I am pleased to introduce Miss Elena Barnes. Miss Barnes, the Duchess of Highbury and Lady Charlotte Grey. Otherwise known as two of the three Furies."

Victoria pinned him with a piercing glare, then seemed to mellow a touch. "I suppose I deserved that last reference to the Furies. Now, Miss Barnes, do sit down—wherever you please," Victoria continued. "Though I do feel compelled to advise you that the Sheraton chair, situated quite close to me here, is, by far, the most comfortable in the entire house."

No, the sisters didn't resemble gargoyles. But Elena would not place any bets on who would come out on top in a boxing match or any other competition among them.

"Well, who am I to refuse a comfortable chair?" Elena

replied, carefully avoiding Lady Mowbray's gaze and
her surely pinched expression as she walked to the chair
and sat.

"I like her already," Victoria announced with pleased
satisfaction, gesturing at Dash to join the marchioness.
"Do sit down, my lord. Next to Bessie makes the most
sense, I suppose, what with her being your favorite."

Dash strolled across the room and settled in next to
the marchioness, crossing his legs and resting one arm
along the back of the chaise lounge. "I was five when I
made the choice, Your Grace. I can hardly be held ac-
countable for playing favorites at such a young age."

"Then you do not know Victoria as well as you might
think," Lady Charlotte replied softly, the merest hint of
a beatific smile on her lips.

"What was that?" Victoria asked, turning her sharp
gaze on her sister.

Charlotte shifted gracefully to the edge of the chaise
lounge and reached for the tea service. "What was what,
my dear? I fear your hearing is not what it once was."

"What of this horse you've come all the way to town
to look at?" Dash interjected, earning a sharp elbow in
the ribs from Lady Mowbray.

"Ugh," he grunted, looking pointedly at the marchioness. "What on earth was that for?"

Lady Mowbray raised an eyebrow and looked at Dash
as though he belonged in Bedlam. "You know better
than to interrupt their arguments. Cross as crabs, those
two," she paused, tipping her chin in her sisters' direction. "If they're not arguing with each other, then they're
bound to start a fight with me."

"Really, Bessie, as though you don't adore a good
brangle now and then," Victoria said crossly, accepting
a cup of tea from her sister.

"Now and then?" Lady Charlotte questioned, contemplating her spoon as she stirred her tea.

Normally, Elena would have found such discord distressing. As an only child, her house had always been quiet and comforting. And as for her acquaintances, other than the one disastrous season, her life had been filled with pleasant interactions and polite conversation. It was all so simple and easy. And Elena had liked it very much.

But surprisingly, the sisters' mild wrangling somehow had a calming effect on Elena's jangled nerves. She'd dreaded coming to their home, sure that thoughts of Smeade would keep her on the point. And the man did plague her mind, his face and the sharp edge of his blade seemingly hovering just at the edge of her vision. But the women's entertaining arguing and banter was slowly dissolving the worry that gripped Elena. She knew she wouldn't be completely settled until Smeade was safely locked away. But right now, in the cheery yellow drawing room, with Dash and the Furies, Elena felt safe.

The noise and vibrant color, light and life that surrounded the three sisters seemed to be exactly what she needed.

Elena looked at Dash and smiled with relief and appreciation. She'd fought his suggestion to visit the Furies, so sure that she knew what was best. When all along, he'd known better.

"And this prime bit of blood," Dash pressed good-naturedly.

Victoria took a swift, efficient swig of tea and returned the cup to its saucer. "Oh yes, the horse." Her face relaxed, coming alive at the mere mention. "Gorgeous chestnut yearling. Son of Wind Dancer and a mare out of Pennington's farm—Springtime Serenade. His conformation is perfect. And from what Lucinda's been told, his disposition is perfectly suited to racing."

"Lucinda?" Elena asked, unfamiliar with the name.

Victoria took a second sip of tea before responding.

"Yes, our niece. One of the most accomplished horse-women in all of England, I dare say."

"And loving mother," Charlotte added. "And of course, wife to the Duke of Clairemont."

Elena remembered the story Lady Mowbray had shared at the musicale. "Lady Mowbray, is this the niece you told me about at Lady Haven's musicale?"

"Yes, my dear," the marchioness answered, picking up her spoon and stirring sugar into her tea. "The very one. I'm so very glad that all turned out well. Of course, I knew it would. But still. There were those who doubted."

Victoria emitted a rather loud "pfftt," setting her Sèvres cup on the silver tray with a decided snap. "No one knew if all would be well. A scandalous duke. A kidnapping. The world was pear-shaped for quite some time, I can tell you that much."

"Kidnapping?" Elena repeated, sure that she'd mis-heard. "I'm sorry, but did you say kidnapping?"

Victoria turned her hawk-like gaze on Elena. "My dear, of course I said kidnapping. Poor Lucinda was taken by a hooligan connected to a rather fierce group of men—"

"A gang, Victoria," the marchioness corrected, then continued. "Les Moines, infamous on the continent, ap-parently."

"Savages," Victoria added, folding her hands in her lap, her eyes brimming with ire. "But the duke did his duty and brought her safely home—thank heavens."

All three of the women held still, as if giving thanks, the only sound to be heard in the room being an ormolu pedestal clock on the mantel.

"And she's well, your niece?" Elena asked, needing to hear so again.

"Oh yes, quite well," Victoria answered simply. "Well, the entire dreadful occurrence was quite a shock, as you can imagine. But eventually, in time, she recovered."

"With her husband's help," the marchioness added warmly.

"Really, Bessie. Still mooning over the man?"

Lady Mowbray raised one eyebrow and smiled dreamily. "Of course. It is perfectly within my purview to do so. Why on earth would I forgo such an opportunity?"

"You are nothing if not predictable, Sister," Victoria pronounced, and then tapped the length of chaise lounge between herself and Elena. "Now, do tell us about yourself, Miss Barnes," she said briskly. "From Dorset, if I remember correctly? Your father was a friend of the late Lord Carrington, I believe?"

Elena felt exhausted, but in the best way possible. If a woman could survive a kidnapping—even resume a normal, happy life after such as their niece Lucinda had done—then there was a chance that Rowena would recover—and perhaps even the memory of Smeade's attack would relinquish its hold on her. Eventually.

There was hope. Blessed, reassuring hope.

"Miss Barnes, are you hard of hearing?" Victoria asked, tapping the settee cushion once again. "I asked after your people in Dorset. I imagine you miss your home and your father most dreadfully. London is nothing compared to the glory of England's countryside, wouldn't you agree? I myself would not set foot in town—if not for the occasional beautiful stepper, of course."

Elena smiled wearily at Her Grace and sipped her tea, savoring the tang of citrus on her tongue. "Well, yes, Dorset has no comparison, truly. But London has a certain charm," she answered, looking through lowered eyelashes at Dash.

"My dear, I feel sure you've not visited Derbyshire, or you would not make such a statement . . ."

Elena knew that the duchess continued to speak, but she couldn't concentrate on anything but the warm tea in her belly and the peace that she'd found amidst the noisy discord of the Furies.

It was wholly unexpected. And exactly what she'd needed.

❧ ❦

Dash leaned back casually in his leather chair and puffed on a cigar. He scanned the Young Corinthians Club's main rooms and exhaled, the smoke drifting in front of his face for a moment, then floating away.

It was half past three in the morning. He'd stepped across the club's threshold some six hours before with the express purpose of ruining Smeade's reputation once and for all.

Dash sat up, leaned toward the low oak table in front of him, and rested his elbows on his knees. God, but he'd done more talking that evening than he'd ever care to do again. And drinking. And gambling. He'd even partaken of not one, but three dinners over the course of the night. Roast beef would not be served at Carrington House for some time to come.

But it had been well worth it. Every member of the club not tied to the Corinthians had eventually listened to Dash tell Smeade's sad story. Why, the poor man had lost a fortune in a shipping venture and was about to be cast out of his home with little more than the clothes on his back.

And for those lords who appeared sympathetic to Smeade's plight? Dash had carefully underscored the man's inability to turn a profit at this juncture, ensuring they understood that making a loan of any amount would be an ill-advised investment indeed.

Smeade was within his grasp. The very idea made Dash salivate. He could taste revenge. And it was sweeter than he'd imagined it would be.

He took one last, long puff of the quality cigar, then stubbed it out in a crystal ashtray. A man entered at the far end of the room and walked toward Dash. The lingering haze of smoke and low lighting obscured his identity at first and Dash relaxed back into the chair, assuming it was a footman.

"Carrington," the man called, his face revealed as he stepped within the circle of light cast by a nearby candelabra.

"Smeade." Dash picked up his glass of brandy and drained the last of the amber-colored liquid, letting the slow burn distract him.

He wanted to murder the man with his own hands. Right there, on the Aubusson carpet. In the Corinthians Club. With no one about to witness the crime but a few footmen.

They'd be easily bribed into silence. Dash was sure of it.

But he couldn't. And the knowledge made his gut roil.

"Fancy a drink?" Smeade asked, sliding inelegantly into the chair opposite Dash's.

He'd clearly been dipping rather deep, his face ruddier than normal and his speech slightly slurred.

"I'm afraid I'm done for the night, old man," Dash answered, doing his best to remain calm. "And you? A bit late, isn't it?"

Smeade waved off Dash's words, sloshing brandy from his glass. "Come now, Carrington. It's never too late for men like us."

Dash realized with satisfaction that Smeade was likely hiding out, the club his last refuge. "Indeed."

"I say," the man continued, pausing to take a lusty swig from his glass. "Did you decide what to do with your father's books?"

Dash was tempted to go to the window and signal for Nicholas to join them, Smeade's inquiry only confirming that he was as desperate as a man could be.

"Books?" Dash asked, toying with the man.

"Well, yes," Smeade replied, his frustration showing.

"I believe it was Lady Mowbray's friend who'd thought to take them. A Miss Barnes, wasn't it?"

The sound of Elena's surname on Smeade's tongue stripped any pleasure Dash had felt earlier from the man's presence. "Oh, yes. Well, you're quite mistaken, Smeade. Miss Barnes did not 'think' to take them. She is, in fact, taking them—no thought required."

"And is that wise, Carrington? Allowing the books to leave the family? Surely your father would have reconsidered such a decision in time. I know that you'd want to do what was best."

Dash could take no more. He planted both hands on the low table and leaned in until his face was even with Smeade's. "Do not presume to know me, nor my father," he said in a low, lethal tone.

Smeade's pallor faded to a grim, gray shade and he swallowed hard.

Dash stood. It took all his cool control to keep his tone amiable. "Come now, Smeade. I was only having a bit of fun with you. But I am afraid the books are a done deal. As am I. Good to see you, though."

"Yes, you as well," Smeade managed before finishing off his drink.

Dash turned on his heels and left. He made for the gambling room and located the large banner where the bet concerning himself and Elena was recorded. He ran his finger down the column of participants until he reached Smeade's signature. Nicholas needed the likeness in order to complete the forged banknotes. Dash had originally planned to secure the signature in a less obvious way. But he could not spend one more moment under the same roof with Smeade.

He ripped the banner from the wall, hastily folded it, and tucked it inside his vest. He'd hand it over to Nicholas outside, then return to Carrington House, where Elena awaited.

17

Bell had delivered a note from Elena to Dash's chamber door late that evening. She asked him to meet her in the library alcove once he'd risen and eaten his breakfast the next morning.

After spending the night tossing and turning, Dash strode purposefully down the hallway, his hair still wet from his morning bath. He'd not bothered with breakfast. Or sleep. Over the last several days, Dash had sensed a shift in Elena's response to him. She'd put space between them when she could, avoided his affection, and kept her thoughts and emotions to herself. He'd felt the loss slowly at first, the change almost imperceptible. But somewhere in the chaos of the days leading up to this point, the emotional chasm had grown vast indeed.

He turned into the library and headed for the alcove, its drawn curtains coming into sight as he passed the now empty bookshelves.

He pulled back one of the curtains and found Elena. She wore a simple blue cotton dress, her hair swept up and pinned on the sides with the length of it unbound and spilling around her shoulders. "Good morning," he said, sitting down on the opposite end of the cushion.

"Good morning," she replied, fidgeting with the cap sleeve of her dress.

Dash was too impatient for such pleasantries. "Please, let us stop this."

"Before your brain is rendered useless?" she asked,

releasing the fabric and folding her hands in her lap. "Not unlike mine, I'll add."

"Your head hurts too, then?"

She chuckled, a low feminine sound of amusement that lightened the weight Dash felt. "And heart." She reached out, taking Dash's hand in hers.

They sat in silence for a few minutes, the tension in Dash's head slowly melting away the longer her fingers touched him. The warmth of her small, soft hand cradling his eased his worry as if by magic.

"I'm sorry for how I've behaved," Elena offered humbly, moving closer to him. "I don't know what I was thinking."

Dash brought her hand to his lips and gently kissed her knuckles. "Perhaps you think too much?"

"Never," Elena answered quickly, emitting a second chuckle. Her eyes softened, lit with mirth.

"Tell me," Dash murmured. "I need to know."

"I feared that I'd let myself become distracted by you," Elena began. All amusement fled, her expression solemn as she spoke, her clear gaze fastened on his. "I could think on nothing else from the moment I arrived at Carrington House. At least not with any real concentration. You consumed me, you see, unlike anything had before. The feelings you inspired . . ." She paused, closing her eyes for a moment before continuing, her fingers tightening on his. "The feelings you inspired in my heart and soul were so unexpected. And enchanting. And true."

Dash nodded solemnly, feeling more vulnerable than he ever had before. He closed the distance between them until he could feel the soft ebb and flow of her breath on his face. He pressed a kiss against her lips before leaning back once again to meet her gaze.

Elena drew a deeper, shaky breath, the tip of her tongue slicking over her lips as if to collect and keep the lingering taste of his mouth against hers, before she continued speaking. "And then Rowena was taken and I blamed myself. If only I'd given her more of my time. If only I'd listened to my instincts when we first met Mr. Brock. So many regrets and very little in the way of what I could do to help."

Dash nodded again, his heart aching for her.

"The Halcyon Society made me believe that I could atone for my part, at least in some small way. And in order to do so, I needed to focus entirely on the endeavor. I had to let go of my own desires. I had to let go of you."

Dash suddenly felt as though he'd been punched in the gut. He gripped Elena's hands in his and held on. "That's not true," he said fiercely. "I want nothing more than to care for you. Your concerns will become mine, don't you see? You are stronger in my arms, as am I, in yours."

She pulled her hands free and cupped his face tenderly. "I know. I simply wasn't brave enough to admit it before. But I am now, Dash. And I'll never let you go."

Her eyes filled with tears, but her honest, exposed gaze did not waver.

Dash kissed Elena's lush, soft lips. "God, Elena. Say it again."

"I'll," she began, and then touched her lips to his. "Never," she continued, kissing his cheek. "Leave," she pressed on, landing a kiss on the opposite cheek. "You," she finished, her lips claiming his with such tenderness that Dash felt his heart respond silently, the last of the heaviness lifting higher and higher until it disappeared altogether.

She wrapped her arms around his waist and rested her head on his shoulder.

Dash placed a loving kiss on the top of her head. He

closed his eyes and cradled Elena in his arms, basking in her love. She was his salvation.

"Elena, I vow I'll never leave you. Though the reading of many books will surely make you go blind and your form will likely cripple from too many hours spent tucked away in the alcove, there is nowhere I will ever want to be but with you."

"You know me so well, Dash," she replied, snuggling in closer.

"Elena?" Dash asked, his fingers skimming circles along her back.

"Hmm," she murmured, arching into his touch.

"This—us, that is. It will never be easy, will it?"

"I suspect not," she replied, her voice low. "And just when we think that it's all been figured out, it will grow even harder. I suppose that is the price we pay."

"Gladly." Dash leaned back and brought her hand to his heart, so that she might know his sincerity in its strong, steady beat.

❧

God, but the man was irksome. Nicholas turned his face to the afternoon sun and sighed with irritation.

Smeade's desperate search for help in dealing with the threat from his employer had led him all across the city—with Nicholas forced to trail behind. Irksome and not short on endurance, apparently.

Nicholas rested against the park bench, situated within viewing distance of the James and Mulroy Merchant Bank.

He's persistent. I'll give him that.

Somehow, the admission did not make Nicholas feel any better.

His bones ached to sleep in his own bed. His stomach growled mercilessly, demanding a real meal. And his mind. God, his mind. Nicholas raked a hand through his unruly hair and decided not to think beyond Smeade and solving the case.

According to his sources, a network of connections that ran from the squalor of Wapping Stairs all the way to Mayfair and St. James's palace itself, word of Smeade's financial situation had spread like wildfire. No one was extending him credit. Not Rundle, Bride, and Rundle, where he bought the fanciest of snuff boxes. Nor Grillon's Hotel, where he dined on the most expensive food to be found in all of London.

Nicholas smiled at the thought of Smeade being turned away everywhere he went. It must be killing him to be treated thusly.

Or at least, Nicholas hoped so.

He crossed his legs and attempted to get more comfortable on the iron bench. None of Smeade's previous visits had taken long, but he'd been inside the bank for nearly an hour now.

This worried Nicholas. If they discovered that the banknotes had been forged, what would happen then?

It hadn't even occurred to Nicholas to consider the possibility. His work had never once been questioned in India, and some of it had been far more difficult than forged banknotes.

India.

For the millionth time since returning to England, Nicholas questioned his decision to leave India.

So many reasons to have stayed there. But if he had, he wouldn't be sitting here now, with Lady Afton's murderer almost in his grasp.

"No, you'd be riding in a palanquin, feasting on rich curries, fed to you by beautiful women wrapped in silken saris," he murmured to himself, shaking his head as if doing so would remove all the warm, happy, dreams from his thoughts.

A slow drizzle began to fall. Nicholas hunched his shoulders and crossed his arms against the damp.

He'd made the right decision. He knew it in his heart, even if his mind refused to see reason.

Monse, the street urchin that he'd employed to keep an eye on Smeade, suddenly burst through the door of James and Mulroy, his scrawny legs moving faster than Nicholas would have thought possible as he crossed the street, dodged a hackney, and careered around an island of rhododendron bushes before reaching the park bench.

"All right?" Nicholas asked dryly, looking the boy up and down.

The youth bent over and braced his hands against his knees, gulping down large breaths of air. "Those coves don't like my type in their establishment, that's for sure."

Of course, Nicholas already knew this. But he'd needed someone who wouldn't immediately consider blackmail if Smeade revealed anything useful. And it hadn't hurt that the boy was extremely slight for his age. No one noticed the poor. And the smallest of the poor? Even less noteworthy.

"They didn't hurt you, did they?" Nicholas asked, having noted no blood on the boy earlier, but aware that bruises would not show themselves for a bit.

The boy stood erect, though he continued to breathe hard. "Those slow blokes? They'd have to catch me first."

"And the man I asked you to keep an eye on?"

He smiled, revealing blackened, chipped teeth. "That'll cost ya, guv."

Nicholas reached into his waistcoat pocket and produced several coins, watching the boy's eyes dance and light with greed. "Four now," he replied, offering four sixpence. "And four once you've told me the details."

"Fair enough," the youth agreed, shoving the coins

into a pouch that hung around his neck, then tucking it
protectively beneath his torn shirt. "Seems the swell is
missing his money."

"That, I knew," Nicholas answered, eyeing the boy
warily. "I do hope you've more. Otherwise I'll be needing my coins back."

The boy clutched at the pouch desperately and held
up a hand. "I'm not trying to pull caps with you. There's
more. Plenty more."

Nicholas gestured for the boy to sit down next to him
and gave him what remained of an eel pie.

The boy accepted it with a tilt of his cap and dove into
the pie, taking an enormous bite. "He's none too happy,
I can tell you that," he began, bits of flaky pastry flying
as he spoke. "Seems he's wantin' to take a trip real
bad—only he needed the blunt for this trip. No blunt,
no travelin'. Kept going on about how the bank had
made a mistake. And the mister in charge kept telling
him that it was impossible. They never make mistakes.
He showed your man some notes, and then added up
what was left in his account."

Nicholas watched as the boy finished the food and
wiped his face and hands with the oil-soaked paper.
"And what was the amount?"

"Cleaned out, sir. Your man's out of money. That's
when the yellin' started. Scared a woman right out of
her hat, it did. Your man screaming that they might as
well have killed him for all the good they'd done. And
the one in charge yellin' back that he'd look into what
had happened if the bloke would just shut his trap. But
your man came right back at him, claiming they'd never
figure it out—couldn't be done."

The urchin looked off in the distance, as if he could
see Smeade's face, hovering before him. "He'd the
look of a dead man, he did. So scared and all. Said they'd

find him facedown in the Thames. Food for the fish, he'd be."

The boy shuddered from fright. "And I believed him. Ain't never seen a man so scared for his life—and I've seen plenty of men scared, sir. Anyway, that's when one of them clerks spotted me. I ran out of there as fast as I could, seeing as I'd be no use to you if they caught me. I hope that's enough to make you happy, sir."

Nicholas dropped the second set of coins into the boy's hands. "More than you'll ever know."

⁂

"You look absolutely beautiful."

Elena peered up from her ledger and smiled expectantly, watching Dash walk out from behind the wall of trunks assembled in the library. He stopped in front of the large table tucked away in the corner of the room and offered her a rose.

Elena uttered an "O" of surprise when she realized it was a wild dog rose and held it to her nose. "Please, say it again."

Dash came round behind her chair and bent down. "You look absolutely beautiful," he whispered in her ear.

His breath teased her lobe and she giggled. "Thank you."

"No thank-you is needed, Elena. I was simply stating a fact." He reached down and gently pulled her from the seat until she was wrapped in his arms.

She rested her cheek on his chest. "But I never believed it before. Not when my father told me, nor when Lady Mowbray said so. But now," she paused, looking up into his face and feeling nothing else but the single most powerful force of love. "Now I believe that I am beautiful—I *know* I am. Because of you."

"Well, I think anyone who knew the truth of the matter would point out how lucky I am to have been saved from my meaningless existence by you—but I will hardly pass up the opportunity to come out the hero in all of this," he replied, smiling down at her.

"Shall we agree to disagree?" Elena suggested, tightening her embrace.

"Absolutely."

"Perfect," she said, clearly pleased. "I do enjoy a good compromise—especially when I am the one who offered it," she added saucily.

Dash lowered his head and brushed a warm kiss against her lips. "You are taking full credit, then?"

Elena pulled him back for a second kiss, boldly running her tongue along the seam of his mouth.

Dash growled low in his throat and his arms tightened, gently crushing her breasts against his chest.

Her mind hazed, the world narrowing to nothing but delicious sensation and rising heat. And then she realized just what the man was up to and pulled back. "Dash, why are you here?"

"Can't a man enjoy a bit of time in his library with the woman he loves?" he countered, attempting to reel her back in.

She placed her palms firmly against his chest and refused his lips. "I believe you're trying to seduce me."

"Well, yes. I would have thought that was fairly obvious," he answered pragmatically, one hand stroking lower to cup her buttock.

The pressure from his palm felt so, so right. She pulsed with a surge of need and lust, then leaned in and grasped his shoulders, a moan escaping her lips.

"No. Wait!" Elena insisted, barely managing to reclaim her wits before pushing him away. "Tell me the truth. Why are you here?"

Dash looked at her as though she were insane.

"Dash," Elena ground out, her frustration growing.

He stopped caressing her bottom and moved his hand

back to her waist. "Are you quite sure you want to attend the ball tonight?"

"Really, Dash. The answer is yes—the same as it was yesterday. And the day before that. The Furies themselves could not keep me from Lord Elgin's ball tonight."

Dash gently rubbed her back between her shoulder blades. "And what of Smeade? Could the man keep you from the evening's festivities?"

Elena closed the narrow space between them and hugged him reassuringly. "Please, Dash. We have been over this time and time again. Nicholas will be following the man the entire time. I could not be safer anywhere than I will be with you at the ball."

"You have no idea what it was like for me, Elena," Dash replied, hugging her more tightly. "If he managed to get his hands on you again . . ."

Elena looked into his eyes, the pain she saw in the intense blue twisting her heart. "I will not tempt fate," she promised, capturing his beloved face with her hands. "I promise."

He lowered his head and took her lips in a tender, sacred kiss.

Elena treasured the feel of him against her, his powerful body a protective, sheltering bulwark. "Lady Mowbray informed me that her sisters will be in attendance this evening, so we've the unified strength of the Furies, should we find ourselves in need of it."

Elena watched his face, amused as he attempted to form a reply.

"Speechless, then?" she asked, caressing his cheek.

"Quite so."

She decided to put to use an academic study from a set of library books she'd found in her father's collection one long-ago summer.

Elena gently kissed his mouth, then trailed her lips lower down his body, landing soft, wet pecks on the strong column of his neck, dipping lower to his chest, where she tugged at his shirt with her teeth.

Dash's breath came faster, harder, his hands lifting to her tangled tresses.

Elena pushed him back against the trunks and reached for his breeches. She fumbled with the buff material and his smalls, then pulled both down until they skimmed the top of his boots. She slowly dropped to her knees and tentatively reached out, running her fingers worshipfully from his trim waist to his muscular thighs.

"Elena," he uttered in a throaty plea, as if begging for mercy.

She smiled up at him, then reached around and caressed the expanse of his skin where his back met his buttocks, dipping lower to playfully score the sensitive area.

Dash started at the unexpected act, his hands moving to brace himself against Elena's shoulders. "You are torturing me; you do know that, do you not?"

"I disagree, my lord," Elena countered wickedly, then leaned in close and licked the velvety tip of his shaft. "The torture is only beginning," she warned.

Placing her hands on his hips, Elena took him in her mouth and swirled her tongue around the length of him.

Dash released her shoulders and frantically reached for the trunks behind him. Finding the leather straps affixed to the sides of the cases, he grabbed tight to one with each hand and held on.

Elena interpreted this as a good sign and continued on, delicately sucking as she moved her mouth up and down the shaft, allowing her teeth to lightly graze the skin. She placed one hand on his testicles, caressing them before gently squeezing.

The trunks behind Dash began to shake from the force of his grip.

Elena quickened her pace, sucking intensely and applying a touch more pressure with her teeth.

Dash's head rolled back against the cases, and he groaned deeply, the sound echoing in his throat.

She released him and sat up on her knees, proudly watching his face contort with exquisite pleasure.

She held out her hand and beckoned for him to join her on the carpet.

He tugged his breeches and smalls up until they hugged his hips, then accepted her hand as he slid down the trunks, coming to rest with his back against the solid leather. "You must tell me, where did you learn to pleasure a man so thoroughly? You are remarkably skilled. And understand that I'm not complaining, mind you." His voice was rough as he pulled her into his arms.

Elena smiled, and then kissed him before settling in next to him. "You're not questioning my virtue, are you, Lord Carrington?"

"Never," he replied. "The thought would never have entered my mind. I'm just curious, is all."

"Books."

He took a lock of her hair between his fingers and twined it around his forefinger. "Books?"

"Yes, books. You know, of course, that reading is an integral part of my existence—as is learning," Elena answered seriously. "And when I happened upon a stash of certain instructional texts in my father's library one summer, well, I wasn't about to let them go unread. You cannot even imagine the information contained within those books—positions and breathing techniques and so much more."

He leaned back to look down at her, his expression stunned. "Are you teasing me?"

Elena sniffed and gave him an offended look. "Absolutely not, my lord. There is nothing that a book cannot teach you—even the ways of love."

Dash's full, firm lips stretched into a delighted smile. "God, Elena. Did you say 'love'?"

Heat bloomed and Elena was sure her face was blushing pink. She lowered her lashes, concealing her eyes.

Dash reached out and gently tilted her chin up until her gaze met his. "Do not be embarrassed, Elena. I love you more than I've ever loved anyone in my entire life. I was simply too cowardly to tell you."

"Do you mean it?" she asked shyly, her lip quivering. "Truly?"

"Truly," Dash confirmed in a hushed tone.

She looked deeply into his eyes, his words giving her strength and courage. "Then let me say it again: I love you, Dash. Truly."

18

"Really, my boy. You need to propose and marry her already," Victoria urged Dash, swatting at him with her silken fan.

Dash rubbed his forearm where the weapon had made contact and continued to watch Elena converse with Lady Mowbray and Lady Mayhue just at the edge of the dance floor. "What on earth are you talking about, Your Grace? And where is Lady Charlotte?"

"At home with a headache." She whacked him a second time. "Now, please. You look at her as though she were a ripe, red apple and you a half-starved horse. Bessie cannot stop talking about the match she's made."

"Match? Made?"

She moved to hit him again, but Dash captured the fan, wanting to break it in half, but resisting the temptation to do so.

"Well, yes. Apparently, she is the reason that you two fell in love. Some nonsense having to do with a number of ton parties," she paused, raising one eyebrow as she considered. "The opera or something. I cannot remember because I admittedly was not giving the woman my full attention, but the opera figures into the story."

"And whom, exactly, has she told this to?" Dash asked, fingering the sticks of the fan with careful concentration.

Victoria looked at him with shock, then thumped his

arm with her hand. "Really, you mooncalf. My sister would not spread rumors."

Dash looked the woman straight in the eye, quirked his eyebrow, and waited.

"Oh, all right. Of course, she spreads rumors," Victoria conceded. "But she would never do so when it came to certain persons, you being one of them."

Dash's brow dropped and he gave the fan back to Victoria. "I suppose you are correct."

She offered him a small, stiff smile, and then whacked him one last time—and with markedly more effort than the first three attacks. "You suppose? Really, my boy. The mere fact that you questioned me to begin with deserves a proper set down, but it looks as though Miss Barnes is coming this way—so I will spare you."

Dash covered his upper arm protectively with one hand and smiled, all too aware that any further argument would be in vain. "Thank you, Your Grace."

"Of course, young man. And now you owe me a kindness. I'll not forget," she replied, watching as the ladies made their way toward them. "Now, do be a gentleman and refrain from drooling, won't you?" She waved the fan in warning.

Dash regretted not having broken the fan when he'd had the chance.

Bessie and Elena joined the two, the marchioness smiling with obvious pleasure while Elena looked decidedly displeased.

"Really, Miss Barnes. You look as though you recently swallowed a spider," Victoria offered in greeting.

Bessie gave her sister a critical glare. "She does not. That is simply how she looks when she is delighted to accept an invitation for tea at Lady Mayhue's home on Tuesday afternoon."

Elena looked at Dash pleadingly while she sipped her punch with a marked lack of enthusiasm.

"Bessie, I thought the two of you had reached an agreement as to how many outings Elena would endure—that is, attend, while in town," Dash said in her defense.

The marchioness pretended to look surprised, but gave up any effort as all three in the group looked back at her with complete astonishment. "Oh, all right. Yes, we decided on a number. But what was I to do? Lady Mayhue was absolutely smitten with Miss Barnes—which, by the way, my lord, is the proper way to refer to her," she said, winking conspiratorially at each of them. "'Elena' is rather too personal—or would you not agree?"

Elena gasped and choked on her mouthful of punch.

"Really, Bessie. Now look at what you have done. The girl might die all because you could not keep your observations to yourself."

Elena coughed a second time and Dash took the cup from her. "Ladies, if you'll be so kind," he began, handing the punch to Bessie while gently thumping Elena on the back. "I believe that I will show Miss Barnes the Marbles."

Elena gasped twice, holding up her hand as she coughed, and then drew several deep breaths and composed herself. "That would be lovely, Lord Carrington."

"Yes, lovely. Here, Victoria, do hold this," Bessie added, shoving the cup toward Victoria. "Though I have seen them before, I always find them quite inspiring."

Victoria refused the cup and whacked her sister on the arm with her fan. "As do I."

Elena elbowed Dash in the side, her brow furrowing.

"Actually, I believe I am in the mood for dancing," he corrected himself.

Elena's eyes rounded and she elbowed him a second time.

God Almighty. I will be black-and-blue from head to

toe after tonight, Dash thought to himself as he placed Elena's hand on his arm.

There was little that could be done now. And besides, surely dancing a good distance away from the two hovering Furies had to be preferable to viewing the Marbles in their presence. Surely.

❧

"A waltz, how daring!" Dash said pleasantly, leading Elena onto the dance floor. "A good excuse to keep my arms around you."

Elena attempted to root her feet to the edge of the floor, but had very little luck against Dash's greater strength and subtly insistent tugging.

"Are you all right?" he asked worriedly, looking about at their fellow dancers, and then searching the crowd beyond. "Has something alarmed you?"

The music began and Dash held out his hand for Elena to take.

"No, nothing alarming," she said as quietly as possible while still being heard.

Dash's jaw relaxed a bit and he smiled. "Good. Now, take my hand."

Elena stared at Dash. "I cannot."

Dash dropped his arm, took her hand in his, and then embraced her waist. "Yes, you can, you see. As simple as breathing."

Elena did not see the point in mentioning that currently, she couldn't do that either.

The couples surrounding them began to dance, elegantly twirling to the music as if they were born to do just that.

Dash looked down at her and smiled. "Are we ready then?"

"No!" she hissed, feeling foolish. "Dash, I cannot dance. I will embarrass both of us. Everyone will stare—

and whisper, if I recall such things correctly. Trust me. You do *not* want to do this."

"Come now," he replied reassuringly. "I am barely proficient myself. We'll muddle through—together. Besides, I am sure that you're not nearly as bad a dancer as you think you are. You just have not had an opportunity to practice in the last several years."

Elena wanted to believe him. After all, she'd not danced since her one season in London. Perhaps it was something that came more naturally as one grew older. Like, well, Elena could not think of one single undertaking that fell into such a category. But that was beside the point.

She smiled affectionately and moved her right foot, allowing Dash to lead her in the first movement. She followed with her left, a glimmer of hope rising in her mind.

Was it possible that she was actually dancing and not simply watching her partner endure a torturous turn about the floor? She tilted her chin up proudly, wishing now that everyone would watch as she triumphantly danced with the man she loved.

And then she promptly stepped on Dash's foot.

She stopped abruptly, managing to nearly cause a collision with other dancers on the floor. "I told you," she whispered, a painful bubble of shame clogging her throat.

She had come so far. And yet, here she was, reminded of her awkwardness and inabilities—and feeling it just as deeply.

"Then we will improvise," Dash replied, squeezing her waist lovingly. "Now, stand on my feet."

Elena looked about at the other couples as they danced around them, their curious faces only making Elena feel worse. "I can't—I won't. Please, don't make me do this."

He pulled her in closer and bent to whisper in her ear. "Trust me. Now, place your feet on top of mine."

Elena was not entirely sure that the situation could get any worse. So she did as Dash asked and placed her small slipper-shod feet on top of his large ones.

He gripped her hand tightly in his, looked down into her eyes, mouthed "here we go," and they did. He suddenly began to move, his feet expertly executing the steps—all with hers balanced atop.

It took Elena a moment to capture her balance, but once she did, she honestly began to enjoy herself. It was something she had never expected to happen.

But wasn't that the theme of her London stay? Everything that she'd assumed about herself, her life—her very place in the world—had been tossed up in the air, blown about in the wind until she'd not known up from down, and then gently settled back on the ground. Some pieces could be found, while others had disappeared entirely, lost in the sky forever.

And this was not a bad thing, she realized with a start. Not a bad thing at all.

"You, Elena, are a brilliant dancer," Dash assured her, smiling widely. "You only needed the right partner."

Elena relaxed her head back for a moment and giggled, the sensation very much as she would imagine flying felt like for a bird.

They twirled again, and then settled into the strong movement of the dance.

She wanted to preserve the moment in time. Tuck it away and pull it out every now and again when she needed reassurance. Because, Elena knew, without a single, solitary doubt, that in the future she would have questions and disbelief, self-doubt and misgivings. And suddenly, that was all right.

The music came to an end and Dash slowed their

pace, finally stopping and gently setting Elena back on her feet.

They clapped politely, and then Dash captured Elena's hand in his and pulled her toward the edge of the room. "Come quickly, before the Furies see us. I want the honor of showing you the Marbles all to myself."

"I could not agree more," Elena replied, holding tightly to his hand.

Dash would have happily watched Elena viewing the Marbles for the rest of his life. Her delight was nothing short of childlike as she gleefully examined each and every detail, her mouth forming an enchanting "O" of awe as she reached out her fingertips to touch the smooth marble, stopping out of respect just short of laying her hand on the art.

"Go on," Dash whispered, looking about to make sure no one was near. "Touch it. We're the only ones here. Who would know?"

Appalled, Elena snatched her hand away as though she'd been burned. "I would know, that's who!"

But her crossness faded almost as quickly as it had appeared when she caught sight of the figure of Dionysus. "Oh, my goodness," she exclaimed, catching up the skirt of her silk dress and hurrying to where the sculpture was displayed near the back of the room.

Dash followed behind at a slower pace, acutely aware of how perfect the night was. Not that he cared a whit for the sculptures. The Greek statues were things to be treasured, but they were nothing compared to Elena.

No, it was that he was there at the Elgin Ball with Elena—and nothing else. And for a moment, he'd forgotten all about Lady Afton. He'd let go of Langdon and Sophia—even Nicholas and his quiet rage. Dash had twirled Elena about the dance floor, thinking only of her comfort and how he would cherish her for the rest of their lives.

He'd glimpsed what his life could be. And he wanted more.

"There you are," a male voice said.

Dash turned away from Elena and looked behind him, seeing Nicholas approach.

He needed more time with Elena. But he could not have it. Not until they dealt with Smeade and put the nightmare behind them.

"Hiding among the Marbles," Dash replied, turning back to watch Elena's rapt contemplation of the marble statues just a little longer.

Nicholas joined him. "From the Furies, more like."

"They are only two this evening, which dilutes their potency a touch," Dash offered, looking wryly at his friend. "But yes, that is precisely what we are doing."

The two men stood quietly, gazing upon a marble centaur.

"I do not believe I have ever witnessed an individual quite so enthusiastic about such things," Nicholas remarked, watching as Elena pointed at various details, posed questions to herself, out loud, and answered in the same manner.

Dash smiled proudly. "She is amazing, is she not?"

"All right, then. Enough with the tender revelations," Nicholas answered sarcastically. "Smeade has made contact with his superior."

Dash blinked hard. The switch from Elena to Smeade was too abrupt. "How?"

"Yesterday, I watched him take a piece of coal and draw an X on the lamppost just outside his townhome. No more than an hour ago, I intercepted a messenger about to deliver a message. The letter was in answer to his request and contained specifics on when and where to meet. I wrote a second letter, of course. Wouldn't want the handwriting confusing Smeade. Then had it delivered to the man."

Dash thought for a moment on Nicholas's words. "The X must be a way to communicate directly with his employer."

"If the signature on the missive is to be believed, that is precisely what it is for," Nicholas replied, widening his stance. "We have very little time. Smeade is to meet the man on the London Bridge in less than an hour."

The two continued to watch as Elena moved to a frieze of a chariot group. "What will you tell her?" Nicholas asked Dash, his eyes remaining fixed on the woman.

Dash scrubbed his hand across his jaw. "You know, of course, that she will want to come."

"That is precisely why I am asking."

Elena's possible inclusion was not even open for debate—the situation was far too dangerous. Dash could not allow Elena anywhere near Smeade nor his employer. She'd played her small part admirably earlier. The information she'd purloined from the bank had been key to cracking the case.

The problem was, how could he convince her she must stay behind?

"You will need to lie. Obviously," Nicholas offered, turning to look at his friend.

Dash met his gaze reluctantly. "I could never lie to Elena. Not now."

"Well, let me put it this way," Nicholas countered, pausing while he looked again at Elena. "You can lie and keep her from meeting Smeade's employer face-to-face. Or you can tell her the truth. It is up to you, of course. But I would like to state for the Corinthian record that I wholeheartedly supported lying in this case. Actually, I wholeheartedly support lying in most cases."

"Do not joke about this," Dash insisted, wishing he could ignore his options.

Nicholas returned his gaze to Dash and slapped him on the back. "You know what you have to do. Now do it."

"Damn it all to hell," Dash uttered mournfully. He walked toward Elena, his feet as heavy as the marble before him—and his heart too.

19

Nicholas narrowly avoided crashing into a coach as he steered his Tilbury carriage down Holborn Hill. His bay tossed his head nervously but pressed on, leaving behind the sound of the coachman's angry yells.

"Why the bridge?" Nicholas asked Dash, seated next to him on the padded leather seat.

His friend shifted his weight in an attempt to put some space between them on the narrowed perch. "That's a good question. It would be hard for one to hide in the middle of a bridge, I suppose. And his employer would have an unimpeded view of Smeade's arrival, thereby guaranteeing that the man arrived alone."

Nicholas flicked the right rein and the bay turned down Bridge Street, one of the carriage's wheels lifting from the road momentarily. The vehicle swayed danger-ously before righting itself. "I suppose that makes sense. Damn inconvenient for us, though."

"Inconvenient. But not impossible."

Nicholas nodded, pleased with his friend's reply. "Tell me," he began, coaxing the bay to pick up its already hazardous pace. "Did you believe this day would come?"

"Of course," Dash answered instantly. "Didn't you?"

Nicholas had long ago given up on ever apprehending the man who'd murdered Lady Afton. He'd just as-sumed that it was to be one in a long line of curses that clouded his life. But he admired his friend's optimism.

And more important, he had no moral objections when it came to lying. "Absolutely."

They careered around a corner and headed for Lower Thames Street. "And your Corinthians? What will they have to say about the matter should they find out?"

Dash gripped the side of the seat as the carriage encountered a hole in the road, holding tightly to avoid being thrown. "I've broken nearly every law within the Corinthian code—and a few outside of it as well. Carmichael could not overlook such things. But I've come to terms with the possible consequences."

"And those are?" Nicholas pressed, a fine misting of rain beginning to fall.

"My expulsion from the Corinthians," Dash answered simply. "But we'll have captured Smeade and his employer. And that's what matters."

The bay's hooves slipped on the wet street, but he recovered and held his stride. Nicholas called reassuringly to the horse and kept his hands firmly on the reins. "Are you sure?"

"What on earth do you mean?" Dash countered.

It sounded to Nicholas as though his friend genuinely wondered at the question, though he found such a thing hard to believe. "Your whole life has been dedicated to the Young Corinthians. How could you surrender it so easily?"

Dash seemed to consider the question while he swiped at the rain gathering on his greatcoat. "Elena."

"Come now. Everything, for a woman?" Nicholas pressed, unconvinced.

"Yes, Bourne. We're capturing Lady Afton's killer not only for justice, but a second chance at life. Elena is my second chance."

It was inconceivable to Nicholas that any man would think it a sound idea to put his entire future in the hands of a woman. But the purposeful look in his friend's eyes made him believe that if someone was going to prove him wrong, it would be Dash.

"I see," Nicholas replied dryly, slowing the bay with a tug on the reins. "Well, as for me, I'm looking forward to a second, third, and perhaps even fifth chance at *life* with Lady Whitcomb. Widows are rather generous, I find."

Dash arched an eyebrow sardonically. "You'll never change, will you, Bourne?"

Nicholas brought the carriage to a stop and jumped down. "Did you honestly think I would?"

Dash joined him on the ground and gestured for the reins. "Honestly?" he asked, tying the bay to a post outside of a butcher shop. "No."

"I didn't think so."

※ ✥

"I must say I am rather surprised by Mr. Bourne's presence here this evening," Lady Mowbray stated, spearing an asparagus tip and delicately lifting it to her mouth.

Elena leaned closer in an attempt to hear the marchioness over the deafening conversation of those packed tightly into the dining room, nearly dipping her bodice in her plate. "And why is that?"

"Well, the man is not known to enjoy polite society."

Elena eyed the grayish roast beef on her plate with displeasure, and then pushed it toward the middle of the table. "Though I find the man not entirely to my liking, I believe he is rather popular with women, is he not? Surely such events as this one tonight would offer ample opportunity to make the acquaintance of many, many, enthusiastic new friends."

The marchioness smiled slyly. "Well, that is true enough. But Nicholas has never had the patience for the prologue, if you will. He appears to abhor suffering through dancing, a mediocre meal, and conversation.

He does not care for the simpering milk-and-water misses, either."

Elena was hardly surprised by the information. Mr. Bourne seemed to care very little for *anyone*.

But if that were the case, why then was he here, at the Elgin ball? He and Dash had escorted her and Lady Mowbray to the dining room and then left for the card tables, assuring the women that they would return when the dancing resumed.

Elena eyed the cold meat on her plate once more, a sense of unease growing steadily stronger. "Lady Mowbray, I believe that I will seek out the viscount in the gaming room, if you do not mind."

"I don't in the least," the marchioness answered, pushing her own plate away. "But I will accompany you. It would hardly be proper for you to wander about the house alone."

Elena rose from her seat and waited while Lady Mowbray walked around the table and joined her. "And is that all?"

"Of course not, my dear," she answered, walking from the room and heading for the back of the house, where the gaming was presumably taking place. "It is a room filled entirely with men. How on earth could I be expected to pass up such an opportunity?"

Elena smiled at the woman, but could not quite enjoy the humor of the situation.

A nagging feeling refused to let loose of her—that she had been lied to. And that she had been fool enough to have believed it.

Lady Mowbray swept into the gaming room as though she owned it, offering a superior nod of the head to those men who were brave enough to question their presence.

The two made a complete circuit of the room, finding neither Nicholas nor Dash.

"Where do you think they are?" Elena asked the marchioness, panic beginning to knot her stomach.

Lady Mowbray patted Elena's shoulder and smiled. "Smoking cigars. Drinking port—really, there are any number of activities those two could be enjoying right now. I am sure they will find their way back to the ballroom at some point."

"But I need to know where they are right now," Elena demanded, her tone as desperate as she felt.

Lady Mowbray stopped abruptly and looked Elena in the eye, her keen gaze assessing. "My dear, is something wrong?"

"Possibly. But I cannot say anything more. Please," Elena pleaded with the woman. "You must help me find them."

The marchioness hesitated for a moment, and then took Elena's arm in hers and headed for the front door. "Victoria will be able to tell us where the two have taken themselves off to. She makes it her business to know absolutely everything about everyone."

"And where is she, exactly?" Elena asked, confused by their direction.

"The mews."

A footman opened the door wide and they stepped out into the cool night air. Lady Mowbray quickly dragged Elena down the stairs and around to the back of the mansion. Carriages and horses filled the area until there was hardly enough room to walk between them.

"What makes you think that Her Grace would be here?" Elena asked as they squeezed between two lacquered carriages.

"Victoria has three passions," the marchioness began, stopping to look about and orient herself. "First, horses. Second, sticking her nose into everyone's business. And third . . ." She paused, spotting a group of liveried drivers gathered in a circle just up ahead. "Gambling.

And by gambling I am not referring to Commerce or Silver Loo. I mean real, hard-and-fast gambling. For money."

Lady Mowbray took off again toward the men, pulling Elena along behind. "Pardon me," she said to one of the servants, gesturing for him to step aside. He complied and the women stepped into the circle, where Victoria stood, holding a pair of dice and blowing on them.

"Just as I told you," the marchioness announced, supremely satisfied with herself.

Victoria glared at her sister, and then blew on the dice a second time. "Hardly a state secret, sister—as though I would let something as inconsequential as male opinion keep me from a quality game of Hazard."

She threw the dice into the center of the circle and watched as they hit the ground. A servant bent to look at the numbers, then announced a pair of twos. The entire circle erupted into excited shouts.

"Drat!" the duchess commented, then turned her attention back to her sister and Elena. "Now, what do you require? And do hurry up about it. I've a losing streak to break."

Lady Mowbray nodded, understanding her sister's need for timeliness. "We are attempting to ascertain Lord Carrington and Mr. Bourne's whereabouts. They are not in the gaming room, nor the dining—"

"Of course they aren't. The two left in Bourne's high-sprung carriage some time ago," Victoria interrupted. "His tiger boldly attempted to join our game, claiming he'd nothing better to do since his employer had flown for London Bridge."

Elena felt a cold, sickening panic grow with each word that the duchess spoke. "I'll need a carriage," she commanded, looking at Lady Mowbray.

"What is going on?" Victoria demanded, stepping in front of the two.

Elena respectfully shook her head. "I cannot tell you. Not now. I must go to the bridge."

"Then we will accompany you," Victoria said plainly, turning to her driver. "Prepare the horses. Apparently, there is not a moment to lose."

❦

"Do you remember shooting the bridge?"

Dash turned up the collar of his greatcoat to the damp, cool night air and looked out at the span of London Bridge from his vantage point near the center of the structure. "How could I forget? I nearly died."

As misguided youths, Dash, Langdon, and Nicholas had procured a ridiculously small boat, ventured out on the Thames during the turning of the tide, and held on for dear life as the water swelled from the powerful natural force and shot them through one of the small arches on the underside of the bridge.

"But you did not," Nicholas replied, looking toward the north end of the span.

Dash folded his arms across his chest and looked out from their hiding place behind the wall of the bridge master's quarters, fighting a smile. "That is not the point."

There were times when Dash wondered how he was alive at all. From the moment Lady Afton had been laid to rest to, well, that very moment on that very bridge, Nicholas had organized far too many death-defying acts to count.

Would this be the last one? God, he hoped so.

Nicholas elbowed Dash and pointed toward where he'd been looking. "Smeade," he said in a low tone, inching back a touch.

The two men watched Smeade walk slowly toward the central span of the bridge, his head turning often to look behind him suspiciously. As he drew nearer, he suddenly stopped and stared into the night directly in front of him. "Is that you?" he called, jutting his head out and squinting.

Dash followed his gaze. A man walked out of the darkness. Dressed in a greatcoat and beaver hat, the shadowy figure strode confidently to where Smeade stood.

"There," Nicholas whispered, tensing to attack.

Dash held tightly to his friend's arm and restrained him. "Wait." He may have spent most of his Corinthian career behind a desk, but Dash knew that waiting for the exact moment was of paramount importance.

Smeade backed up two steps, gaping at the man who stood in front of him. "I did not request a meeting with some errand boy," he ground out, his voice thick with forced indignation.

The man slowly began to unbutton his greatcoat, his eyes never leaving Smeade's. "Really, Mr. Smeade. Did you truly believe that we would take your summons seriously? The Bishop does not have time for you anymore, I'm afraid."

"I beg your pardon?" Smeade faltered, backing up further.

A pistol appeared in the man's hand and he pointed it directly at Smeade's heart. "It seems rather simple, even for the likes of you, Mr. Smeade. You failed to kill the Barnes woman. Your services are no longer needed."

Smeade held up his hands defensively. "Lord Carrington interrupted my attempt. What was I to do?"

Dash fisted his hands at his sides, willing himself to remain concealed.

"Your job, Mr. Smeade. You are far more trouble than you are worth."

"Surely my history counts for something," Smeade shouted, his voice quivering. "I demand to see the Bishop, right now."

The man cocked the gun, the sound making Smeade jump. "You are in no position to make demands. No, the only *someone* that you will be seeing is the Lord God Almighty—if you are fortunate enough."

Smeade suddenly lunged at the man, throwing him off balance. Then he turned and made for Fish Street Hill.

The man righted himself, pointed the gun, and fired off a shot.

Smeade fell forward, stumbling, tripping on his own feet, and hit the bridge deck, hard.

"I'll take Smeade, you see to the shooter," Dash told Nicholas. The two men exploded forth from their hiding place and ran with all that they had.

Dash passed up the shooter as he headed for Smeade. He looked back to see the man run toward the west railing of the bridge, Nicholas changing his course and following.

Dash reached Smeade and fell to his knees, turning the man over on his back. He was still alive, gasping for breath as small, round bubbles of blood slipped from his mouth.

"Tell me who you work for. Tell me who ordered Lady Afton's death," Dash demanded, looking down into the dying man's face.

Smeade managed a blood-frothed smile. "You. Really, Carrington. I didn't know you had it in you."

Dash wanted to kill him with his own hands, but he needed to know the truth. "Tell me, Smeade. Now. You have nothing to lose at this point."

"The sad truth is, I can't tell you because I do not know," he answered, his breath becoming shallower. "I took my orders from the Bishop, but never met the man face-to-face. And the bastard who shot me? Not the Bishop, unfortunately."

A gurgling noise sounded from the man's throat and set off a steady stream of blood. "Find the Bishop. And then you'll find the King," his voice rasped, his words barely discernible.

"Who is this King? We're not playing a bloody game of chess. Is the Bishop our man or not, Smeade?" Dash ground out, grabbing his coat collar and shaking him. "This is not enough."

"But it is all that I have," Smeade answered, his body suddenly wracked with uncontrollable coughing. Blood spurted across Dash's coat as Smeade convulsed. The killer reached out and gripped his arm, his eyes widening in fear and alarm, then he slumped, his body suddenly quieted and stilled.

Dash looked to where he'd last seen the shooter, just in time to witness the dark figure jump over the railing and disappear into the black water of the Thames below. Nicholas bent over the side of the bridge, but quickly abandoned the chase.

He turned back and ran to Dash, stopping beside him. He peered down at Smeade's body. "Is he dead?"

"Yes," Dash answered, looking down at the corpse.

Nicholas kicked the body and shouted, "Dammit! Did he tell you what we need to know?"

"We have a lead, Bourne," he said quietly.

"Then your answer is no?" Nicholas pressed, his voice thick with emotion.

"My answer is no."

Nicholas stared at Dash, his eyes hard and cold. "I knew it. This nightmare will never end." He kicked Smeade a second time and roared, the sound coming from his mouth more animal than man. He turned and strode away toward the end of the bridge, the rain and the darkness quickly swallowing his figure up until Dash could no longer see him.

※ ※

The carriage hit the bridge hard, throwing all three women up in the air, then bouncing them back down with a thud. Elena opened the coach window and peered out, the sight of Dash walking straight for the carriage making her scream.

"Stop the coach!" Victoria demanded, thumping the roof as hard as she could.

The driver obeyed, pulling up the horses with marked force. The women held on as the coach rocked to a halt and finally stopped.

Elena threw open the door and leapt out, pulling up her skirts as she ran toward Dash. Just as she reached him he opened his arms, catching her in an embrace. She felt a sticky wetness and looked down. Blood stained his shirt and smeared the front of her dress.

"Oh, my God, Dash," she gasped, terrified and struggling to remain calm. She pressed her palms to him, seeking out the wound. "Please, my love. Please stay with me."

He caught her hands in his to still the frantic search. "I am not injured, Elena."

"But the blood," she began, straining against his hold.

"It's Smeade's—not mine," he assured her, gently kissing each gloved hand, then closing his eyes.

She looked past his broad shoulders to where a man lay on the bridge. "I thought it was you," she began, her words thick with tears. "I saw the blood and I . . ." Elena could not finish her sentence.

Instead, she burrowed deep against Dash's chest and began to cry long, soulful sobs of relief. "Do not ever leave me again. I could not bear it. I cannot live without you, Dash."

"Nor I you, Elena," he answered, resting his chin against her soft curls.

A scream came from just behind them, followed by the telltale sound of a slap.

Elena looked over her shoulder to find Victoria glaring at the scene while Bessie tenderly held her cheek.

"Are you injured, my boy?" Victoria barked, eyeing the blood.

Dash allowed Elena to ease back a step in his arms and looked down at his shirt. "Despite appearances, I am not."

"Thank God!" Bessie wailed in tearful relief, stepping gingerly away from Victoria's tense form.

Victoria drew a deep breath and nodded abruptly. "And the man on the ground there. Who is he?"

"Smeade," Elena answered, looking at the still, lifeless form.

"Good God, though I daresay, choosing between you two," Victoria replied, "I would much rather it be Smeade than you, dear boy."

Dash nodded.

Victoria took Bessie's arm. "Come along, then. This is most likely the one time we'll be given the chance to see a corpse. And I, for one, will not pass up such an opportunity."

Bessie patted Dash on the shoulder, pausing briefly. "Do not frighten her so again. Ever."

The two sisters walked on, though Victoria appeared to be pulling Bessie toward the grisly scene.

"Did he tell you what you needed to know?" Elena asked, looking at Smeade a second time.

Dash's arms tightened around her. "No."

"I'm so sorry." Elena looked into his eyes and realized with absolute confidence that nothing mattered to her more than Dash. If only he felt the same way. "You'll continue to search, then?" she asked, though she felt certain she knew what his answer would be.

Dash enveloped her in his powerful arms and pulled her protectively closer until she was pressed against him from head to toe. "No."

"I'm sorry," she faltered, sure that she'd misheard him.

He placed a soft, soul-searing kiss on her forehead and sighed deeply. "*You* are all that I need, Elena. I know that now. But what about you? Is Brock's capture and Smeade's death enough?"

Elena turned her chin up and captured his mouth in a grateful kiss. "It is," she said with conviction. "Never let me go, Dash. Promise me."

"I promise, Elena. I will never let you go."

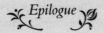

Epilogue

Everything in Dorset was calm, even tranquil, Dash thought. He breathed in the crisp night air and looked out over the lake from his vantage point in the folly. A full moon illuminated the dark water, the fringe of trees separating it from the fertile land beyond casting fanciful shadows across the waves.

He pulled Elena against him and wrapped his arm about her shoulders. "Are you tired, my love?"

"Yes, but in the best possible way," she replied, resting her head on his chest. "And Rowena has been such a help. The Dorset branch of the Halcyon Society is almost ready to receive the first of our Verwood residents."

Dash smiled at the news and an overwhelming sense of pride filled his heart. Elena had worked tirelessly since their wedding and subsequent move to the rented estate that bordered her father's. She'd overseen the renovation of the home that would house the society. And she'd asked Rowena to assume the role of headmistress, which had pleased the now fully recovered maid greatly.

Dash hadn't found the individual who'd ordered Lady Afton's killing, but he'd discovered Smeade—and, in the end, brought him to a justice that he deserved. It was enough for him now.

He looked down at Elena and realized he had more than enough. She'd brought the peace he'd been desperate for most of his life when her love settled deep into his heart and soul.

Bourne would take up the reins and continue the quest for the Bishop. Dash felt confident his friend would succeed. Whether he would do so within the confines of the law was another question entirely. But if working with Nicholas had taught him anything, it was that laws were merely a suggestion, not a dictate.

"It's heaven, isn't it?" Elena asked with a satisfied sigh.

Yes, Dorset suited Dash perfectly. "It is, my love. But I believe it's time to return to the house. Your father will be worried."

She snuggled closer to him. "Is that so? Or is it perhaps that you're worried?"

He hoisted Elena into his lap, settling her in with a sweet kiss. "I've absolutely no idea what you're talking about," he answered, looking meaningfully at her belly.

"Why do men think of pregnancy as an illness?" she retorted, reaching inside his waistcoat and pulling out a missive from the hidden pocket.

Dash looked at his wife pointedly. "How did you know that was there?"

"Shhh," she urged him, placing a finger on his lips. "My ways are best kept secret."

Elena winked, knowing that she'd won, at least that round, anyway, and broke open the seal. "Lord Carrington, as you know, your service to the Young Corinthians is integral to our ability to perform our duties to Country and Crown," she read out loud, stopping to add begrudgingly, "true enough," before picking up where she'd left off.

"That being said, the desire for a life outside of service is an understandable one, made even more so by your wife's legitimate concerns for your safety. Therefore," her voice faded, but her eyes continued to scan the words, her expression changing with each line, until tears overflowed and slowly began to trickle down her cheeks.

"You did this?" she whispered, folding the letter until the two halves of the seal met again.

Dash had told her about his involvement with the Young Corinthians the night Smeade had died, needing to have nothing between them but absolute love and honesty.

He slipped into his familiar guise, pasting a vapid smile on his face and shrugging his shoulders dramatically. "Did what?"

"Stop that this instant," she demanded, her fingers tracing over his features as if to wipe away the fool's look completely. "This is a serious consideration, Dash."

Dash obliged and looked at his wife as he knew he would for the rest of his life: with love, admiration, and respect. "If by 'this,' you are referring to the fact that I asked to only be contacted should the Corinthians have no other options, then yes, I did."

Elena kissed him, harder this time and with an intensity that stirred Dash's soul and heated his blood. "Thank you. I couldn't ask you to quit—wouldn't, actually. I know how much your work means to you. But I wasn't sure what I was going to do if you were ever in danger again. When I thought you'd been shot on the bridge . . ." she paused and buried her face against his neck. "It was the end of the world for me. Everything went black, Dash. Everything." Her tearful words were muffled.

"Never again, Elena," Dash reassured her, wrapping his arms about her protectively. "I promise."

They sat that way for some time, the silence soothing their nerves and reminding both that the past was just that—not forgotten, but certainly gone. And the future?

"Besides," Dash began, kissing her hair. "I'd hardly

have time to continue my Corinthian work, what with a son on the way."

Elena poked him in the stomach with her finger. "A daughter. But yes, you will be busy, I would imagine."

"I still wonder at how lucky we are. Surely you conceived the very first time we made love."

Elena picked up her head and looked at Dash seriously. "Oh, it has nothing to do with luck. I consulted the *Philosophical Transactions of the Royal Society* just yesterday. Apparently, scientists believe that one in every ten children was conceived in the very same way. We just happen to be in the minority, is all."

"Have I ever told you how fetching you are when you quote statistics?" Dash asked her, kissing just along her jawline.

Elena chuckled low in her throat. "Of course you have. Why do you think I do it so frequently?"

"Lord, I do love you," Dash replied, glancing about to discern whether they were truly alone.

Elena closed her eyes and lay back in his arms, a satisfied and altogether beguiling smile curving her lips. "No more than I love you. I've proven it—the equation is in the house, if you'd like to see it."

"Elena," Dash growled, cupping a firm, ripe breast in his hand and kneading it.

She moaned and let her knees fall open. "You've no need of a proof, Dash, nor do I."

Dash leaned forward and caught the hem of her dress. He slowly drew the fabric up, revealing her shapely legs. "God, Elena. What I did to deserve a woman such as you—well, I'll never know."

She toyed with his cravat. "Well, you seem rather handy with mathematics. Surely there's an equation that would apply—"

He captured her mouth in a hard kiss, then scooped

her up and carried her down the steps of the folly. "You torture me, Elena."

He laid her down in the soft pennyroyal and rid her of the bothersome clothing.

She wound one leg around him and reached for the buttons of his breeches.

Dash grabbed his cock and pulled it free of the fabric, then slipped his finger into her core, groaning when he found the exquisite wetness. "I want you. Now."

"Then take me," she urged, tipping her hips up and sliding his cock into her. "Deeper, Dash."

He wound an arm around her and succumbed to the heated, dizzying desire that drove him on.

Her other leg hooked around his waist and she arched her back.

Dash closed his eyes and held on to Elena as though his life depended upon it. The sweet, spicy mint scent from the pennyroyal, the distant, night noises of the country—everything vanished until there was nothing but Dash and Elena. And their desire. And their love.

Elena clenched his hair with both hands, her buttocks coming off the ground as she writhed with pleasure. She leaned in and sank her teeth into his shoulder.

The feel of her teeth on him pushed Dash over the edge and he finally let go, his body shattering into a million minute shards as he came.

Elena wrapped her arms around him tightly and spread tiny kisses over his throat.

Dash rested his head against hers, their foreheads touching. "It's true, my love. We're never stronger than when we are in each other's arms."

ACKNOWLEDGMENTS

Lois Faye Dyer for her fantastic fabulousness.
Randall for his superlative support.
The Girls for their crazy coolness.
Junessa Viloria for her epic editorial work.
Jennifer Schober for her awesome agenting.
Franzeca Drouin for her righteous researching.

Read on for an exciting sneak peek at

THE SCOUNDREL TAKES A BRIDE

Stefanie Sloane's next Regency Rogues novel

Coming from Ballantine Books
Available wherever books are sold

"Lady Sophia, can you hear me?"

An unpleasant, sharply medicinal scent filled Sophia's nostrils, and her eyes flew open in response. "What on earth is going on?" she demanded, bracing her palms against the cushions of a striped settee and pushing herself upright.

"I am afraid you fainted," Dash's wife Elena answered from where she sat on the Aubusson carpet at Sophia's side. "Dash told me you had an aversion to weddings, but this seems rather much. Not that I would blame you. it is my own wedding and I find myself in need of a quiet room and a good book. But fainting? Stroke of genius, if you ask me," she said wryly.

Though thoroughly confused, Sophia couldn't help but smile at Lady Elena's dry humor. "It does seem rather drastic, doesn't it?" She glanced about her, taking in the room and its furnishings, recognizing it from a childhood game of hide-and-seek. "And I see I've been spirited away to the countess's quarters, no less. My, I do know hot to draw attention. I must apologize, Lady Carrington. I had no intention of ruining your wedding celebration."

"There is no need to apologize. First, you managed to extract me from the festivities, which, as I mentioned before, was not a wholly unwelcome thing. And second—and rather more important—you received some rather disconcerting news—and with little preparation, unfortunately. Though from what I understand, you gave Dash very little choice in the matter."

Lady Elena was not angry with Sophia, that much was clear. But she appeared to be a woman who thought very little of beating about the bush. A quality Sophia valued.

"He would not bend," Sophia countered. "Therefore, it was necessary to encourage a break, if you understand my meaning."

Lady Elena nodded thoughtfully. "I suppose there is some merit to your methods, though as it happens, you needn't have labored quite so hard—nore risked fainting and the possibility of acquiring a sizable lump on your skull. Dash had every intention of telling you about the events of the last weeks; but not in the middle of our wedding celebration. There are considerations to be made, after all. Considerations best taken under advisement with a touch more solitude and privacy, if *you* understand *my* meaning."

"Then you know what Dash is keeping from me?" Sophia asked, her heart beginning to pound with equal parts anticipation and dread.

Lady Elena nodded again. "That is why I am here—and why Dash is currently keeping your Langdon at arm's length. Not an easy task, as I am sure you are aware. He all but insisted on carrying you up to my room and staying by your side until you were fully recovered. He is a most congenial man in all matters, with the exception of you. Dash found it necessary to enlist Lady Elizabeth in the effort. She is a resourceful woman, but I fear it is only a matter of time until he is pounding on the door, demanding access. Which is why we must be quick."

Sophia felt a twinge of unease at her use of "your Langdon" but let it pass without contemplation. She needed to know what Dash had uncovered concerning the mystery of her mother's death.

"Then tell me, Lady Elena," she replied with resolution, swinging her legs from the settee and settling her slippered feet firmly on the floor. "Tell me what you know."

Lady Elena rose from the deep green patterned carpet and sat next to Sophia on the settee. "Very well. As you know, I came to Carrington House shortly after the death of Dash's father. As it happened, my arrival coincided with the discovery of the late earl's journal—wherein specifics concerning the man who murdered your mother were contained. Dash enlisted both my and Mr. Bourne's help in pursuing the killer—"

"Your help?" Sophia interrupted, sure that she'd misheard.

Lady Elena turned to Sophia and grimaced. "Yes, though I should mention that my assistance was not precisely 'enlisted.' Actually, the issue was fought rather fiercely to the bitter end. But a situation arose for which a woman was needed. The men had no choice."

"I disagree. They should have come to me," Sophia countered, indignation rising in her chest. "If any one woman was to participate in the capture of my mother's killer, it should have been me. Surely you see that."

Lady Elena reached out, her upturned palm a tentative offer of peace and silent request for understanding. "Lady Sophia, you do know how dearly Dash cares for you, do you not?" she asked gently.

Her tender tone tempered Sophia's growing anger. "I do," she answered, accepting Lady Elena's hand in hers.

"Then you must recognize what a difficult position

this put him in. Though very aware of your desire for revenge, he could not, in good conscience, put you in harm's way," Lady Elena explained. "Besides, I believe he felt sure you would see the logic at play once the killer was captured."

Sophia jumped up from the settee, nearly falling from a swift return of dizziness. "I must see this man at once. Where is he being held?"

"Do be careful," Lady Elena protested, popping up from her seat to take Sophia's arm. She pointed to the settee. "Sit."

Sophia was not about to do anything of the sort. "How can you expect me to sit calmly when the man who murdered my mother has been found? Do you have any idea how long I have waited to see his face? To ask him why he would commit such a brutal, senseless act? If you did, you would not ask me to wait. Truly, you would not."

Lady Elena continued to hold tight to Sophia's arm, gently but implacably keeping her from rushing out of the room. "No, I would not—not for all the world. But he has not been captured, Lady Sophia."

"But the late earl's journal," Sophia pressed, looking at the closed door.

"It is complicated," Lady Elena began. "The murderer's name was not supplied, only his code name and a few other pieces of the puzzle. Dash and Mr. Bourne made temendous progress, but they were not able to completely unravel the murder plot."

Unable to be still, Sophia shifted her weight from one foot to the other, trying to make sense of Lady Elena's words. "And that is why Nicholas decamped for the Primrose?"

"Yes," Lady Elena replied plainly. She carefully took Sophia's other arm and steadied her, calming her restless movement. "And why Langdon cannot be told. He could not keep such information from the Young Corinthians. And, as you well know, the Corinthians will hardly allow the four of you to be involved in the case."

"Then why tell me now?" Sophia asked, the fierce, bright hope for resolution that had filled her soul only moments before flickering out.

Lady Elena gestured toward the settee once more and waited until Sophia was settled. "You should know that Dash has made several trips to the Primrose in an attempt to persuade Mr. Bourne to leave. His visits have been met with very little enthusiasm on Mr. Bourne's part—and that is putting it mildly."

"From what I understand of such trips, Nicholas likes nothing more than to steep himself in brandy and brood," Sophia answered, still confused. "But that is neither here nor there. This still does not explain why Dash is finally willing to share this information with me now."

"He needs you to convince Mr. Bourne to take up the case again," Lady Elena replied. "He cannot ask Langdon. And there is no one else but Nicholas now."

Sophia stared up at her, the sudden urge to shake Lady Elena silly censured by the realization that it was, after all, her wedding day. "Then there is still the possibility that my mother's killer will be brought to justice?" she said carefully, determined to not misunderstand the true situation.

"Lady Sophia, let me be frank. I suspect that we are very much alike. Which is why I know that you are currently strategizing how you might join Nicholas in the apprehension of your mother's killer. But I can tell you from quite recent experience that Mr. Bourne is amply equipped to take on such an endeavor on his own. And beyond that, he will not stand for your participation. In fact, he will do everything in his power to make sure that you stay as far away from the case as possible."

Lady Elena spoke the truth. Precisely how Nicholas had spent his time in India over the last few years was a mystery to all. It was, however, abundantly clear that whatever it was he'd done had not involved manners, nor morals, nor perhaps anything that could be misconstrued as legal. Nicholas Bourne had returned from his travels a much more dangerous, mysterious man. But Dash's new wife had miscalculated when it came to Sophia. Nothing would stop her from finding the man who had killed her mother, especially not Nicholas.

"Then it is settled," Sophia replied, leaning into the settee cushions as if overcome with relief. "I will travel to the Primrose and do my best to convince Nicholas of his duty."

Lady Elena eyed her suspiciously, though her own relief at having finished such a challenging conversation was evident in the sign that escaped her lips. "Thank you."

Pounding sounded just on the other side of the countess's door, followed by Langdon's voice demanding entry.

"The excitement of the day became all too much and you fainted," Lady Elena suggested to Sophia, eyeing the door with worry.

Sophia nodded quickly, then laid down on the settee. "We women are such delicate creatures, are we not?"

"Hardly," Lady Elena replied, "but man's general ignorance of such things does come in rather handy at times."

❦

The Honorable Nicholas Bourne could not decide which was worse: the rattle of metal rings over the curtain rod as the rough linen hangings were pulled back, the excruciatingly loud crash of the shutters slamming against the outer stucco and timber siding of the Primrose Inn, or the sudden flash of blinding sunlight.

"Mrs. Church, are you trying to kill me?" he asked the innkeeper's wife in a low, even tone as he willed the relentless pounding in his head to stop.

Something soft yet painfully unwelcome landed on his face in response to his query. Nicholas cautiously opened his eyes but could see nothing through the folds of his linen shirt. "I see no need for clothing at this juncture, my good woman, as I intend to stay abed for at least another two hours. Now, off with you. I'm sure there are other guests who would welcome your attention."

"I am neither Mrs. Church nor am I trying to kill you. Not yet, anyway."

Nicholas startled at the sound of the woman's voice. He grabbed the bedcovers, yanking them higher over his bare chest as he levered himself upright. "Sophia?"

Lady Sophia Afton stood in front of the open window, backlit by the late morning sun. The warm golden rays silhouetted her graceful form against the gloom and dark of the rented room. All about, empty bottles of brandy and cognac, sheets of parchment and discarded quills, and Nicholas's clothing were carelessly tossed hither and yon—the evidence of a messy and misused life.

And in the middle of it all, Sophia stood still. The faint pink of her rosebud-printed gown appeared to be the exact hue of her full lips. Her hair, gleaming like autumn's burnished oak leaves, was artfully pinned up, a few stray curls expertly arranged about her face. And below the feathered arch of brows, her eyes were the deep green of emeralds, framed with dark lashes and spaced just far enough apart to give her an exotic air. One could get lost in those unfathomable depths, a fact Nicholas knew all too well.

Sophia stole his breath away. She always had. And without even knowing that she did so. He'd long ago learned it was useless to fight the fascination. His obsession with her would pass, eventually. And his sanity would return again.

"Surely you're not surprised," she said, slowly walking toward the bed until she stood within touching distance. "Someone had to fetch you."

Nicholas fought the urge to stare at her beautiful, honest face, painfully aware that the sight would only make his heart ache as much as his head. "Well, *someone* usually means Carrington or my brother. How on earth did you draw the short straw—and where's your Mrs. Kirk? This is feeling more scandalous by the moment." He gestured abruptly. "Turn around, Sophia, while I get decent."

With an unfathomable glance from beneath her lashes, she did as he bade her, turning to face the opposite wall.

Nicholas tossed back the covers and swung his bare feet to the plank floor. He unearthed his shirt from the pile of clothing flung carelessly on the edge of the bed and pulled it over his head, tugging it into the place.

"Mrs. Kirk is waiting in the hallway so that we may speak privately," Sophia replied, her back to him as Nicolas buttoned his breeches. "As for Dash, he's celebrating his wedding trip."

"Dammit," Nicholas cursed under his breath. "I thought he was to be leg-shackled on the 24th."

Sophia turned back to face him, pity pooling in her eyes. "He was, Nicholas. Today is the 31st."

He froze, staring at her. He'd lost a week. In the past there had been a day here or there that had disappeared into the ether, consumed by drink and Nicholas's own need to forget. But never so many days in a row. Too many days.

"And my brother?" he asked lightly, desperate to maintain some sense of dignity though he knew it to be a pointless struggle. "Your betrothed is busy with Parliament, I suppose?"

Sophia crossed the room to where a slat-backed chair stood. She turned it around and clasped the worn wood, tipping the chair onto two legs and dragging it toward the bed.

Nicholas winced as the scrape of wood against wood set hammers pounding inside his skull.

"I suppose," she began, situating the chair across from where Nicholas sat, then taking her seat to face him. "But you know as well as I that he could not be involved in this business. The Young Corinthians would put an end to our involvement, and we cannot allow that to happen."

Nicholas narrowed his eyes over her. "What are you up to, Sophia?"

"Do you promise to listen?" she implored, extending her arm, her palm up in silent plea.

Nicholas scrubbed his hand across his unshaved jaw. "Are we seven years old again, then?"

"Do you promise, Nicholas?" Sophia pressed. "Or have I come all this way for nothing?"

"Honestly, Sophia," Nicholas muttered, reaching out and taking her hand in his.

Sophia laced her fingers with his and squeezed, just as she'd done countless times during their childhood. "Say it."

"I promise to listen, Lady Sophia Afton. There, will that do?"

It killed him to touch her, her soft, small hand in his akin to torture. But he wouldn't let go. He knew he would never be an honorable man. Never marry nor know the joys of family. But he would take his love for Sophia to his deathbed. Even if it destroyed him, which, he ventured to guess, was precisely what would happen.

"Thank you, Nicholas." She sighed, relief easing the strain from her countenance. She squeezed his hand in hers one more time, then let go.

Nicholas lowered his arm, the tips of his fingers still tingling from where they'd gripped Sophia's mere seconds before. "Well, out with it, then. What is so important that you've come all the way to the Primrose to tell me?"

"I need you, Nicholas. You're the only man who can help me."

Nicholas stared hard at the one woman he'd ever loved. He'd often imagined what it would feel like to hear Sophia say such words to him. And the emotion was nothing like the growing sense of unease that crept up his spine now.

※ ✈

Sophia folded her hands in her lap and stared at Nicholas. When she'd thrown back in the curtains earlier and turned to look at him, she'd been stunned, frozen into stillness and too distracted to move or speak. The sunlight had arrowed through the window behind her directly onto the bed. In that brief moment before Nicholas recognized her, she'd been shocked at the powerful, dangerous man sprawled on the rumpled bed. The blankets were pushed to his waist, his upper torso bare. Though she'd known him since they were children, he was suddenly a stranger. She'd been unable to look away from the flex and smooth ripple of well-defined muscles in his chest and arms as he pushed himself upright. It was only the sound of his sleep-roughened, deep voice as he spoke her name that broke spell that held her and she was able to move again.

Now that she was nearer, she could see that deep crease marks from the crude Primrose Inn bedding ran the length of the left side of his face. He'd been abed for some time. But the dark crescents beneath his eyes intimated exhaustion.

An air of dissipation and soul-deep weariness shrouded his handsome countenance. She wanted badly to know why he felt driven to drink when it only led to this: a dank room in an unremarkable inn, surrounded by nothing that could hope to bring him any peace. But despite their long-held friendship, she felt a reluctance to question him. It wasn't her place to ask.

He scrubbed at his jaw for the second time in as many minutes, the muscles beneath the unshaven skin rigid. "Shouldn't you be asking my brother for help?"

He was clearly exhausted, but there was more. There always was with Nicholas. Her presence at the Primrose wasn't merely an inconvenience: Was he angry? Or perhaps embarrassed?

"Langdon would refuse me aid. And as much as I chafe at the very idea, I cannot do this alone," Sophia replied honestly.

Nicholas captured her with a look of abject disbelief. "I'm sorry, Sophia. I don't believe that I heard you correctly. Did you just say that you could not accomplish something on your own?"

His eyes glinted with sudden amusement. There he was, the Nicholas she knew best. Flirtatious. Irreverent. Fun. He was the only man who could always make her laugh, no matter the circumstances. "I missed you terribly while you were away in India. Do you know, I believe I didn't laugh once while you were gone," Sophia countered, an affectionate smile curving her mouth.

His brow, cocked jauntily for effect only a moment earlier, lowered, his expression smoothing into indifference. "And I missed you as well, you—all of you," he answered, the light-hearted sarcasm gone from his voice. He crossed his arms over his chest. "Now, tell me what you've come for."

And just that quickly, the brief glimpse of the Nicholas she'd once known was gone. She should have known better than to attempt such easy conversation with him. When they were children, it had all been so simple. But the death of her mother had changed everything; how could it not? Once a dear and trusted friend, Nicholas was not someone whom Sophia desperately cared for, yet couldn't get near. Not in any real sense. Not any-more.

Sophia peered down at the planked floor. She missed her friend. But she couldn't ask Nicholas to come back to her—no more than she could move the sturdy, strong wood beneath her feet. "Very well," she began, looking up and fixing him with a somber stare. "Dash told me what you've been up to. And now that he's married, someone will need to continue the search for my moth-er's killer. I want in."

Nicholas uncrossed his arms and propped his elbows on his knees, frowning at her. "You want in?"

"That is correct," Sophia confirmed earnestly. He hadn't refused immediately, causing the slimmest twinge of hope to take root in her heart.

"You want to traipse about London looking for a man who thought nothing of murdering innocent people—and would do so again given the chance?" Nicholas continued, raking both hands through his hair until the rumpled black locks stood up on end.

Sophia fought hard to hold onto the fledgling hope, fortifying it with the constancy born of every day lead-ing up to this point. "I understand the danger, Nicholas. It's precisely why I did not ask for Langdon's help. He never would have agreed to—"

"But you think I will? Am I that careless, then?" Nich-olas interrupted bitterly. "So careless as to risk my brother's bride for revenge?"

Sophia instinctively reached out for him, her breath catching involuntarily when Nicholas jerked away to avoid her touch. "No, you've misunderstood me," she assured him, needing to make him understand. "This revenge you speak of, it's mine as well, you know. My entire life has been spent waiting for this very moment. You can understand that, can't you?"

"She was your mother, Sophia. Of course I understand," Nicholas curtly replied, balling his left hand into a fist, then releasing his fingers slowly.

"It's more than that—and you know it," Sophia said with quiet conviction. "We're alike, you and I. Somehow Dash managed to escape. And Langdon can see a future—in the distance, true. But it's there. And the two of us? We can't let go of the past. And we'll never be able to until my mother's killer is captured."

Nicholas continued to flex his fingers as he contemplated the floor. "Don't do this, Sophia. You know I cannot agree to such a thing. Even if what you say is true. I will not be responsible for endangering you."

He would not meet her gaze. His discomfort was palpable. But Sophia could not surrender. "I am afraid you've very little choice in the matter."

Nicholas slowly raised his head, bringing his deep umber gaze level with hers. "This is not a game."

Sophia flinched at the mix of anguish and hard conviction in his eyes but continued to hold tight to her hope. "No one knows that better than me, Nicholas. No one."